medics who advocated brain surgery as a cure for the psychic scars of service. If that seems an outrage today, Llewellyn's achievement in this tender period piece is to evoke an incendiary sense of scandal, while avoiding all trace of we-know-better-now smugness.'

'Llewellyn has taken the harrowing subject of PTSD and used it to produce a haunting debut novel . . . The level of detail in the book is remarkable.'
Eithne Shortall, *Irish Sunday Times*

'Reminiscent of Pat Barker's *Regeneration*, and its portraits of damaged soldiers from an earlier conflict, this is a novel that matches Barker's work in its exploration of the trauma wars inflict on those who fight them.'
Nick Rennison, *The Sunday Times*

'Llewellyn's considerable gifts keep us gripped to the end even when the pain described becomes almost unbearable. The beauty and skill of her own writing is the best testament to her belief in the redemptive power of art.'
Martina Evans, *Irish Times*

'Quietly self-assured [and] deeply touching'
Elizabeth Lowry, *Fiction Book of the Day, Guardian*

'Writing about a hospitalised and traumatised poet is to invite comparisons to Pat Barker's *Regeneration* trilogy about shell-shocked First World War poets. Llewellyn's shocking and moving debut can hold its own even in that celebrated company.'
Antonia Senior, *Book of the Month, The Times*

'A moving novel exploring the effects of PTSD post World War II.'
Emerald Street

Sheila Llewellyn

Walking Wounded

SCEPTRE

First published in Great Britain in 2018 by Sceptre
An imprint of Hodder & Stoughton
An Hachette UK company

This paperback edition published in 2018

1

A CIP catalogue record for this title is available from the British Library

Paperback ISBN 9781473663107

Typeset in Sabon MT Std by Palimpsest Book Production Limited,
Falkirk, Stirlingshire

Printed and bound in Great Britain by Clays Ltd, Elcograf S.p.A.

Hodder & Stoughton policy is to use papers that are natural, renewable and
recyclable products and made from wood grown in sustainable forests. The logging
and manufacturing processes are expected to conform to the environmental
regulations of the country of origin.

Hodder & Stoughton Ltd
Carmelite House
50 Victoria Embankment
London EC4Y 0DZ

www.sceptrebooks.co.uk

To Ken

Something has gone wrong inside my head.
The sappers have left mines and wire behind;
I hold long conversations with the dead.
Casualty – Mental Ward, Vernon Scannell.

As far as treatment is concerned, one might well say that everything we do here is treatment.
'Introducing You to Northfield' (Pamphlet produced by patients for new patients, 1945).

Some years ago, I expressed my view that leucotomy was the worst honest error in recent medical practice, and I am often asked whether time has led me to alter my view. Actually it has not.
D.W. Winnicott, British Medical Journal, *1956*

Author's Note on Sources

This novel is a work of fiction, set in the context of real events which took place in 1940s psychiatry. David, the Burma veteran, and Daniel, his psychiatrist, are fictional characters who interact with several real figures from that period. I thought the reader might be interested in some of the sources which both inspired and informed the story. The first known leucotomy on a Second World War veteran was written up by William Sargant and C.M. Stewart, in 'Chronic Battle Neurosis Treated with Leucotomy', *British Medical Journal*, 29 Nov. 1947. Wylie McKissock detailed several 'civilian' case studies in his article, 'Prefrontal Leucotomy – a Further Contribution', *The Lancet,* 20 Mar. 1943. McKissock also provided a description of a leucotomy in 'The Technique of Pre-Frontal Leucotomy', *The Journal of Mental Science,* April,1943.

Northfield hospital was an influential military psychiatric hospital during the 1940s, and Tom Harrison's fascinating account of the psychiatrists and patients who were there at that time was invaluable: *Bion, Rickman, Foulkes and the Northfield Experiments: Advancing on a Different Front,* (2000). For the Burma campaign, I am greatly indebted to Major General Julian Thompson's *Forgotten Voices of Burma,* (2009). This moving collection of memories, based on Imperial War Museum sound archives, did much to confirm the details in the private journal, poems and letters home, and rare anecdotes from my father, who also fought in Burma. David Ayerst's book, *The Manchester Guardian: Biography of a Newspaper,* (1971), provided details of the *Manchester Guardian* in the pre and post war years.

Vernon Scannell's three volumes of autobiography informed my imagination of his character in the novel: *The Tiger and the Rose: An Autobiography,* (1983), *Argument of Kings: An Autobiography,* (1987), and *Drums of Morning: Growing Up in the Thirties,* (1992). Andrew James Taylor's *Walking Wounded: The Life & Poetry of Vernon*

Scannell, (2013), also illuminated other aspects of Scannell's life which influenced my portrayal.

Numerous other books provided insight into the war in Burma, the development of war time psychiatry, and the social context of immediate post war Britain. Special mention should be made of Robert Lyman, *Kohima 1944:The Battle that Saved India*, (2010); Fergal Keane, *Road of Bones, The Epic Siege of Kohima, 1944*, (2011); S.H. Foulkes, *Introduction to Group Analytic Therapy*, (1948); David Kynaston, *Austerity Britain*, (2007); Alan Allport, *Demobbed*, (2009).

David

The mule has a world-weary look about it of an animal that has seen it all. It stands impassive as the two muleteers approach. The men pull it to the ground and one of them sits on its head to hold it down. The Doc moves past me and presses a chloroform rag over its mouth and muzzle, then injects something into the soft flesh of its throat. It kicks a little, then lies still. The Doc hands me the rag. He takes out a knife, cuts into the mule's voice box, severs the cords and swabs the wound with disinfectant. The smells from the chloroform, the blood and the disinfectant overpower the man sitting on the mule's head and he slides off, retching.

The mule comes round and staggers to its feet, glassy-eyed.

It's fit now for jungle combat.

De-braying, the Doc calls it.

The muleteer who was sick wipes his eyes with his sleeve and sniffles.

'Poor little bugger. It does everything we do, goes everywhere we go, with more than a hundred and sixty pounds of mortars on its back. Then we do this to it. Poor little bugger . . . poor little bugger,' he croons, stroking the animal's long nose.

The mule tries to voice its protest, its pain, but can only manage a dumb show.

Daniel

Northfield Military Hospital, 1943

PREFRONTAL LEUCOTOMY —
A Further Contribution

G.W.T.H. FLEMING   WYLIE McKISSOCK
MRCS. DPM   MS LOND. FRCS
Medical Superintendent   *Neurological Surgeon*
Barnwood House   *to the EMS*

The results of pre-frontal leucotomy. 15 cases operated on from August 1941 to January 1943.

Technique

Cases 1 and 2 were both done under a local anaesthetic. The patients found the experience terrifying in the extreme, so that local anaesthetic was abandoned. In both cases for months afterwards, the terror was still a vivid memory.

Case Histories

Case 1. Housewife, aged fifty. Melancholia. Duration of condition – two and a half years.

Aug. 23, 1941. Leucotomy. Barnwood House Hospital.

Oct. 11, 1941. Returned home to the care of her husband. Showed some post-operative headaches and impairment of memory for recent events. No rectal or urinary incontinence. Depressed for a while and was given amphetamine. Recovery slow.

Feb. 6, 1943. Husband reports that his wife is 'very well indeed, but not quite perfect'.

—Published in the *Lancet*, 20 March 1943

Housewife, fifty, Melancholia. She'd haunted Daniel for months after Barnwood. Those eyes full of terror, full of protest. Then full of nothing. The profound silence when it was all over.

Part One

Northfield

June – July 1947

I

The gates are Asylum-Gothic and locked. Beyond them, a tree-lined drive stretches uphill to a blur of buildings on the horizon. At the east end stands a campanile, its verdigris dome outlined against blue sky. I point through the leaves of a wrought-iron clematis, and shout over my shoulder to Louie. 'That's the tower we could see all the way across the fields.'

He switches off the engine, lifts my suitcase out of the sidecar and comes over.

'Christ! That drive's about a mile long. Still, with all those fields and trees – looks more like bloody Chatsworth than a hospital.' His voice sings false.

I want to turn to him and say, *Take me home, Louie, please take me home*. But then he says, 'They'll get you right in no time,' and I hear a true note now, one of desperation. They've all tried to get me right – Louie, Beth, my mother, George – but I've left them confounded.

He stands next to me, rubbing his chin with his forefinger, looking down at his feet.

I wait for him to say something, anything, but he turns and looks back at the bike, so I can't see his face.

My mind begins to tumble. 'We can't stand around here all day.' I pick up the suitcase and head for the metal box set in the wall at the side of the gates. A peeling painted sign above it says: *Northfield Military Hospital. Ring for admittance*, and the telephone inside has a handwritten label stuck on it – *dial o*.

'Someone will be down in ten minutes,' says a woman's voice, business like.

A plank across two rounds of sawn oak forms a makeshift

seat and we sit with our backs against the wall, feet resting on the suitcase on the scrubby grass. The early June heatwave has gone, but it's still hot, and the midday sun saps us. We slump, heads lolling, chins on chests like two old men dozing after a morning's labour.

I can't keep still for long and go back for another look through the bars. A spot appears at the top of the drive. It shimmers then grows bigger, the shimmer changing to a wobble.

A man on a bike freewheels down the hill, then slows down as he pedals on the flat towards the gates. He props the bike against the wall and mops his brow with a khaki handkerchief.

Louie brings the suitcase over.

'Reece?' The man looks at Louie then me. I spot the three chevrons on his sleeve.

I nod, placing my hands flat on the bars, fingers upwards. I look like I'm surrendering.

'Corporal Reece?' He eyes me up and down, frowning at my civvies. 'That is, Corporal Reece, as was?'

'Yes, Sergeant, that's me.'

'Right you are, Corp . . . Mr . . . Corporal Reece.' He settles uncomfortably on the military rank. It's probably what he knows best; maybe it's all he knows – he has the air of a long-service man to me. He produces a bunch of keys from the knapsack slung across his chest, unlocks the gate and beckons me through. 'In you come.'

Louie shakes my hand. 'They'll get you right,' he says, his voice throaty this time.

Those blue eyes of his – I look into them but can't read what I see there.

'I'll try not to let the bastards grind me down.' I smile at him, take the suitcase and turn away. Don't give him time to say anything else. Don't look back. Walk through the gates.

'Welcome to Northfield,' the sergeant says. 'Up the hill. Follow the gravel path. Report to the guard room.' The directions sound like a stream of orders.

Guard room? It's a hospital.

The gates clang back, the sergeant locks up, the clematis entwines its leaves again, looking like it's never been prised apart. It occurs to me that the lock isn't to keep strangers out; it's to keep strangers in.

The sergeant pedals past and puffs: 'Remember, guard room to the left.'

Don't look back. The words bounce round my head to the rhythm of my steps. If I look back, I might turn back, blub against the gates, like a boy on his first day at school. It would have been less painful if I'd let my mother and George bring me here. Lying to them came easily – *army regulations, Mother, everyone takes the train to Birmingham and the hospital lays on a bus from the station to Northfield*. What was one more deception? Then I arranged with Louie to bike down to Birmingham and have him pick me up at the station. I hear him kick-start the engine and the rumble as he manoeuvres round, then the higher revs as he sets off. I can't bear the thought of seeing him getting smaller, further away. I don't look back.

He's right, the grounds do have an air of the country estate about them. Horse chestnuts and copper beeches in full leaf, fields at their June greenest, rolling away west and east. A great oak stands about halfway up the drive. I focus on it and decide I won't change hands to carry my suitcase until I get there. But my gaze keeps drifting up to the tower. A bell tower. A clock tower. Maybe even a watch tower. I reach the oak and put the suitcase down.

The sergeant has long vanished from sight round the side of the buildings. I change hands and trudge on, feeling the pull in the back of my legs as the incline grows steeper.

It's another half-mile before I reach the hospital, a low run of red brick stretching on for ever. It lies marooned in a sea of grey gravel separated from the driveway by a border of white-painted bricks, angled on their sides like shark's teeth. Close up, the tower turns out to be a water tower, looming over the hospital entrance.

I stop at the border. The main doors are closed. No signs of life. No patients being loaded or unloaded. No nurses scurrying on or off duty. Everything hidden from view round the back. It reminds me of something, this building, but whatever it is hovers on the edge of my remembering. I can't reach it and struggling to bring it back only saps the little energy I have left. I shut down my thinking and step lightly onto the path, trying not to scuff the gravel, but scuffing it anyway, and make my way round the back to the guard room.

2

Daniel Carter stood at the bay window in the doctors' tea room, watching the man make his way up the driveway and pause at the great oak. They all stopped there to get their breath or to take stock of the incline, but mostly, he supposed, to gather their nerve. The figure was no more than a dark brushstroke dwarfed by the smudged leafiness of the tree.

There was something different about his outline – it didn't go in and out like an army blouson, or have trousers tucked into boots, and there was no military cap or beret. The man flexed his arms, took up his case and trudged on. As he came nearer, Daniel saw he was wearing a suit. Apart from that, there was nothing exceptional about him. Average height and build, dark hair with a hint of Celtic curl about it.

'Is that the deserter?' A voice cut across his thoughts and Daniel turned to see Hunter's bony face next to him, extended from the neck like the muzzle of a pointer as he manoeuvred himself into the bay window to share the view.

'No. The deserters have to wear their uniforms. Technically, they're still in the forces. Anyway, the deserter scheduled for today isn't due until later.'

'What's this one doing in civvies then?' Hunter moved away to the long mahogany table in the middle of the room, finding a place to angle his elbows among the files and dirty cups.

'He must be the civilian from the Manchester Clinic. Demobbed in '46.'

'Demobbed? So why's he coming to us?'

'Not sure, I've only skimmed the first page of his notes. Got himself in a spot of trouble in civvy street. Chap who did the initial assessment in Manchester thinks it might be army-service related – he's ex Burma Campaign. Suggested sending him here.'

'Dumping him here, more like.'

'He's a bit of an experiment, apparently.'

'Aren't they all, these days?' said Hunter. 'They're sending us too many like him, if you ask me.'

'Like him?' Daniel instantly regretted his words. Why did he always rise to the bait?

'Thugs who were thugs before the war. They come home, slip back into their old ways, black marketeering or some such' – his voice went up an octave in contempt – 'get caught, claim a spotless war record and get off with a caution from some newly appointed socialist magistrate. It's a bloody insult to our real patients.'

'He doesn't sound like a thug. Not from a quick look at his file anyway.' He was annoyed with himself again for bothering to answer, and as Hunter droned on, he went back to watching the man as he stopped at the brick edging of the gravel path.

Daniel had a little theory about how the men tackled this demarcation between driveway and path. It was a borderland, their own known territory behind them and just a little strip of sharp-stoned no-man's-land in front, separating them from . . . what? The unknown? The last resort? The enemy? They all hesitated before they stepped over.

It was surprising how the way they dealt with those next few moments gave a clue to how they'd react to their stay in hospital. Some of them would start to shake. Their hands would tremble as they tried to soothe themselves by running their fingers through their hair. Others would square up to the building and march on round to the guard room – there weren't many of those. A few of them cried, wiping their noses on their sleeves, like little boys.

This man stood for what seemed like an age, head on one side, studying the building like an architect, then picked his case up again. No tears or trembling. But anxious, cautious.

Treading lightly on the gravel as if he didn't want to leave any footprints.

He became dimly aware that Hunter had asked him a question. 'Sorry?'

'I said, he's one of yours, then.' Not a question; it was a statement of fact.

'Yes, I'll take him.'

'You can take the deserter as well, if and when he gets here.'

'I'll read his file, then we can decide.' Daniel cursed inwardly as he heard the weak attempt at asserting himself. He was older, with slightly more seniority and more time served at Northfield, but technically they were the same rank. Both majors, a fact Daniel knew was more about him having ground to a halt, than about Hunter's rapid rise through the ranks, filling the post-war gaps. So here they were, both hovering on the same level, spending an increasing amount of time sparring about the allocation of patients.

'I'm chock-a-bloody-block.' Hunter pinned down each word with a nod.

'Aren't we all, these days?' Daniel was conscious of echoing Hunter's earlier sarcastic tone, but he also meant it as a genuine observation. Yet another psychiatrist was finishing at the end of the week, leaving yet another patient quota to be shared out.

'They both sound like yours rather than mine,' Hunter persisted, cocking his head in an even more emphatic nod on 'yours'. This time, Daniel didn't take the bait. He knew Hunter meant they didn't sound like 'real cases', bona fide anxiety states or hysterics or long-term severe depressions. For conditions like these, Hunter specialised in physical treatments – deep narcosis and electro-convulsion, mainly. He'd made it clear he had no truck with psychotherapy. On his arrival last year, he'd dismissed Daniel's enthusiasm about the experimental group therapy sessions set up by Michael Foulkes, Daniel's much missed colleague. 'I'm a doer, not a talker,' Hunter said, with that supercilious sniff of his. Daniel often wished he had

Foulkes's way of not allowing people like Hunter to get under his skin.

He was one of the new breed, Hunter, recently qualified, rapidly promoted and deeply browned off at having drawn Northfield in its declining months. By the end of 1946, all the big guns had gone – Bridger, Main, Foulkes. They'd all made their reputations here but they'd taken those reputations with them. Daniel couldn't blame them. The place was in chaos.

It was heading for closure as a military psychiatric hospital in less than a year's time, and was to be absorbed into the new National Health Service. The problem was, no-one yet quite knew how. There were too few doctors, too many patients and too little direction.

Hunter spent all his spare time back in London, 'keeping up', as he called it. Daniel suspected this was a euphemism for ingratiating himself with the powers that be. He was the sort to find himself a pair of coat-tails to hang on to back in London, then he'd be off. At least, Daniel hoped so.

He tuned in again. Hunter had set off on another rant.

'It's not our job to help the demob lot out in civvy street,' he said. 'There are civilian hospitals for that. The demobs are the lucky ones. They made it through. They should bloody well just get on with it and leave us to work with the poor sods who genuinely need our help.'

'I'll let you know about the deserter,' Daniel said, heading for the door.

The letter from Foulkes was waiting for him when he checked his pigeonhole after supper. Strange that it should come after his ill-tempered spat this morning with Hunter. His spirits lifted. He sometimes fancied Foulkes was still hovering around, looking after him. Back in his room, he slumped down in the baggy chair next to the bookcase and lit a cigarette, smiling as he studied the distinctive Germanic script on the envelope – the loopy 'D' and the 'e' that looked more like a sharp-angled 'n', in 'Daniel'.

He'd never figured out why Foulkes had taken to him. They made an odd pair. Foulkes, who'd trained in psychoanalysis in Vienna and studied with Adler – he'd even met Freud himself way back – and Daniel, three years out of medical school and still floundering. Maybe they shared a sense of having to make the best of it. The war had changed the flow of their lives and deposited them both at Northfield, like so much flotsam. But there was a serious job to do here, treating the military, even if it wasn't what they'd planned, and they'd worked well together, Daniel learning much from the man he came to think of as his mentor.

He looked around the room while he finished his cigarette, feeling the tension ease from his body. The room had been Foulkes's, a perk as one of the senior psychiatrists. It was shabby, but Daniel had always liked it. When Foulkes left last year, he made sure Daniel got it. Split in two by a chintzy curtain, it served both as a consulting area for patients and a private space, with a few sticks of furniture and a bed for sleeping over. Foulkes being Foulkes, he'd preferred to consult patients in a side room off one of his wards, an innovation that got up the noses of some of the others. As if he wasn't unpopular enough – *more accessible for the patients*, he said – *too bloody accessible, there is a limit*, they said.

A small coterie of psychiatrists made it clear from the start they didn't like him. Whether it was because he was German, or Jewish, or because he kept aloof, Daniel couldn't say. Tillotson, chief rumour-monger in the tea room, had connections in Exeter where Foulkes had worked before enlisting in the army, and within a week of Foulkes's arrival, he was reeling off information like it was an intelligence briefing. Foulkes, Sigmund Heinrich – Tillotson emphasising the German Christian names and ignoring the more English sounding 'Michael' that Foulkes actually preferred to use – father of three, fought in the German army in 1917, came to England 1933, divorced first wife 1937, remarried 1938 and in the same year became a British subject, changing his name in the process.

'From Fuchs to Foulkes in five years,' Tillotson said, after enlightening those who chose to listen, 'and now he's as British as you or I, gentlemen.'

Foulkes had always seemed impervious to such animosity. Daniel suspected he missed nothing, but had decided to treat them all like an interesting group for observation.

He stubbed his cigarette out and opened the letter. Typical Foulkes, he'd never been one for small talk. A brief greeting, a hope that Daniel was in good health, then straight to the point. His private practice in London was doing well and he was developing group analysis at Barts. Not at all like the military men at Northfield, but stimulating and inspiring.

There were many others who were now professing an interest in the approach. So much so, he'd been encouraged by his colleagues to write a book on the subject – how to run sessions, how they develop, how the dynamics shape the groups and the individuals within them. And most importantly, how group analysis could be used for therapeutic ends. *More than ever, Daniel, I am convinced that this approach deserves a central place in psychotherapy.*

His last paragraph ended in a request. He'd gathered a wealth of material both from his present work and from the early experimental work they'd undertaken at Northfield. Would Daniel send him his observations on some of the work they'd done or discussed together? The sessions he'd found most interesting, perhaps, whether group or individual. It would be invaluable material for the book.

Daniel thought back to when he'd first started working with him. Foulkes had arrived at Northfield a month after him, in April 1943, and had hit the ground running. Within six weeks, in addition to his full caseload of individual patients, he got grudging permission from the Commanding Officer to hold his first group therapy sessions, but only in his own time and at weekends, and restricted to his own ward patients. *It's a start, Daniel, it's a start*, Foulkes said, pragmatic as ever, when Daniel agreed to assist him. He knew little about the new approach but was intrigued by the idea of it, and Foulkes's commitment to it was infectious.

He'd kept a journal back then, on Foulkes's advice, covering the sessions they'd run from 1943 to 1945. It was gathering dust in the bookcase between Freud and a copy of Moreno. He decided he'd set aside some time later in the week to go through it and see if it contained anything that would be useful for the book.

It might do him some good to remember Northfield before its decline. Then again, it might only serve to highlight the state of decay it was in now. But at least it would take his mind off Hunter.

3

Checklists. I'm ticked off countless checklists at Reception by a cheerful captain and a sour-faced nurse. Then Corporal Tait comes to collect me. He mutters, 'Reece, David, Corporal,' checks my name on his list, his face expressionless as he takes in the civvies.

'We'll soon have you kitted out in the Blues, lad,' he says, and guides me down a short corridor to the kit store. He wears khaki and has two white chevrons fastened with safety pins to his sleeve. His small head sits badger-like atop his barrel-shaped body, his dark hair already streaked grey, yet he can't be more than thirty. He's a patient, too – all part of the Northfield way, the captain tells me, 'Our chaps showing you new chaps around.'

The storeman hands me my kit. Jacket and trousers of blue serge. Red skinny tie. White flannelette shirt. I'm struck by the brightness of the blue. Cornflower blue? Campanula? More delphinium, I decide, and I think of my mother in the garden, staking tall, belled towers.

Corporal Tait says I must trade my Oxfords for plimsolls – brown canvas with elasticated insets at the front, rather than laces.

The storeman piles pyjamas on top of the Blues. 'There's no cord in these,' I say.

'None of 'em 'ave cords,' he says, checking off the items on his list. 'You'll soon learn to keep 'em up without.' He puts an enamel plate on top of the uniform pile, places an enamel mug on the plate and drops a fork and spoon in it. No knife.

Corporal Tait collects a battered trolley like a child's small cart with a long steering handle from a row parked neatly against the far wall. 'Take what you need from your suitcase, put it in this, leave the rest. You get it back when you get out.' I pick out a package wrapped in brown paper. George had handed it to me as I'd got on the train, mumbling, 'Something to keep you company.' His kindness had left me numb. I hadn't been able to look him in the face.

I add my writing paper and sketch pad and pencils to the cart, then some odds and ends, spare vests, underpants and my leather case with my shaving things. Corporal Tait picks the shaving case off the top and hands it back to me. 'You only need your brush out of this lot,' he says with a well-practised, reassuring air. 'Everything else is on the house.'

I put the shaving case back in the suitcase together with the dressing gown my mother packed for me. I can't imagine pottering around here in a dressing gown.

'Wait there.' He points to a bench next to the carts. 'There's another lad just arrived, you can go through together.' He ambles off down the corridor leading back to the Reception office. The storeman busies himself with his lists, getting another pile of Blues ready.

When you get out, Corporal Tait said. Not 'when you leave', or 'when you're discharged', like they say in hospital. That's prison-speak, 'get out'. No laces, cords, sharp objects – that's mental asylum security. I'm imprisoned in a mental asylum. I examine this thought like a disembodied object I'm about to draw, twist it this way and that, check out the shape of it, the weight of it. It's my reality, this thought. It's me. It's what I am. I've no idea what will happen next and no energy to care. I suddenly feel a little light-headed and close my eyes to stop the dizziness.

'Christ! You're not expecting me to wear that?' A pleasant voice cuts in.

I open my eyes and see the back of a tall, broad-shouldered man, dangling one of the delphinium jackets by its collar on the end of his fingers. He's in uniform and sports the Glengarry cap of a Scottish regiment, but his accent is plummy English, difficult to place.

'Khaki's bad enough, but this!' he says, grinning at Corporal Tait who sighs and fetches another cart.

'Everyone wears the Blues to kick off with,' says the corporal, weariness in his tone as he explains the system yet again. 'It's Treatment first, so that's the Blues. Then, when you get better, you're transferred to Re-training and that means back to khaki – see?'

'Treatment means the Blues,' echoes the storeman, with no trace of irony. He stacks up the enamelware on the pile of clothes and pushes them along the counter.

'I'm sure you're right.' The man picks up his kit and turns to place it in his cart.

He notices me. 'You too?'

I nod, taking in the angular face, the soft mouth, the wariness about the deep-set eyes.

He goes ahead of me with his cart and as he passes, he says, 'John Bain.' I think I detect a slight hesitation in his voice as he introduces himself.

'David,' I say, 'David Reece.'

'Bloody awful dump.' He shakes his head.

I nod. My tongue is thick and dry and is stuck to the roof of my mouth.

'Right, lads, follow me.' Corporal Tait leads the way and we trail after him like two school kids, wheeling our carts. He doesn't amble this time – he sets a fast pace for a fat man – and we have to speed up to stay with him. We manoeuvre our carts through a door opening out on to a stone-floored corridor.

'Petticoat Lane,' says the corporal, gesturing in front of him.

The corridor must be over two hundred feet long, stretching off into the distance, with doors leading off to the left and right at intervals. The carts jump over the cracks in the flags, rattling forks and spoons round the enamel mugs. There is a strange mixture of smells: decay, disinfectant, damp. And something else, long seeped into the walls. Despair. If despair has a scent, this is what it smells like.

We hit a T-junction and turn right on to another corridor. Both John and I draw a quick breath of disbelief. The corridor is at least three hundred feet long in front of us, and when we look back, as we do automatically, it's another three hundred feet behind us.

'Christ!' says John.

'Pall Mall,' Corporal Tait says. 'You'll soon get used to it, lads,' but his eyes tell the lie.

The corridor is lit by weak bulbs, twenty-five watts at most, muzzled by wire grilles on the ceiling. I count my steps to the first light bulb. Forty. And forty to the next. And the next. I give up counting. I have this sense of walking deeper into a labyrinth. Only we're not letting out any thread. The wheels of my cart begin to squeak and the squeaks ricochet off the flags on to the walls, echoing round the corridor. No-one speaks.

We reach the end, turn right again and come to a halt in front of a locked door with a small reinforced glass pane. Corporal Tait rings the bell. A face appears like a waxing moon in the window. The moon smiles. There's the rattle of a key and the door opens and an orderly dressed in a white coat over khaki lets us in. Corporal Tait walks ahead of us, turns and signals for us to catch up. We edge our carts forward.

The dormitory is small with high ceilings. Eight iron beds range down both sides. I'm dazzled at first as we move from the dimness of the corridors into the natural light streaming through the windows. They're an elegant shape, these windows, running the length of one wall, their sills finishing halfway down, out of reach. My gaze goes first to the curved tops with their daisy-petal panes, then takes in the narrow glass rectangles below and the vertical iron bars welded over them, casting fat slatted shadows across the dull parquet flooring.

'This is part of Charles Ward . . . the . . . secure ward.'

Corporal Tait almost whispers this information. 'We use this end as the Reception Ward.'

'We're locked in?' I gesture back to the door.

'You probably won't be here long – just until the Doc's seen you, then you'll be moved to one of the open wards.'

A man in his pyjamas is sitting on the second bed along from the end wall. He's statue still, hands clasped on his knees, and is staring at the blank wall at the end of the dormitory. Corporal Tait goes over to him and places a hand lightly on his shoulder.

'A bit of company for you, Freddie,' he says, gentleness in his voice. The man doesn't move, stays silent. 'Freddie's been with us a week. He's not up to talking much,' Corporal Tait adds.

He gives Freddie another gentle pat, then points at the beds either side of him.

'Those are yours. I'll show you the baths. You get one a week, so you can have yours now, then change into your Blues. After that, I'll show you where the day room is.'

I head for the corner bed. All I want to do is flop down, but I empty the cart on to the bed then stand at the foot of it and wait. John piles everything neatly on the bed on the other side of Freddie.

Something on Freddie's locker top catches his eye, some sort of regimental badge, a black bull with red horns and hooves, woven in cloth, frayed at the edges, in a cheap wooden frame. It sits on top of a Bible with a roughened leather cover. John stares at the badge, then rummages in his pocket and brings out a packet of cigarettes. He offers Freddie a cigarette but doesn't say anything, doesn't smile. Freddie looks up at him, then takes one and nods. John waves the cigarette pack at me over Freddie's head. I mouth *no thanks*.

'Ready when you are, Corporal.' John sorts out some clean underwear from his pile.

As we make our way to the bath house, I look back at Freddie. He's smoking his cigarette, still staring at the same spot.

*

'Treatment means the Blues, the man said.' John stubs his cigarette out in a fire bucket of filthy sand standing outside the bath house entrance. 'Never a truer word, I fear.'

The baths turn out to be a real luxury, five lined up in a row, our two with six inches of hot water, and no-one's used it before us. Corporal Tait stays in the changing area, so John and I are the only ones there. We sit splashing water over our backs, John humming tunelessly.

He breaks off mid-hum. 'So what outfit were you?'

'Signals. Burma.'

'Burma? Christ. One of my mates was with the Chindits.'

'I wasn't a Chindit. I count myself lucky. They had the worst time of all of us.' I can feel myself begin to tense up. No swapping war stories, please.

He lies back, resting his head on the edge of the bath. 'I was with the Gordons. North Africa. Then Normandy, like Freddie, by the look of it. Poor sod.'

'How do you know that? Was it the badge?'

He nods. 'Black Bulls. 11th Armoured. They were in Normandy with us.'

He falls silent and I relax a little. He doesn't come across as the war story type.

'Just so as you know,' he says, his voice quiet but matter-of-fact, 'I'm a deserter.'

'A deserter?' I can't keep the surprise out of my voice.

He turns his head towards me and gives me a half-smile. 'I scarpered on VE Day, '45. Decided I'd done my bit. And I knew they wouldn't be demobbing me any time soon. So that's why I'm in here, not because I'm a loony – no offence intended to you, my old lad.' The smile fades and he turns away again. 'I thought I'd tell you, as you're the first person I've met in this dump and we might well go through the system together, at least to begin with. It'll be on the jungle telegraph soon enough anyway.'

He slides down a little, resting his feet on the bath taps, perfectly at ease.

I don't know what to say. Men deserted in Burma, but they were either never seen again, or caught then jailed back in India. I'd never met any. But here was one sitting in the next bath along. The water is cooling now, but I lie back, trying to digest what I've just heard. It's slowly beginning to dawn on me that Northfield might house not only mental cases like me, and Freddie, by the look of him, but also misfits like John and God knows who else. It's not so much a hospital, more a receptacle for army rejects.

John begins his tuneless hum again.

I'd like to ask him why he deserted, but the hum sounds like a strong signal that he's closed down, so I decide to say nothing.

I breathe in a faint smell of lavender from the flannel my mother packed for me. A furry-leafed wave of silver-blue edging down the front garden path drifts into my memory. It was the last thing I saw as my mother and George helped me to the car when I left home to come here. I hold my breath, trying to hang on to the perfume. But I have to breathe out. As I breathe in again, the memory is overpowered by a thick soup of smells hanging in the damp air. I can pick out the throat-rasping carbolic soap Corporal Tait gave us, mixed with sour undertones of disinfectant and urine from the lavatory block we can see off to the side of us.

Each lavatory has a single panel of hinged wood across it, like the top half of a stable door, but highly polished and set lower down. It strikes me as incongruous, this luxury item of well-cared-for wood in such a stinking, utilitarian place.

I'm still pondering on this when Freddie shuffles in, helped by the orderly, and takes the end cubicle. We can see him from our baths. The bottom of the door stops short at his knees and the top is level with his chest when he sits down. The orderly leans against the lavatory doorpost, reading his paper.

After a few seconds, Freddie grunts and a frown flits across his face. The orderly looks over the door at him. 'You done, Freddie? Good lad. Remember to wipe. That's it.'

I look away, feeling slightly sick, but mostly I feel ashamed – ashamed for Freddie, for the indignity of it. I hear the lavatory flush, and look across. Freddie is being led out, clutching the waist of his pyjama bottoms in his fist.

'You'd think there'd be a bit of privacy in the bloody lavatories,' I whisper to John.

'They need to keep an eye on you. In case you top yourself.'

'No razors, no cords. It wouldn't be easy.'

'Bed sheets. Tear them into strips, wrap them round your middle under your uniform, find somewhere to take the weight, knot the strips together.'

He sounds like he knows what he's talking about, as if he's seen it done. 'Of course, it would be more difficult here – they've got modern flushes. No cisterns to hang from.'

I look across at the lavatory where Freddie had been, and see a body hanging by a twisted sheet from a cast-iron cistern. I push the image away and get out of the bath, wrapping a khaki towel round my waist. John follows suit. Corporal Tait reappears from the changing area and hands us a razor and some shaving soap. He takes them from us when we've finished. We put our Blues on, John cursing under his breath as he buttons up his jacket.

The corporal leads us back to our dorm, pointing out the day room en route.

'See you at 0900 tomorrow to take you to the Doc.' He walks away quickly. Like everyone else, he can't wait to get out of Charles Ward.

Freddie is curled up on his bed, eyes closed.

John whispers, 'I could do with a pint. We could just make it before lunchtime closing.'

'We're locked in, remember. Until we see the Doc.'

'That wasn't much of an obstacle at my last hospital. Granted, that was an ordinary hospital, not a loony bin. Anyway, getting out isn't the problem. It's getting bloody well back in again, after lights out – that's the tricky bit.'

'I think I'll pass this time.' My head is beginning to buzz.

He turns on his heel. 'Fair enough. I'm off to do a recce – see if there's any way out of this place,' and he walks back in the direction of the day room.

I lie down on my bed, turning over the events of the day. Those bloody endless corridors. The straight lines of them. The stone-flagged floors and dreary walls and dimly lit ceilings, all converging at a point hundreds of feet ahead. I see myself walking towards the vanishing point but I never quite reach it.

My breathing becomes more laboured and I have to place my hand on the wall to steady myself. My footsteps echo, but I look down and think, how can they be my footsteps, I'm wearing soft-soled canvas plimsolls. I stop. The footsteps don't. They get louder and a meaty hand comes down on my shoulder from behind and I find myself moaning as I wake up to find John gently shaking my shoulder. The dorm is in evening shadow. I must have slept for seven hours straight. I'm lying on my stomach, soaked in sweat, my palm pushed against the side wall. But the moaning goes on and I realise it's not me.

I turn over and see Freddie on the floor half under his bed, rolled up in a ball, arms covering his head, whimpering. He's trembling so badly, the framed badge is shaking on top of the Bible on the locker. John kneels on the floor next to him.

He touches his arm lightly. 'It's OK, Freddie, it's OK.'

The orderly is sitting at his desk in the corner, illuminated in a pinpoint of waxy light. He doesn't even look up. Moaning is woven into the regular night sounds of the ward.

John gently props Freddie up against his locker now. My eyes close again. This time, there's no vanishing point. Freddie's still making little animal noises but more quietly and John's still comforting him – 'It's OK, Freddie, it's OK.'

But it isn't OK. I can't see how it will ever be OK again. Not for any of us loonies and misfits in here.

And I don't care if he's OK or not. I just wish he'd shut up.

I keep my eyes closed. The moaning carries on, then goes quiet.

4

Daniel settled himself into the captain's chair at his desk, determined to spend the afternoon catching up with the paperwork for the latest admissions. A faint breeze came in from the open window, cooling the back of his neck. He picked up the top file, put his glasses on, and winced – he was new to reading glasses and these wire-rims needled him behind the ears.

Corporal Freddie Simm. Already here two weeks, most of it in the secure ward, and not yet fully assessed. Veteran of D-Day. Even though the Normandy Invasion had been three years ago, there'd been an increase in D-Day-related admissions since the beginning of May. The memories could be triggered off any time, but the third anniversary of the 6th June landings last week had meant a surge of remembering. Daniel added Simm's file to the D-Day pile. Hunter could take that one on, chock-a-bloody-block or not.

Three files on, he came to one with *Non-Military?* scrawled in red across the front. He'd already skimmed it briefly in the admissions office. David Reece. The man in civvies he'd watched arriving last week. The local doctor in Manchester had initially treated Reece, then referred him to the psychiatrist who in turn referred Reece to Northfield. The doctor was apparently a life-long friend of the family and had written to the psychiatrist informally, filling in some of the personal background as well as his own initial diagnosis.

David Reece. General information. Only child. Father deceased. Called up in 1941, aged eighteen. Posted to Burma early 1942. Fought through until the end in 1945, then kept out there for extra duties. Demobilised November 1946. Took up a position back at the *Manchester Guardian* – had been employed there as a messenger boy until 1941.

Referral background. April of this year, Reece presented himself at the surgery with a damaged right hand, several cuts and bruises to his face, and badly bruised ribs. Obviously involved in some sort of incident, but has always maintained he can't remember it.

Physical injuries healed. However, his mental state deteriorated. He has developed acute anxiety, palpitations, insomnia, sleep disturbance, including dreams and nightmares related to his service in Burma (although he will not elaborate), and exhibits symptoms of depression.

The doctor had added handwritten comments at the bottom of his referral letter.

I'm of the opinion that a general psychiatric hospital is not the best place for David. He would do better in a military psychiatric hospital, where they will be familiar with his symptoms and with the context of longterm active service associated with them. I sit on one of the Advisory Committees for the proposed new National Health Service and I am aware that most military psychiatric hospitals are going to be phased out, or absorbed into the new Service as general hospitals, from next year. At present, the boundaries are, shall we say, in a state of flux. David, as an ex-service man barely six months out of the army, might be admitted into a military institution with minimum fuss.

Daniel thought back to his exchange with Hunter about Reece being a bit of an experiment. General psychiatric hospitals were admitting more men who'd been demobbed. Their symptoms were typical of battle neurosis, but they were civilians now, so

28

their problems were classified as civilian. Not the responsibility of military hospitals like Northfield.

Then again, the doctor in Manchester had a point. Boundaries were blurring in all areas of life. Why should the military be any different? In Reece's case, there'd obviously been a certain amount of string-pulling and rule-bending by the doctor and psychiatrist in Manchester. And now here Reece was at Northfield. Leaving Daniel with the problem of what to do with him.

He doodled on the blotter as he thought. What would be his aim in treating a man like Reece? It wasn't so clear-cut any more. Whether you liked it or not – and Daniel had always struggled with it – when the war was on, the job had always been to get the men back to the fighting as soon as possible. You knew what you were aiming for.

The army is your patient, not the individual. Who'd said that? Tom Main, probably; it was the sort of thing he would say.

He thought of Main, back in 1945, lecturing the latest intake of student psychiatrists. He'd taken one of them to task – Daniel couldn't remember his name – who'd questioned how any real therapeutic work could be done in the space of a six-week turnaround.

Main had turned on him with that stare of his, fixing him to the spot like a hapless rabbit cornered by a fox. 'In here,' he barked, 'you help a man to recover his poise. That lasts him out in the field for a month. One month. And you accept that as a satisfactory therapeutic result – you have to, in an army fighting for its very life, even though you know that a result like that would not be worth having in civilian life.'

That's what we've been about, all this time, thought Daniel – nothing much more than helping men 'recover their poise' – a typical Tom Main expression – so they could go back to situations where they could be killed, or severely wounded, or end up worse mentally than they were when we first saw them here. Not only that, we could send them back so they could do the same thing to the enemy – kill them, maim them, break them mentally. And we'd help them back to all that while we stayed here, safe. In his lowest moments, he'd ask himself how far he was responsible for the death by proxy of others, on his own side and the enemy's.

A bad case of non-combatant guilt, that's what you've got; it comes to us all in this job, Foulkes had said, after Daniel had confided this anxiety.

But now, he said to himself, I can't even rationalise it as non-combatant guilt. I'm not sending them back to war; I'm sending them back to civvy street. That should mean I can get back to practising psychiatry as I think it should be. The individual, not the army, should become important again. There should be time to practise longer term psychotherapy. But there wasn't. It was one session every two weeks for six weeks, if he was lucky. Sticking plaster stuff. And the group therapy sessions had been abandoned – there weren't enough psychiatrists left committed to group therapy to make it work throughout the hospital. Foulkes had been the driving force. The motivation for experimentation had fizzled out after he'd left.

The most Daniel could hope for was persuading the men to join activity clubs like woodwork or music. These used to be part of the group therapy sessions, getting the men to cooperate on projects and interact together. Laurence Bradbury in the Art Hut still did good work along those lines. But the other clubs were mainly ways of killing time. Much as Daniel didn't want to admit it, Hunter was right. The Great British Soldier was expected to count himself lucky he'd come through it and just get on with it.

Wallowing. He was wallowing. He looked down at the doodles. They were a circle of question marks, some hooked on to each other, some standing alone, all of them thick-lined and drawn with a heavy hand. He forced himself to concentrate and started a new pile with Reece's file. For now, he'd call it 'the undecided'.

He needed a break. He took off his glasses and swivelled himself round to face the window. The view was another reason for Daniel being grateful to Foulkes for this room.

It was directly above the tea room, so he could enjoy the landscape and look down the drive as far as the halfway oak. But there was a practical advantage too. He'd arranged his desk so that the patients got the view. It interested him to see how they avoided eye contact when they needed to, and stared past him out of the window. He would ask them sometimes how they felt when they looked out and saw the gates. To some of them it was frightening. The idea of going back into the outside world was too much. They needed a lot more time and the hospital didn't have it to give to them. Others changed gradually and grew in confidence so that getting out held fewer terrors. Those were the cases that made the work worthwhile, but they didn't happen enough, these days.

The initial enthusiasm to get through all the admissions had ebbed away. That was it for the afternoon. Most of the backlog had been cleared. That was an achievement. Worth a small reward. He got rid of the wire rims for the day, massaging the soreness behind his ear lobes, then made his way through the curtain to the wardrobe. He rummaged under his dirty linen bag and brought out the Black Label. He poured two fingers' worth into the glass on his bedside table and sat down on the bed, working his shoes off at the heels without undoing the laces, then swung his body over on top of the quilt, propping himself up on the pillows.

He held the whisky up to the light, admiring the depth of the old gold colour. It was a gift from an officer patient who'd left last Christmas. The whisky was black market. The first sip was always the best and he took it slow, rolling it round his mouth before swallowing. He reckoned it tasted better for being illicit.

The patient, a Captain Green, had been part of D-Day and the Normandy Campaign and had gone right through, on to

Berlin – 'without a scratch, physical or mental', Green had joked on his first session with Daniel. But then there was Belsen. That had been the tipping point. He'd got through the first few weeks of the initial liberation of the camp. Then one morning, he found himself driving out of the gates not knowing or caring where he was going, blinded by tears, and landing up in a ditch.

Daniel had only seen him three times at Northfield. He'd sat through the sessions quietly, giving answers Daniel thought were meant to please him. He'd been discharged after six weeks, to clerical work at a London depot. The day he left, he handed Daniel the whisky and as they shook hands, Green said, 'It has helped. Being here at Northfield, I mean. Talking to you. All that . . . stuff . . . that therapy stuff. I enjoyed talking to you. You've always been decent to us, all the chaps say so.'

Daniel smiled and said, 'Good.'

He remembered how his heart had sunk at what Green had said. *All that therapy stuff.* Daniel knew it probably hadn't been one jot of help. If the sessions had felt like a pleasant chat, it hadn't worked, or only enough to help Green function until he was finally discharged from the army. Another of Main's 'helping them to regain their poise for a month'-type successes.

He was wallowing again. 'Thou shalt not wallow,' he told himself, swigging down the last of the whisky. New commandment for all military psychiatrists.

5

Corporal Tait picks us up at 0900 hours, marches us to the
Doc's room, has a word with the nurse and marches us back to
the dorm. It's been the same every morning for almost a week.

'Bit of a log jam, lads. I'll be back tomorrow, same time,'
and off he scuttles.

Freddie's bed is empty. The orderly said he'd gone to see
another doctor for treatment.

We head for the day room. Men are dotted around, playing
cards and dominoes at scruffy tables. We sit on our own at the
table nearest the door. There's a hatch in one wall where a pair
of disembodied hands dispenses mugs of tea. John goes across
and gets us tea and toast with what passes for strawberry jam
but looks like runny blood.

A few people look across at us and one of them, red-haired
and round-shouldered, who everyone calls Chalky, gives John a
mock salute, then goes back to his cards.

John finishes his tea. 'Right, I'm off for a game.' He gestures
towards Chalky. 'Then it's follow the yellow brick road to the
Crown for a lunchtime pint.' He grins at me and makes his way
across to the card school.

Chalky had shown him the route that first day, the unofficial
route that is, good for late nighters sneaking back after curfew.
No invite for me, this time. He's not asked me to go with him
since the first day. I get the feeling there are no second chances
with John. He makes a move towards you, you don't take one
towards him, and that's it. You've failed some sort of loyalty
test. Weariness washes over me. I must be more worked up
than I realised about the possibility of having to see another

psychiatrist, and this on/off business with our appointments isn't helping.

Back in the dorm, the weariness turns to heaviness in my limbs. Freddie is curled up as usual on top of his blanket, eyes closed. I flop on my bed. I'm dog tired, but don't want to fall asleep. I stare at the wall, picking out scuff marks and greasy handprints and drab olive paint flaking round the edges of the cracks.

It comes to me then, the memory I was grasping for on the day I arrived, when I was facing the shark's teeth border for the first time.

'What's he called this one?' My mother leans towards the painting to check.

I step back from it to give her more room. '*The Empty House*, Mother.'

We're in front of L.S. Lowry's contribution to the Manchester Exhibition. All the best works have been packed off to some secret destination for the duration, but the Gallery is determined to keep going. It's July 1941. I've been called up and leave for the army in two weeks. This is my last outing with my mother. I stand on one side of her. Leo Marwick, the Gallery Director, stands close to her on the other. He's a genial man, easy to tease. He's also a widower, was a close friend of my father's and is hopelessly in love with my mother.

'Between you and me, Ginny, I can't see what the fuss is about with Lowry,' he says.

'Owen would have liked him. He thought he was the coming thing.'

As my mother mentions my father, Leo takes a fractional step away from her.

'He's got something, I suppose.' He's not quite able to mask his reluctance. 'They like him down in London. But then, they probably think his version of the North is quite exotic.'

'He's very modern,' my mother says.

34

'Yes, well, he asked a very modern price for the last one, thirty-one guineas if I remember rightly.' Leo rolled his eyes. 'But I beat him down to sixteen. That was nearly five years ago, mind you. If we want this, we'll have to pay the full price.'

'It would be worth it.' My mother is all innocence. 'Owen would certainly think so.'

He sighs. 'At least there are no dogs in it.' He winks at me as he says this.

'Dogs?' My mother looks at him, eyebrows raised.

'He's getting a reputation for putting dogs in all over the place. Spot the dog.'

'Maybe he just likes dogs.' My mother smiles at him and he melts. 'What do you think that signpost means?' She picks out the wooden signpost pointing left and right, stuck in the foreground in front of the wasteland surrounding the house.

'A way out, maybe? A choice not to cross that wasteland?' I say.

'It's a bit bleak.' She shakes her head. 'No people. Not like his earlier works. They were full of people.'

'Stick people,' Leo sniffs.

She shakes her head. 'All that emptiness. The house looks so abandoned, so desolate. Owen used to say you should try and look into the soul of a painting.' She leans towards the painting again. 'The soul of this one – it's full of melancholy. A study of loneliness.'

'I think that's the point, Mother.' I sound priggish to my own ears.

The scuff marks and handprints and paint flakes begin to shift, slowly re-composing themselves into a landscape slightly out of kilter. An empty house with long, low buildings and a campanile on one end of it, punctuating the sky, and a two-way signpost to nowhere stuck in a gravel no-man's-land at the front, guarded by shark's teeth.

I spend the morning dozing and then the rest of the day

35

wandering between the dorm and the day room. I don't speak to anyone. No-one speaks to me. I haven't felt this low in weeks. John slips into the dorm just before lights out, breathing beer fumes over the beds.

Freddie whimpers in his sleep. I keep my face turned to the wall.

Vinny comes back. And the Japanese boy. It's the first time they've paid me a visit since I've been in here. But only their faces this time. Vinny with his slicked-back hair and insolent eyes. The Japanese, his skin stretched like translucent parchment over starved cheeks and sharp-angled jaw bones. Each face fading in, fading out, but always ending up with the Japanese boy. I wake up, blood pounding in my ears, gulping for breath.

It's five thirty in the morning. John is already up, in the morning gloom, smoothing out his top blanket. It takes me a moment to realise that Freddie isn't there between us. His bed is freshly made. The Black Bull badge and the Bible on top of his locker have gone.

John looks across at me. 'They've taken him to the Acute Treatment Ward, whatever that is. Poor little sod, let's hope it does him some good.'

He finishes making his bed and thumps his pillow so hard the seam splits, and a single dirty feather frees itself and floats to the floor.

6

This was his only off duty evening for the next week, so he settled down to sort out the journal work he'd promised himself he'd do for Foulkes.

The entries for 1944–5 were mostly sketchy and scribbled in haste. There'd been so little time back then. Casualties started to come in after D-Day and the Second Front in Europe, and numbers leapt up from roughly 700 in June 1944, to over 1,700 by October.

And then there were patients from other theatres of war, like the Chindits. Daniel found the entries for them and felt sure Foulkes would be interested in the work he'd done with them. They were a unit who'd fought in the Burma Campaign and had been repatriated in early October 1944. They were such a unique group and had affected everyone in the hospital so much, that he'd made more detailed observations on them than usual. And in particular, there was Spence, the Chindit who'd taught him much about the terrible secrets of war.

3 October 1944

Patients from the Chindit second expedition into Burma are due to arrive this week. All we know about them is that they are from a special unit and have spent five months behind enemy lines, fighting in joint operations with American forces. We watch a film of the Chindit first expedition shot in 1943 by Public Relations, Indian Command, hoping it will give us some idea of the conditions the second expedition has been fighting in.

INTO BURMA. Dramatic music. Film title comes up over scenes of jungle terrain.

Shots of men, equipment and mules at the side of a river, unnamed for security reasons, but most likely the Chindwin. A man smiles as his elbow is bandaged by an (Indian?) major. The Chindit Brigadier, Orde Wingate ('a regular soldier with unconventional ideas'), is shown on horseback. Men do personal chores in the jungle; one is shaving while another scoops up water in a mess tin and others wash by the side of a stream. They all look rather lean, but fit, and smile a lot.

A line of men and mules passes by the camera in shadowy silhouette – on their way, the commentary says, 'to harass the Jap from behind his lines, to sabotage his railways, blow up his bridges, smash his roads, raise the oppressed against him and drive him back from whence he came'. The film fades to more dramatic music.

We know relatively little of the campaign in Burma. Europe gets most of the attention. But the Chindits are fast becoming a legend. There's something *Boy's Own* about them: far away in an alien, hostile environment, fighting in a daring, new-fangled way – long-range penetration behind enemy lines, aided by the Air Force ferrying troops and dropping supplies. Even their badge is exotic – the Chinthe, a mythical lion-like beast, that stands guard outside the monasteries and temples of Burma. The story is that Wingate chose it as their symbol but mispronounced it as Chindit, and the name stuck. He also led the second expedition but now he's their dead hero, killed in an air crash in the third week of it.

5 October 1944

First group of Chindits arrive, around ninety men all told. I watch from the tea room window as the convoy of lorries lumbers up the driveway through the autumn mist and then queues to swing round in front of the entrance doors, open for once. The orderlies are waiting there with armfuls of blankets. The hospital is already bursting at the seams. No-one was expecting so many Chindits all at once, and there are more to come. The CO says they should all be kept together, so a large tent has been erected for them in the grounds.

The driver comes round the back to drop the tailgate. A man in khaki uniform appears and levers himself off the back of the lorry, flinching as he straightens his legs. He is tall and bone-thin, his jacket ballooning loose over his belted waist. I can just make out the flash of the Royal Army Medical Corps on his sleeve. A stretcher appears out of the lorry and he helps the two men who are carrying it to manoeuvre it out and down. Four stretcher cases in all, the patients quite still, obviously in a drug-aided state of oblivion. The rest of the men appear, one by one, a few of them jumping down, others taking it in stages, helped by the medic if they need it.

They stand quietly, wrapped in the khaki blankets the order-lies have given them, keeping close to each other. They are all abnormally thin, their faces still bearing the remains of a Far Eastern tan, mocking the pitiable physical state they are in. And yet even from this distance, I can see there is a closeness among them, a sense of unity I've not seen before in group arrivals at Northfield. Most men, even those from the same units, retreat into some private space in their heads in those first moments of getting here.

But these men are different. They struggle to stand as straight as they can, holding their heads up, trying to form and keep some sort of uniform shape. They touch each other with a gentle familiarity as they help with blankets slipping from shoulders. And they look directly at each other as they speak. These men know each other inside out.

When they are all off, the men set off for the tent, an orderly leading the way. The next lorry pulls up and the process begins again. Half an hour later, the last group heads off, the medic at the front.

10 October 1944

A terrific thunderstorm tonight. Lightning, torrential bursts of rain. The Chindit tent blows down. I help to ferry the patients into the hospital. One of them doesn't move out with the others. He sits on his bed, in a corner of the tent left standing. He has one boot on and laced up and is struggling to tie the laces of the other. The medic is with him and as I make my way over to them, he looks up and mouths, *It's OK*. He has his sleeve rolled up as far as the Chindit lion badge, revealing the remains of a huge ulcer on his lower arm. It's the size of a jam jar lid and roughly healed over, its deep centre ridged like a miniature volcano.

He helps the struggling man to stand. 'Up you get, Gerry,' he says, 'easy does it.'

As they make their way out, I notice Gerry has difficulty walking – he has had injuries to both legs, by the look of it.

Later, the orderlies organise tea in the Mess Hall. I see the medic sitting on his own at a table and go over to introduce myself. He says his name is Spencer. The lads call him Spence.

The men are on mattresses on the floors of corridors or dorms. Spence says they'll be OK. His face is grey under the sallow tan. He can't be more than mid-twenties but looks in his forties.

He tells me he's been with them throughout the campaign. He's worried about Gerry; he thinks he needs to be in one of the wards for the more severe cases. His mate was killed next to him in a mortar attack around one of the landing strip strongholds and Gerry had broken both his legs. The only way they could evacuate him for treatment was to get one of the light planes, a single seater American Lysander, to come and land. It could only take one passenger at a time so they took the splints off Gerry's legs and strapped him to the back of the pilot, piggyback style. 'The American pilots did that a lot,' he says, 'they were fantastic, the best.' Gerry is OK physically, although with a permanent limp. But mentally he's lost it. He and his mate had gone through the whole campaign together.

I think of the *INTO BURMA* film and wonder.

13 October 1944

There is no way these men will go back into active service. They are physically wrecked and emotionally fragile. Most of them were down to seven stone when they came out of Burma and some are still not back to a healthy body weight. They were hospitalised for two months in India, but many are still recovering from the after-effects of a range of diseases like malaria, dysentery and tropical ulcers like Spence's. And injuries not properly healed. They wander the hospital grounds, picking up conkers and marvelling at them like children. Some of them are so vulnerable, if someone does something for them, as simple as lending them an extra jersey, they are prone to burst into tears.

I offer three group sessions, over two weeks, but only for half an hour; that seems to be their limit before they become agitated. It's not therapy. I'm not sure what the purpose is – maybe the men will show me. The group meetings evolve into a place for them to sit quiet. Feel physically safe. Take in that they have survived. So many of them didn't.

16 October 1944

Spence brings eight men to the session. Never speaks on his own behalf.

I tell them they can talk about anything they like.

One of them says he keeps thinking about the mules. When we set out, he says, the brigadier told us there were 4,000 of us and 700 mules strung out over 65 miles from end to end.

And that sets the men off, slowly at first, but all chipping in:

—Poor little buggers.

—The terrain was so bad, we had no choice, we walked single file with the animals.

—First line mules – they were big. 160 pounds on their backs.

—Wireless sets. Mortars. Ammunition boxes. Machine guns.

—Second line mules – they were smaller, but they still carried 80 pounds or more.

—They were all a bloody handful, big or small. Smell water, they'd be off like a shot.

—Slogging up hills steep as the side of a house, then sliding down ravines.

—Hang on to the mule's tail and it'd pull you up.

—Hang on to it on the way down, it'd stop you going headlong.

As they speak, they shake their heads at each other and some manage the odd wry smile. But one by one they fall silent. It's taken it out of them to remember. Then the man who first spoke sets off again, and the others join in, their voices quieter.

—They came out of the jungle in a worse state than us, no spirit left in them.

—They have shiny coats, mules. But the coats they had when they came out . . .

—Scabby. Matted. Ribs showing.

—Cut up to buggery. Deep gashes in their backs and flanks from their packs.

—They got awful galls – stank to high heaven, putrid, bad as a rotted corpse.

—We shot the worst wounded for meat . . .

—We had to, we ran out of supplies.

—They were our lifeline. We'd never have made it without them.

—Poor little buggers.

Reading through the notes he'd made, Daniel recalled how their voices had gradually faded to a whisper as they talked. It was as if caring for their mules, trying to keep them safe, kept them in touch with their own humanity.

He'd wondered how much of the lament was also for themselves. Everything the mules went through, they went through. But they couldn't bear to say that. Describing what happened to their animals was as near as they were going to get.

20 October 1944

Spence doesn't have an appointment but he comes to my room and asks to speak to me. His eyes are full of worry and he holds himself unnaturally still, as if moving might break his will to do what he's brought himself here to do. He breathes in deeply and says, 'I need to tell you something, and I need you not to interrupt. I need you to listen.'

And then he comes out with it, hardly pausing for breath. 'There's a rumour going round about some of our casualties, about what happened to them back in Burma, about how one of the units had to retreat – they held off as long as they could, but the Japs were almost on top of them, so they had to retreat – they got the blind to safety, they tied them to each other with bandages and led them out and the stretcher bearers carried out those they thought still had a chance. The rumour is that they left the rest – the badly wounded – their injuries were catastrophic, they had hours at most. So the decision was made to leave them behind.'

He pauses, keeping his gaze on me. I'm conscious of an absolute silence in the room.

'The rumour is that the doctor asked the officer what he should do; he said he couldn't leave the men to the Japs. There wasn't enough morphine to go round all of them.'

All the time his eyes are searching mine, as if on the alert for the slightest sign of revulsion. 'The rumour is that the order was to give a dose of morphine to those who still had their eyes open. Then they were all shot. All of them.'

He doesn't stop searching my face. 'The Japs would have

tortured those who could still speak, see if they could get anything out of them. Then they'd have bayoneted them all.'

His face suddenly loses all its tension and his body crumples.

I stand up and move round the desk and place my hand lightly on his shoulder.

He looks up at me. The worry in his eyes has softened to immeasurable sadness.

'You tell yourself it's the sacrifice of the few for the many. But it breaks you.'

His voice is almost a whisper now. 'I needed to say it out loud. I know I should never speak of it, and I've promised myself I never will again. But I needed to say it to someone. Just once. I thought, maybe one medical man to another . . .'

He clings on to my arm as he pulls himself to his feet. 'Now I need to bury it somewhere.' He tries to straighten up, but remains slightly stooped. 'God knows where.'

He walks out.

I go to my window and fix my gaze on the halfway oak, trying to assimilate what he's told me. The truth of it feels like a ton weight. If it feels like that for me, what must it feel like for him?

Even now, nearly three years afterwards, Daniel found himself affected by the memory of this ravaged company of men, and particularly of Spence. His desperate need to care for those who'd survived. The compassion he showed them. He wondered if he'd ever found a place to bury the rumour, if he'd ever been able to find compassion for himself.

He thought of David Reece. Since the troops had come back from Burma in 1946, their story had slowly begun to be told. The state of the prisoners of war had added to the horror. Burma was fast gaining the reputation of being the worst posting of the war. Reece wasn't a Chindit or a POW. But he'd spent over three years fighting an alien, terrifying enemy in hostile terrain, knowing what could happen to him if he were caught.

What did that do to a man?

7

Carter says it might help if I try to remember things. Correction. Dr Daniel Carter, psychiatrist, gets me to say *I* think it might help if I remember things.

He looks up from his notes. 'Perhaps you could tell me what brought you here?'

For one stupid moment, I think he means I should tell him about Louie bringing me here on the motorbike – what does he want to know that for?

He must see the puzzled look on my face because he smiles. 'I mean, what happened to you? I only have limited notes from your doctor.' He taps the notes gently with his fingertips. 'It says here, you were "involved in some sort of incident" that you said you didn't remember. If you'd been in the army when it happened, there'd be more in the notes, but there isn't.' He sits back and looks directly at me. 'Anyway, it would be more helpful to hear it from you.'

The Japanese boy's face flashes into my mind's eye, then vanishes.

'I don't think I can talk about it, sir.' I squeeze the words out through the panic.

He leans forward over his notes again. 'OK. We'll save that for later. But it would help if you could bring yourself to think about how you came to be here. Even if you don't want to talk to me about it, it could help straighten things out in your own head. 'You said last time you were troubled by dreams and nightmares.' He waits, then says, gently, 'It might be useful if you could tell me about them.'

He has a habit of making a statement and turning it into a

question. My mind races to remember anything about last time. I'd waited a week before I eventually got to see him and that was two weeks ago. John said it was deliberate; a week locked up in Charles Ward was enough to make you do anything you could to get out, anything that would please the powers that be. At least we're now in an open ward with a normal dorm, or what passes for normal in here. No word of Freddie yet, other than that he's not back in Charles Ward.

I have a vague sense that when I did get to see him that first time, he did most of the talking, telling me about the activity groups. There was a hospital band. Did I play an instrument? I shook my head. Had I seen the Art Hut in the hospital grounds? I said I'd think about it. Then he went on to how was I feeling, now I'd had time to settle in. I think I said I was having difficulties sleeping. Dreams. Nightmares. Or not sleeping at all, just lying there, remembering. I didn't tell him I felt I was going mad some of the time.

'The dreams and nightmares – can you remember what happens?' He cuts across my flitting memories now and brings me back to his last question.

'Sometimes. But then other times I can't remember the details or I can't remember anything at all – I just wake up feeling low.' I wake up crying sometimes, but I don't mention that either. He listens, head on one side in that birdy way he has, and I have a sense he knows what's been going on, anyway. He's probably heard all this before.

'And sometimes I'm in limbo, neither awake or asleep. That feels bad.'

'Because?'

'That's when the dreams feel real.'

He nods as he removes his glasses and rubs behind his ears with his thumbs.

We both fall into silence. Then I hear myself say, 'The memories are the worst. They're almost worse than the dreams and nightmares.'

'In what way are they worse?'

'Because they *are* real.'

He nods again. 'Perhaps you'd like to tell me more about them.'

'I'm not sure I can. They're different. Fragments. They slip into my mind from nowhere. Mostly I see them, but it's the daftest thing – I hear something or even smell or taste something, and the next second, I'm somewhere else, somewhere in the past.' I've never spoken like this to anyone. He must think I'm nuts.

'Can you give me an example?'

How many do you want? I think. But my mind goes blank.

'Take your time,' he says.

Images rush in, jerky, split-second, like those old-fashioned end-of-pier Mutoscopes with their flip-book pictures. If I say that's what I'm seeing right now, he really will think I'm crazy. Then my mind goes blank again. 'One minute I'm here, doing whatever I'm doing, the next I'm back at Kohima.'

He waits, and I hear myself mumbling, 'I know I need to forget, but I can't.' It sounds so lame.

'It might be more important for you to remember.' There's a small silence, a breathing space, as if he's giving me time to absorb this idea, before he adds, 'At least, at first.'

'I thought the idea is to try and forget bad memories, bad experiences? That's what everyone's been telling me – put it behind you, get on with the rest of your life.'

I can hear the voices of my mother, George, Beth, even Louie, echoing in my head as I say this. I look past Carter's head, out of the window, my gaze following the drive to the oak, and on past to the locked gates. This is it. This *is* the rest of my life.

Now it's Vinny's face that drifts in and then out.

Carter leans on his elbows, steeples his hands and taps his forefingers against his lips.

'Our mind plays tricks on us. It drags our memories into the present, convinces us that what you experienced in the past is happening now.'

'Surely it's better to try to forget, and not let the mind play tricks?'

'It's not so much about trying to forget. It's about allowing the memories to come.'

He hesitates, then says, 'If we can do that, we can work out how to deal with them, so they don't disturb us so much. We need to remember what happened, even if we don't want to – so we can try and make sense of it.'

'There *was* no bloody sense in it – in any of it,' I snap back at him. 'How can you make sense of some of the things that happened?' I feel a sudden spurt of anger at him, sitting there – a *base-wallah*, probably never been in a fighting unit in his life.

He gives me a lopsided smile, more of a grimace. 'I'm sorry, I maybe expressed that badly. I meant make sense of why one particular memory is so important to you, what it means to you.'

'So I have to remember in order to forget?'

He doesn't react to the sarcasm. 'Something like that. And it might help you if you can pin down when they come back. What kind of thing seems to lead to the memories. You mentioned seeing something or hearing, tasting or smelling something – that can be enough to trigger them. What sets them off can be as important for you to recognise as the memory.'

'You make it sound like I can treat these memories like thoughts. That I can take my time. I can't. They sneak up on me, ambush me, wallop me round the head, then they're gone. All in the space of a split second. Leave me wrung out, most of the time.'

'It's not easy, I know.' He pauses while he puts his glasses back on and looks down at his notes. 'I see you worked for the *Manchester Guardian*?'

'Yes.' What's that got to do with anything? I think.

'So you like working with words, you like writing?'

'Yes. Well, I did. I had plans. The war put paid to that. Now, I'm just a clerk. Or I was.'

'I was wondering,' he says, in a tentative tone of voice – as if he doesn't want to impose an idea on me, although that's exactly what he's doing – 'if you could write your memories down, catch a little of them, so you can work on them. That way, *you* begin to manage *them*, take some control over what *they* do to *you*, not the other way round.'

I shrug, hoping it looks non-committal. 'I'll think about it. It might help. Maybe.'

'Good.'

We finish soon after. I walk away from his office, still irritated. I don't believe all that guff about memories. Catch them, write them down, control them? Like it's a game.

I don't believe I could ever control those shards of memory, the way they pierce my mind. Vinny and the Japanese boy come back to me when they please, not when I want them to. They won't let go and there's nothing I can do about the pain of it.

But there's no way I'm going to tell Carter that.

8

'William Sargant's leaving the country.' Hunter breathed this information across the tea room table. The low voice was unnecessary; he and Daniel were the only ones there. He leaned forward conspiratorially and carried on: 'Off to America, Visiting Professor of Psychiatry, university in Baltimore. Dukes. Or is it Duke? Or should I say *Dook* à la John Wayne?'

It wasn't like Hunter to crack a joke; he must be really excited about something. Daniel wondered if Sargant's coat-tails were the ones Hunter had been trying to attach himself to on his keeping-up trips to London.

'Off for good?' he said. He almost added, 'Let's hope so' – there was too much of the zealot about Sargant for his liking – but he held back, not wanting to engage with Hunter more than was absolutely necessary.

'Not sure.' Hunter fixed his gaze on a dusty portrait of the King above the mantelpiece. 'He'd be such a loss if he did go for good.' Up went the chin a fraction more. 'Before he goes, he's giving a paper – a sort of valedictory lecture – to bring everyone up to date with the latest developments. A follow-on from the tremendous success of his book, I believe.'

Daniel shrugged, determined not to react to the pointed remarks about Sargant's book. He had a sudden memory of Foulkes throwing a copy of it on the table in the tea room, sighing. *Read it and despair, Daniel.* Its publication a couple of years ago had caused a stir.

With his usual arrogance, Sargant had denigrated both psychotherapy and psychoanalysis. They may have some incidental use he implied, but physical treatments were undoubtedly the most effective methods for psychiatric disorders.

He was a major advocate of chemical sedation, and continuous sleep treatment or deep narcosis, and also had a whole chapter on electro-convulsion therapy, or ECT, as it had come to be known. The book had become something of a bible for the likes of Hunter, and had done Sargant's reputation no harm at all within the influential medical establishment in London.

Whether you agreed with him or not, he was impossible to ignore.

Hunter interrupted his thoughts. 'You should come along to Sargant's lecture. Get it straight from the horse's mouth, as it were.' He lifted his eyes way above the King to the ceiling. 'Lots of interesting people will be there. Wylie McKissock for one.'

Daniel looked up sharply. McKissock. He shot a quick glance at Hunter to see if he'd caught his reaction, but Hunter's gaze was still focused upwards.

'McKissock?' Daniel tried to sound casual. 'What's he got to do with Sargant?'

'They've been working together recently. I think that's what the paper is about.'

'Working on what?' Daniel instinctively knew the answer before asking the question.

'Leucotomies. Formidable partnership, when you come to think about it – Sargant and one of our top neurosurgeons with all his experience in psychosurgery.'

Daniel swallowed hard, as if trying to rid himself of an unpleasant taste. Back in 1941, he'd been invited to observe one of McKissock's earliest leucotomy operations at Barnwood mental hospital, then an important centre for experimental physical treatments. The whole idea of surgery for mental disorders was anathema to him, but he'd reasoned that if he attended, he'd be able to comment on leucotomies from a position of having actually seen the operation performed. In the end, he'd had to admit to himself that he was just plain curious.

The surgery was based at best on an unproven hypothesis, developed in the 1930s, that the brain had an emotional centre which was separate from, but linked to, its intellectual functions. In particular, the theory suggested that the frontal lobes played a role in regulating tension and anxiety. Surgeons experimented with a procedure for cutting through white matter tracts in the frontal lobes to sever connections between them and other brain structures. They maintained this would cut out abnormal emotional functions or, at the very least, weaken them. The location of the surgery on the frontal lobes gave the operation its original name of lobotomy, still favoured by the Americans, who were at the forefront of developing the technique. The British still preferred the term leucotomy.

Daniel remembered one of the professors of surgery at St George's coming into the lecture hall, back when he was a medical student, with the latest edition of an American journal. Freeman and Watts, the most famous of the American lobotomists, had a paper in it. Lobotomies, they said, 'would remove the sting of certain mental disorders'.

The professor had brandished the journal above his head, declaiming: 'Oh, Brave New World indeed, gentlemen! Now we have psychosurgery! Apparently, we can now treat mental disorders with the knife. A lobotomy, our American colleagues call it. As easy as a tonsillectomy!' Daniel and the rest of the professor's students had laughed.

We're not laughing now, Daniel thought. Leucotomies were being done all over the world. Over a thousand in Britain by 1945, if the grapevine was to be believed, and McKissock would have been involved in a significant number of those.

Hunter's drawl faded in. 'It does no harm to be seen with people like that. It's where the most exciting work is going on, and let's face it, we'll all be looking for something else, soon enough. This place is on its last legs.' The contempt as he said *this place* was palpable. He lowered his nose to the point where he could look down it at Daniel. 'You should make the effort. Come to the lecture. See the future.'

Daniel had the sudden urge to be as far away from Hunter as possible. Thinking about McKissock had unsettled him. Memories he thought he'd dealt with were beginning to bubble up and he had to tamp them down. He still had a backlog of patient admissions to do, and needed to put some distance between this conversation and the rest of his working day.

Hunter didn't seem to notice his exit. He was back to staring at the ceiling, as if McKissock and Sargant might be painted on it, like God and Adam in the Sistine Chapel, exchanging the spark of Creation.

He got through the next few admission files quickly until he came to John Bain's.

The deserter. He remembered Hunter's contemptuous tone of voice.

As he read, he summarised the gist. *Gordon Highlander, wounded in Normandy, repatriated to hospital with a broken leg, absconded 1945 <u>on VE Day</u>. Two years AWOL.* Daniel smiled a little at the underlining and the Colonel Blimp-ish outrage it conveyed.

He was about to put Bain on the D-Day/Normandy Invasion pile until a detail at the bottom of the page caught his eye: *1943 – also absconded in a forward area at Wadi Akarit: sentenced to three years, to be served in the Military Prison, Alexandria, Egypt. Released after six months, on suspended sentence, for return to action in Europe.*

So Bain had served in North Africa as well as in Normandy – and had deserted not once, but twice. And had been imprisoned by his own side for it. He'd treated deserters before. But a double deserter was something new.

He sat back to think, wiggling his head, trying to unkink the muscles in his neck, then set his glasses down on the desk. He needed them to check the notes, but he'd noticed recently that when he was with his patients, he'd begun to keep the glasses on for whole sessions, a habit that made him feel uneasy. It could be about not wanting to engage with a particular patient. Some of them were difficult to like, but that went with the job. You saw past that to their fear, their vulnerability.

Maybe he'd been watching men crumble in front of him for too long. Keeping the glasses on meant that what he saw was blurred, softened. Maybe the next step was to find himself going selectively deaf, so he wouldn't be able to listen to their experiences, either.

Glasses back on, he re-read Bain's notes through quickly. He decided he'd see him for his preliminary assessment, then think again, before making a final decision about him. He put the file to one side.

Reece and Bain had been the only two undecided. Interesting, Daniel thought. Outsiders, and misfits, from the sounds of them. Fetching up in a system that obviously wasn't right for them. He wondered what Foulkes would have made of the fact that Daniel had picked them out. *Over-identification, Daniel – you must beware of over-identifying with your patients.*

And not for the first time, he realised how much he missed Foulkes and his wisdom.

Thinking about his friend and colleague, he decided he might as well spend the rest of his afternoon finishing the journal work he'd started for him.

He had to smile to himself as he read the first words of the first entry for 1945. They were positively cryptic. He remembered how problematic that group had been from the start.

6 January 1945

Side ward. New group. Silences. Fix me, Doc! Foulkes gives his 'white coat' introduction. Watch out for Sister Graham.

Foulkes: 'I want you to imagine me wearing a white coat, not

54

an army uniform.' Sister Graham, who's in charge of the ward and has no time for Foulkes and his 'groupy things', snorts as she earwigs from the corridor outside. Foulkes's wordy explanation that group work is another form of treatment is met with silence. No, not silence, with hostile muteness.

Then one of the men says: 'But it's not treatment, is it, begging your pardon, sir, it's just talk. I want medicine. I want you to give me something to make me feel better.'

After the session, I go for tea in the tea room. Tillotson is there with a few others. As I enter, he slips into a thick German accent: 'I'd like you to imagine I'm wearing a white coat, not a uniform.' He speaks just loud enough for me to hear: 'It's damned ridiculous. He's in the army, like the rest of us, and so are the men he's treating.'

I marvel at how quickly Sister Graham must have hot-footed it back to them all to report on Foulkes's 'groupy things'.

It was heady stuff back then, setting up group work with Foulkes. Not even Sister Graham's slyness, or Tillotson's contempt, could dampen their enthusiasm. Daniel had seen immediately the potential of the approach. Dealing with one patient had always been intriguing, but dealing with a group was a different challenge altogether. Like trying to navigate a river, a single organism in its own right, but propelled along by a myriad of unknown forces lying beneath.

Foulkes fostered a small band of enthusiastic followers. They'd had to learn on the hoof. Run sessions then review them in ad hoc seminars. *What did we learn from that session?*

That was Foulkes's favourite question. Slowly they built up a working methodology based on their discussions. What criteria do you use to select groups? What is the therapist's role? Do you concentrate on the individual in the group or the group as an entity in itself? What do you do about silences, about reluctance to participate, about resistance? What do you do about those who are scapegoated and those who do the scapegoating?

They would be exhausted from their full caseloads of standard psychiatric work, but somehow the experimental group work re-energised them. Foulkes drove them on, encouraging them to experiment, adapt, always with the benefit of the patient in mind.

Then in January 1945, Major Bridger arrived at Northfield and the focus of the work changed. The number of psychiatric casualties had increased so much that the War Office put pressure on the hospital to return the men back to military service, in some form or another, as soon as possible. They sent Bridger to oversee this task. He set about revitalising the whole hospital, both in training and treatment.

Foulkes was his usual pragmatic self and worked with him on this. He realised there was always going to be a tension between being in a military context and wanting to practise experimental psychotherapeutic approaches. And after all, they were in the middle of a war, in a military hospital, not an academic institution. So he satisfied himself with just getting the groups to work together, solving practical problems, and then studying the dynamics of that.

It was an unpromising partnership, Foulkes the maverick psychiatrist, Bridger the ex-artillery officer. But they sparked off each other – in fact, Daniel recalled, as he read the entries on the group they came to call the Stage group, sparks began to fly all over the place.

23 January 1945

Session 1 Stage group
Background info.

Eight group members. Arrived between December 1944 and January 1945. Foulkes used their admission dates to select them. Average age is twenty four. Most of them come straight from active service in the most dangerous areas of France or Holland. They're typical of the new intake of psychological casualties. All suffering from acute anxiety, depression, sensory and motor hysteria, mainly after witnessing direct hits on their tanks and seeing comrades burned to death, or fatally injured from shell blasts.

28 January 1945

Session 2
Practise what we preach, says Foulkes. We're all part of groups.

Bridger has this vision of 'the hospital as a whole with its mission'. So we are all here with the Stage group: me, Foulkes, Bridger, social therapists from the training wing, ward orderlies. And Sister Graham, who looks thunderous. Bridger has made it clear they must all attend some of the group sessions to listen to what the men say they want to do – no more basket weaving or embroidery, he says with a meaningful look at the social therapists. Everyone will have to change how they go about things.

We meet on the dilapidated stage in the hall, not on a side ward. The group have requested this – they don't like being in the ward, it makes them feel like patients. They want to do up the stage so they can have concerts and plays.

Bridger listens to what they say, then pauses for a moment. 'You want to restore the stage,' he muses out loud, 'so that's the task.' Then he asks them a simple question:

'If this hospital were your military unit, what would you like to do about that task?'

They hesitate, then begin to come up with suggestions. Between them they discover they have carpentry and electrical skills. Everyone will muck in and slap on a coat of paint.

Foulkes says later he thinks the session was positive. 'Interesting dynamics, Daniel.'

Session 3
Bridger ploughs on with 'the hospital as a whole with its mission'.

They elect a clerk to keep notes – materials required, tools to be borrowed. They suggest asking the Art Hut group to make posters for an opening concert on the new stage.

Two groups communicating and working together – Foulkes and Bridger are delighted.

Session 4
Living together.

At the end of the session, Bridger tells the group they can take over eight beds in the same ward so that they are all together. This will emphasise the fact that they are a unit. This works well. Living together like this seems to improve their morale, and their behaviour in the hospital as a whole is exemplary. They are fast becoming known as an elite group.

NB *Dr Foulkes's precious group.*

Sister Graham comes to see me. Thinks it's ridiculous the amount of attention the group is getting. Special dispensation to choose their sleeping arrangements! Requests for paper and pens, not to mention precious materials like wood and paint. Telling everyone they are a unit. They are stirring up the others.

Throughout, she refers to the group as 'Dr Foulkes's precious group'. Rumours get back to me that she has spoken with matron and with the social therapists in the training wing, who are also not happy. Lines of authority are blurred. No-one is sure any longer who does what, who is responsible for what. Admin staff say patients' files are passed around by so many people they are getting mislaid.

Tillotson and co. in the tea room are apoplectic. The idea of having to listen to what the lowly ward orderlies have to say – they aren't even highly trained nurses – not to mention the patients themselves, who now have their own ward representatives – it's totally unacceptable.

The ward orderlies aren't too keen either. It is far too much responsibility for them to handle, and they don't get paid enough.

Foulkes is fascinated by the 'compelling psychodynamics of so many groups in action'.

Session 5
The khaki question.

Foulkes and I alone take this session. He compliments them on their hard work. They've finished the repair and refurbishment of the stage and the hall is ready for its first concert. The group itself might not be around for this event as Foulkes tells the men he's just received notification that they are going to be transferred to the Convalescence Depot, a halfway house between the hospital and transfer back into the army. It won't be for some weeks, and he's written to the psychiatrist in charge there to request that the men in the group be transferred as a group to the Depot. He's stated that it would help their further rehabilitation if they could be kept together as regards their sleeping accommodation, work and training.

The men are pleased. Then they bring up the khaki question. They hate the Blues. They want to wear khaki. They maintain they're working, and therefore in training, not treatment. Their success as a group seems to have given them the confidence to bring the topic up.

Foulkes asks if it's something they all want. There is universal agreement.

'Then I'll sign you all off.'

By the end of that day, the uniform chit is signed for them all and they are walking around the hospital in khaki.

Foulkes sums this up as progress. 'This is what we're aiming for, Daniel. Individuals in the group interacting with each other, learning from each other, growing as individuals. They don't consider themselves as belonging to us, rather they use us for their own purposes.'

NB Sister Graham collars me in the corridor. She is incandescent. Dr Foulkes is beyond the pale. He knows how all the men hate the Blues. But he also knows the rules about khaki.

'What rules? I don't know of any rules about khaki,' I say.

She says the rules state that only ten per cent of a ward can be in khaki at any one time. This group are together in one ward as Dr Foulkes's special group. Getting signed off the Blues as a group like this means all the available khaki places have gone to them. Her ward is now up in arms.

The whole hospital gets to know of the incident. The CO calls in Foulkes. Tells him in no uncertain terms he's flouted a major military rule of the hospital. There must be discipline and procedure. Foulkes apologises but holds out for the men. They are leaving in a few weeks. He'd appreciate it if things could stand as they are, and they could keep to the khaki.

Bridger backs him up. The CO reluctantly agrees.

'I'm pleased for the men,' says Foulkes.

Daniel skimmed through the next few pages of his journal. There'd been a follow-up to all the goings on and he'd noted it down somewhere. He found it under a hastily scribbled heading: *Foulkes and the postal order.* A month after the Stage group left, Foulkes received a letter from the man who'd taken on the job of clerk for them. The letter sent greetings from 'the Stage group' and enclosed a postal order for 13/- which he said he owed Foulkes for the project expenses – he hadn't got the money on him when he'd left.

Thinking back to Foulkes getting the letter, Daniel was reminded that it was the only time he'd seen him get emotional. He'd choked up on first reading it. None of the men had to be discharged from the army, although they'd not been assigned to active service again. Foulkes had confided to Daniel that he considered it to be one of his most successful groups so far, even though he knew he'd not won over Sister Graham and the CO. 'It felt like we were treating the hospital as a group in its own right. The psychodynamics were particularly complex and intriguing.'

Daniel decided he'd send Foulkes the notes for the Chindits and his account of the Stage group. He tore the pages out of the journal and added his reflections at the end. He wondered what Foulkes would make of Sister Graham's comments about his 'precious group'. But Foulkes always knew how antagonistic towards him and his work she was. Daniel was sure he'd see her as merely another interesting example of resistance, useful for his seminars.

He felt strangely disorientated when he'd finished. The process of revisiting those days made him realise that the group work was, for him at least, fulfilling an emotional need.

The fundamental drive within him to help men recover from their trauma was at the heart of what he did every day, both back then and now. But if he was honest with himself, the group work and the way in which it had been conducted within the military context had satisfied a personal need as much as a professional one. It felt like the world outside was slowly destroying itself and full of threat, but inside the Northfield experimental bubble, the work on groups had felt creative, full of hope, not fear.

They'd got a reputation as a group of 'Foulkes worshippers', but Daniel had never cared about that. They'd all learned new ways of doing things, Foulkes included, Daniel thought ruefully – by mid-1945 he'd abandoned his white coat analogy.

For that short period of time, working with Foulkes and the others, he was able to forget the uncertainties of the future and concentrate on the small triumphs of the present. Now the war was over and the sense of fear had gone, but so had the sense of achievement. Northfield was crumbling round him and the future felt as unpredictable as ever.

But most of all, looking back to that time had made him admit how much he missed the group of psychiatrists and medical staff he'd worked with. They'd all been his colleagues and his friends. Now, with the exception of Laurence Bradbury in the Art Hut, who chatted with him over tea occasionally, it felt like all he had was Hunter nipping at his heels.

He hadn't realised how lonely he'd become.

9

'He got you good and proper.' John shakes his head at me. 'But then, that's what they do, trick cyclists, manipulate you into thinking you've worked it all out for yourself.'

I've just finished recounting an edited version about my session with Dr Carter. I'm careful to adopt the necessary eye-rolling and nonchalance, colluding with the scepticism required when discussing the doctors, at least with John.

He carries on. 'I kept schtum, my very first session with him.' He emphasises the 'I'.

'It annoyed him a bit.' He smiles at that. 'He sat there. I sat there. We both bloody sat there. He droned on about activity groups. I looked out of the window most of the time. All I could think of was walking down that driveway and out through the Pearly Gates to heaven.'

I think back to looking out of Carter's window, down to the gates, and feeling nothing but despair. John offers me a bottle of Bass, saying, 'Courtesy of Mavis, God bless her and all who sail in her.' He has a way with women. Mavis is the barmaid at the Crown and one of a number of women in thrall to him, inside and outside the hospital.

We're sitting on the floor, leaning against the bookshelves in the junk room, a small, windowless room at the back of the library used as a dumping ground for old box files and discarded office paraphernalia. A few battered-looking reference books lie about on the mostly empty shelves. I didn't like it when we first came here – those empty shelves reminded me of the last time I was in George's bookshop, and it was enough to send me sinking down.

But I've got used to it now. John spends a lot of time hidden away here, usually drinking something or other. It's as close to joining the library group as he's prepared to go.

It's after hours, but he's charmed the spare set of keys to the library from one of the admin clerks. We come here on occasion for no other reason than it's out of bounds. It seems important to John to find ways of subverting the rules.

'He's not bad,' I say. 'He apologised to me, said he'd not explained something clearly.'

'And you fell for it?' Now it's his turn to roll his eyes. 'That's the biggest con going, an apology – gets you thinking he's human, just like you – he makes mistakes but he's big enough to admit it. Elementary interrogation techniques, page one of the manual, *make your prisoner think you're on their side.*' His voice sounds harsh.

'It felt genuine enough to me. Besides, he's not an interrogator, he's a psychiatrist.'

'Hard to tell the difference sometimes.' The harshness is still there.

'Maybe.' He's probably right, it's best not to trust anyone. The thought depresses me. I need to trust someone, anyone who might help me shift the weight.

He must have seen my face fall, because he says, 'Alright, he strikes me as one of the better ones, I'll give you that.' He takes another sip of his beer, then looks thoughtful.

'The trouble with memories is that they don't do what you want them to do. They have a life of their own. They stay and haunt you. Or they fade or they change shape, so you forget the important bits, the bits you need to remember in order not to make the same mistakes.'

He hesitates, then gets up, turns to the shelves and dislodges a couple of large dictionaries, furry with dust. 'Nobody ever uses these,' he says, feeling behind them and bringing out a battered box file.

He sits down again, places the file on the floor next to him and opens it. A couple of books lie on top of sheets of hand-written stuff. He lifts one out, flipping through it until he finds the page he's looking for. He reads a bit out in a low, slow voice:

> 'Entrance and exit wounds are silvered clean,
> the track aches only when the rain reminds . . .
> . . . Their war was fought these twenty years ago
> and now assumes the nature-look of time.'

He closes the book and lifts it up to show me. 'Robert Graves. It's from *Recalling War*. That's what I mean about remembering and forgetting.'

'I'm not well up on Graves.' I suddenly see George waving *Goodbye to All That* across the table at me at the back of his bookshop. He and Graves had been in the Royal Welch Fusiliers in the Great War but hadn't met. I'd never taken the time to read the book.

'He was right,' John says. 'We forget what war was like – or we refuse to remember. Maybe we need to do that, maybe we need to refuse to remember, whatever Carter says to the contrary. Otherwise we'd all go insane. But that's the catch – because if we do forget, we let ourselves get drawn into the whole bloody business again.'

He strokes the cover of the book. 'Just think about it. Graves goes through the Great War. Takes twenty years before he writes a poem like this, gets to the truth of it, about what happens to the memories of war, any war. Then his own son is killed, in Burma, with your lot.'

'I didn't know that.' Sadness touches me, knowing it now.

We sit lost in our thoughts. I lean back, nursing my beer against my stomach, looking across at him. He takes a swig of beer and catches me staring at his hand round the bottle. I've always been fascinated by hands, and his are extraordinary – wide-spanned, long, sturdy fingers, the knuckle of his right ring finger as big as a peach stone, raised above the others.

'Boxer's hand,' he says, wiggling it. 'It's always the ring finger that takes the blows.'

The mood between us lightens a little. 'You? A boxer?' I'm surprised, but as I think about it, the more sense it makes. He has the build and there's a natural agility about him, as if he knows his body well and is comfortable with it.

He nods. 'Tried to make a living at it when I was on the run. Mainly around Leeds. Welter, middle, cruiser weight. Didn't exactly rake it in, but it kept the wolf from the door.'

It's the first time he's mentioned being on the run since our conversation in the baths. The gossip had got round the hospital. He's not the first deserter here. No-one seems to care.

'I earned enough at it to keep me while I was at the university,' he says casually.

'You were at university?' I can't hide the squeak of disbelief.

'Not officially,' and he grins.

I laugh. I should have known. Nothing about John would ever be official.

He tells me about living in London when he first went on the run, then moving up to Leeds. 'Did a bit of private tutoring. Lied about my qualifications – I never even finished grammar school. Kept one step ahead of my pupils. Then I met some Leeds University types in a pub and one thing led to another. I ended up meeting the Professor of English and a few others. I asked if I could attend some of their lectures and they said yes.'

He jinks his head towards the library. 'I can't concentrate in this bloody place, but back then, I was reading like mad – Auden, Eliot; novels too – Dostoevsky, Hardy, Melville. Soaked everything up like a sponge. It was one of the best times of my life.'

There's a spark about him I've not seen before. Those hands of his are open-palmed, gesturing, animated as he speaks.

He gives me that sizing-up look of his. 'I was writing too. Poetry. None of it much good. I've got the rejection slips to prove it. But this one made it.' He rummages about in the box file and pulls out a copy of *Tribune*. 'First one I had published, last year,' he says, turning the page and reading out loud: '"One Who Died.".' He passes it over, his hand wobbly.

I read it through, but not with much care. I'm taken aback he's shown me his work.

> . . . the flesh decaying;
> The bones grown brittle in anticipation
> Of the ultimate disintegration.

I notice the name under the poem. *Vernon Scannell*. I frown at him.

'Vernon Scannell?'

'That's me,' he says.

'A poet, a boxer and a *nom de plume* – you're full of surprises,' I say, smiling.

He snatches the magazine out of my hands. 'It's not a bloody *nom de plume*. It's me. It's who I am. It's who I am now.' There's raw anger in the way he tosses it back in the box file, slams the top down and drops the file on the floor beside him.

We sit opposite each other for what seems like an age, my knees drawn up in front of me, his long legs sprawled out. I've learned to keep quiet when he's like this. He's prone to monsoon cloudbursts of rage, sudden, overwhelming, that dry up as quickly as they come on. They've been directed at other people until now.

'This fucking place!' His voice is a hiss in the silence. 'It brings the worst out in you.'

It's the closest I'm going to get to an apology, but it's enough.

He taps the file, the peach-stone knuckle finger leading the staccato rhythm.

'I changed my name,' he says. 'After I deserted in '45. My real name is John Vernon Bain, that's what I was christened, so Vernon is one of my real names. John Bain was the name I had to use when I enlisted in the army when I was eighteen.' He takes another sip of beer. 'But when I landed up in London, a friend got me some identity papers for a man called Scannell, so I changed my name to Vernon Scannell and I've been Scannell ever since.'

'To fool the Military Police?' I say it with a degree of coolness, but I'm still taking in the fact that he knows the kind of person who could conjure up new identity papers for him.

'That was what I told myself at the time.' His hand clenches, relaxes then re-forms a fist on the file. 'But it wasn't that. John Bain was someone I wanted to leave behind. It was my old man's name for a start.' His voice thickens with contempt when he mentions his father.

'When the bastards caught me, I thought, fuck it, they could have John Bain, he wasn't me any more, anyway. But they weren't getting hold of Vernon Scannell.'

He moves suddenly, making me jump. He gets up and goes over to the shelf with the file, carefully hiding it again behind the dictionaries.

'So, in here, I'm John Bain. The army can have him back to play with a bit longer.' He turns round to me and points towards the door. 'Out there, outside this fucking hospital, I'm me. I'm Vernon Scannell.' His voice becomes lighter. 'But as far as you're concerned, my old lad, I'm John Bain. That's the name you use. I don't want anyone else knowing.'

I nod, but I'm confused. He's just told me more about himself in half an hour than he has in the last four weeks. The junk room has become a confessional and I suddenly feel the weight of the secrets he's handed me. I can't work out how this new picture I have of him fits in with him being a deserter, but then nothing about John is straightforward. It makes me feel closer to him, as if I can take a risk. Ask him why he deserted. God knows, we'd all thought about doing it. But that was when we were fighting. When he did it, the war was over. What made him actually walk away? Run away?

I'm about to ask him but something stops me. The look on his face says that's enough of the personal, so far and no further.

Another shut-down signal. Those eyes of his are at their most unfathomable.

As if to emphasise the full stop, he picks up his beer bottle from the floor and raises it. 'A final toast – here's to *not* recalling war.'

He drains the bottle and wipes his lips with the back of his hand. 'Right. My turn to go a few rounds with Carter.' He strides towards the door, light and lithe, as if he's limbering up.

This will be tough going, Daniel thought, glancing across at Bain. The first session with him had been full of silences – it had been a busy session, as far as silences went. Bored silences, mocking silences. Hostile muteness, mainly. All useful stuff – you can tell as much from silences as you can from what is said: *you must feel what the silences mean, Daniel, and let them have their say.* Foulkes again.

He was aware of the limited time they had. He had a good idea of what to do with Bain but needed to confirm the course of action he thought would be best.

He looked up from his notes. 'I'd like you to explain something to me.'

Bain put his head on one side and waited. His face was impassive.

'It says here you "absconded from a forward area in Wadi Akarit"?'

'Correct.' Bain straightened his head up and answered in a quiet but firm tone.

'What does that mean, exactly? "From a forward area"?' Daniel leaned back.

Bain sighed and folded his arms across his chest. He had long, strong fingers, Daniel noticed, the knuckle of the right ring finger as large as a walnut shell.

'It means I deserted' – Bain emphasised the word – 'after we'd taken some ground.'

'So you were in action? You were going forwards? The enemy had retreated?'

Bain nodded, a bored look on his face.

'You could say that, technically speaking, the Germans were actually retreating, so you didn't . . . abscond in the *face* of the enemy?' Daniel chose his words carefully, reasoning that 'abscond' didn't have the detrimental overtones of 'deserter' so Bain might respond better to it.

'You could say that, yes.' The look slipped from boredom to a sly half-smile as Bain mimicked Daniel's intonation. 'You could say . . .' – he paused as if he was also giving careful consideration to what he was going to say next – 'you could say that, technically speaking . . . all things considered . . . it was more in the *arse* of the enemy.'

Daniel smiled. 'Yes, technically speaking, that would be more accurate.'

'And I didn't abscond,' Bain said quietly. 'I deserted.'

'Would you like to say a bit more about that? About what drove you to . . . desert.'

'I've no fucking idea. I'd just had enough. I looked around me, saw what was going on and I thought "fuck it". So I walked away.'

'And what was going on?'

Bain stared past Daniel out of the window, then dropped his gaze. 'The same old thing was going on. Bloody chaos. Men got killed. I didn't.'

A long silence. He must have seen men killed before, Daniel thought. So what was different about Wadi Akarit? He wouldn't push him, he wanted the general picture first.

'And when they caught you, you ended up in prison in Alexandria?'

'Correct.'

'What was that like?'

'What was what like?'

'Prison.'

There was a slight pause. 'A bit like here, only with more sun thrown in.' Bain smirked, but tightened the grip on his arms, his knuckles whitening.

Daniel watched as Bain's body tensed up. So prison was traumatic too. No surprises there – Egyptian military prisons didn't bear thinking about.

'Would you like to say a bit more about being in prison?'

'No.'

More silence.

'And then, in '44 you ended up in Normandy?'

'That was the deal. My get-out-of-jail card.' That half-smile again. 'They came to the prison and said if I promised to be a good boy and not desert again, I wouldn't have to serve my sentence. I could rejoin my old battalion back home. There was still heavy action in Europe and they needed me.'

'So you promised to be a good boy.'

'I would have promised anything to get out of there.' His jaw tightened.

'So prison was that bad?'

'Yes, it was that bad, and no, I wouldn't like to say any more about it.'

Bain looked directly at him, then unfolded his arms and let his hands drop to his knees, the broad span of his fingers gripping them like gnarled tree roots.

Daniel looked at his notes. 'So that takes us to Normandy, where you broke your leg?'

Bain nodded. 'Easy ticket back to Blighty.' Glibness slid back into place.

'And you deserted a second time?'

Bain laughed out loud. 'Correct. I "absconded" from Hamilton. Bloody Hamilton! Godforsaken convalescent depot in Scotland. Worse than any bloody "forward area".'

'And that was in May '45?'

'VE Day. As you already know.' Bain nodded his head at the notes. 'That was it, as far as I was concerned. The war was over. I'd kept my part of the bargain. But I knew they could send me overseas again if they liked. So I walked out of the depot and hitched a lift south.'

'But you were still on suspended sentence for your first desertion?'

'Correct.'

'And you were on the run for two years. What did you do all that time?'

Bain stared out of the window again, his eyes squinting as if he were focused on a distant target. He leaned forward a little, massaging his knees with his tree root hands, the walnut knuckle rising and falling in a slow rhythm.

The silence stretched out between them. Then Bain shifted his gaze and looked straight at Daniel. 'I became human again.' He nodded, as if to confirm the truth of it to himself, then said slowly, 'It's taken me two years, and I'm still working at it, but that's what I've been doing, trying to get the fucking army out of my system, becoming human again.' His face dropped with exhaustion. He sank back in the chair, his hands still.

Daniel let the silence settle. All the tension had gone out of it now, the quiet was almost soothing. The time for the session was up, so he said the usual things to bring it to a close. Bain shrugged and got up and headed for the door. His hand on the doorknob, he looked back at Daniel and hesitated as if he was going to say something. But he turned away and went out.

Daniel felt physically drained. It had been like swimming against a strong current with Bain. He wasn't mentally ill, that much was obvious. There was anxiety around his memories, but that was normal, considering what he'd gone through. He was hiding a lot. Nothing unusual in that either, they all were. Whatever had happened at Wadi Akarit – that seemed to be the key. There were serious problems around that. Daniel could spend time on it, but it was long-term work. Longer than the time he had left with him. No point in opening it all up then not having the time to help Bain come to terms with what had happened.

He turned to look out of the window and thought of Bain looking out down the driveway too, talking angrily about Wadi

Akarit. The anger had masked something else, as it usually did. Guilt? Shame? He'd felt a hot spot within himself as he'd listened, and he'd struggled to keep the focus on his patient. Reflecting on that now, he realised that he'd tapped into his own anger about Barnwood and McKissock. It had been rumbling around inside him since his conversation with Hunter. Like Bain, there'd been guilt there too.

He swivelled back to the desk and shook his head ruefully. Patients come along who do as much for you as you do for them – more, sometimes. He could imagine the sly half-smile on Bain's face if he knew that was what he'd done.

It was obvious he wanted to be released from the army, wanted his ticket out. Many men here did. And he'd already gone a long way in building a new life for himself. The trick was to get him out without him having to serve the rest of his suspended sentence. If he could keep his head down during his time here, Daniel could arrange for a Medical Board. It would be a formality; the army wouldn't want to hang on to the likes of Bain, and since the amnesty for deserters last year, they were even less interested him. They'd only sent him here to save face. They'd hear his case, Daniel would support it. He'd be discharged.

He felt a certain relief as he finalised his notes. Although his experience told him that Bain would have emotional problems further down the line, the last place for him at this point in his life was Northfield. Getting back to what he'd already started, that was what he needed. Getting back to becoming human.

A sudden need took him over to fill his head with something other than patients, past or present, to clear out all his toxic thoughts about Sargant and McKissock, if only for a moment. He went over to the gramophone on top of the chest of drawers. There were two neat stacks of records nearby on the floor. The first was mainly classical, some of them early recordings of the Brandenburgs. Foulkes had given them to him – *When the angels in heaven have receptions to organise, Daniel, Bach is what they play.*

But today, it had to be something from the other pile. He spotted the red and gold Decca label and slid the record out of its sleeve. He held it by its edge with the pads of his fingers, then tilted it, checking for scratches, the light glinting off the finely ribbed black shellac.

He'd been a reluctant convert to jazz. But Ian, his brother, had worked on him. 'Think of it like this,' he'd said to Daniel once, in that earnest way he had when he was talking about something he was passionate about, which was everything – music, politics, his latest relationship – 'in jazz, the theme you play at the beginning is the territory – what you play after is the adventure.' That was Ian all over, seeing music as an adventure.

There were just the two of them since their father had died in 1939. Daniel was older by eight years, but his brother often made him feel ancient, and he was conscious of acting the father with him at times. Ian said as much when he'd given him the record for his birthday. 'You're getting positively avuncular,' he'd teased him. 'Try this, it'll take years off you.'

He was right, Daniel thought, wiping the record lightly with a cloth. It wasn't so much that the years faded away; it was more that when you gave yourself up to the music, you fell into a space where time didn't matter, where you didn't matter, only the music. He placed the record on the green baize turntable, positioning the needle arm with great care. He waited, counting down to the intro. 'Sweet Georgia Brown' set off, Django pulsing straight in.

Immediately, Daniel felt his mood lift. He always found it impossible not to get caught up in the beat, he had to chug out loud with it – 'chug-chugga-chug-chugga-chug-chugga-chug,' following the rhythm, the power, the certainty of la pompe pounding out, then the glorious unpredictability of Django surging through, juggling notes, making the guitar sing. Those chords, those impossible jags and stops and ripples climbing up from the fretboard to the headstock, lightning quick, then shimmying down again, those

74

shivering *b-r-r-r-rs*, the pings of the high notes like the chink of good crystal glass. The sense that just when you thought you knew what Django might do next, he somehow managed to do something completely different, time and time again. Then Stephane Grappelli coming in, going wild, and Django shouting, 'One more Steph, one more!' then 'Yeah!' towards the end.

Daniel put the record on again, moving away from the player in case he made the record jump. He stomped the floor in his stockinged feet, like an Indian chief lost in a ritual dance, shaking his head from side to side, joining in with Django and shouting at the top of his voice, 'One more Steph, one more, yeah!' Then the end. Silence outside his head, and a wonderful thrumming inside, the final chord bouncing off the insides of the bones of his skull and fading slowly away like a struck tuning fork.

He moved over to the bed, sweat on his eyelids, prickling behind his ears, trickling down the back of his neck. He rested back on the pillow, enjoying a rare moment of simple pleasure. Maybe Foulkes was right. Bach might be what the angels played on important occasions in heaven. But surely, Django was what they played when they were off duty.

Freddie's come back to the open ward with us, he's been back a week, after a long stint in the Acute Ward. He's one of Dr Hunter's patients, so he's been getting special attention.

'The Doc says I'm a bit of an experiment,' he says. 'He wants to see how I get on.'

He does a little woodwork – a small bookcase for the wife is taking shape. We're all supposed to sign up to groups. I drift in and out of the Art Hut. I haven't done any painting yet but it has an energy I haven't found anywhere else in the hospital. Men are busy painting or drawing or just watching. Music plays in the background. The men take it in turn to choose the records. It's almost civilised.

I've no idea how John occupies his time. We've not been in the junk room since he went to see Dr Carter two weeks ago. He'd come back to the day room after the session and I took one look at him and realised we were in for a monsoon or two so I kept quiet. I thought he'd open up when he was ready. But he's been closed down, at least with me. It's hard to fathom. I wonder if it's because he thinks he's let slip too many secrets. Like people do on a train journey, sharing personal details in the general conversation, and then when they get to where they're going, it's as if they've never spoken to each other and they wish they hadn't.

When Freddie first reappeared, John took him under his wing. He doesn't fuss, doesn't mollycoddle him, just makes sure he's settled and gets to meal times and his woodwork classes. We're left to our own devices in the afternoons. Freddie spends all his time sitting in the corner of the day room. The open ward isn't much different from Charles Ward except there are no locks. Same dreary dorm. Same mind-numbing routine. John usually appears about four o'clock. I fetch the tea for the three of us from the hatch and claim my corner seat alongside them. John and Freddie play dominoes, like two regulars in some nicotine-stained corner of their local.

Since his treatment, Freddie has been more able to look after himself. He doesn't remember that once he had to be told to wipe his backside when he went to the lavatory.

At least we don't think he remembers. It's no bad thing if he doesn't.

He's begun to talk at last. Mostly about his family, his wife, his son and daughter. 'Little smasher, my Avril,' he says, showing us a photo. A curly-haired child, about nine or ten, in a white dress, sits on a rug in a park squinting into the sun for the photograph.

'Lovely,' says John. 'How old is she, Freddie?'

Freddie looks at the photo. 'She's . . . she was born . . .' and he trails off. He's not good on dates. Perhaps he never was. It's hard to say, because he never spoke before his treatment.

Then today, out of the blue, he says, 'I can't remember things since he put me to sleep.'

John looks at me, then looks at Freddie. 'Who put you to sleep, Freddie?'

'Dr Hunter. He said it was like first aid for my mind – he would put me under, for a long, deep sleep, then they could start to treat me properly. I said anything that would help me not feel so bloody terrible was alright by me.' He manages a small smile. 'Jungle juice. That's what they gave me. I don't know what it was but it knocked me out for two weeks.'

'Two weeks?' John sounds gentle, but incredulous.

'Funny old time,' says Freddie. 'They told me I was supposed to be asleep for twenty hours a day for two weeks. They wake you up to feed you, then you go back to sleep again. You sort of wake up, but you don't – it's like seeing everything through a veil. I think I remember them feeding me from one of those long spouted mug things.' He nods his head slowly. 'Funny old time, alright. When I did come round properly, I was in this darkened room, lying on this mattress. No sheets or blankets or anything. I . . . I didn't have any pyjama bottoms on.' His pale face blushes. 'They said it was better for them if you were like that, because when you were under, you couldn't stop yourself going to the toilet then and there.'

He shrugged. 'A bit embarrassing, that.'

'Was that it, then, Freddie?' John frowns. 'Was that all they did, let you sleep for a fortnight?'

'There were quite a few of us, all lying there on our mattresses. We didn't look at each other, didn't talk. The nurses called us the Sleeping Beauties. Then they took us to another ward and cleaned us up. Gave us a blanket bath and a shave.'

He looks vague. 'It must have worked, though, the deep sleep thing. I felt calm, more relaxed – better than I'd been when I first came in here.'

'I thought you had electric shock treatment?' John hesitates, as if he doesn't really want to remind Freddie of what he went through.

'I did,' says Freddie. 'I was OK at first, after I woke up, then I dipped down again. Had a bit of a relapse.' He shakes his head. 'So Dr Hunter said they'd try ECT.' He pauses, then says, slowly, enunciating each word with care: '"Electro-convulsion therapy" – that's its proper name. A right mouthful. The Doc says to me, "Your mind's in a bad state, Corporal, where everything feels too much for you. And it feels like you'll never find your way out." He got that right, that's just how it felt. "This will help," he says, "a bit of ECT will help to sort things out." So that's what I had.'

He sits there, docile.

'What was it like, the ECT, Freddie?' John asks, keeping his voice even.

Freddie places his fingertips on his temples. 'They get you to lie down on this padded couch and give you an injection to calm you down. Then they put a sort of a green jacket on you, with straps hanging off it, and you have to cross your arms and they strap you down because they say you might thrash around and hurt yourself.'

He massages his temples with his thumbs. 'Someone holds your head down so you don't bang it. And they put a rubber gag in your mouth, so you don't bite your tongue. Then they put wires on your head, and they press a switch. It jolts all the bad thoughts out.'

He nods at us. 'Gets rid of all the bad memories. I felt much better after I'd had it.' He drops his voice. 'I know I shouldn't say this, but before, when I first came here, I sometimes wished I was dead. But now, after the treatment, things don't bother me so much. It's the electricity. It's the electricity that cures you.' He frowns. 'I might have to go in for a top-up if I dip down again. Maintenance fits, they call them. Dr Hunter says it will keep me normal.'

I'm left wondering what it feels like to have electricity passed through your brain.

Freddie seems to drift off somewhere in his head. Then he says, 'My brother was here.'

'I didn't see you with him, Freddie.' I think he means here for Saturday visiting.

But he's oblivious to both of us. 'They brought him here . . . January, 1945,' he says, searching for the date and finding it this time. 'He was a tank commander, like me, our Alan. He didn't want me to go in for tanks, but I had no choice, I was selected. "Make sure you make it to tank commander," he said, as if I had a choice about that too, silly bugger. But if you're a commander, see, you have time to get out.'

It's like he's speaking to someone across the table we can't see. I open my mouth to say something that might take his mind off what he's saying, but John shakes his head. *Let him talk*, he mouths.

He sits straight in his chair and speaks quietly but clearly, as if he's giving a training lecture. 'When you get hit, the shell hits the metal of the tank and blows it inwards. White-hot metal, it is. People think it's the shell exploding in the tank that does the damage, but it's not. It's the white-hot metal hitting the ammunition inside the tank.' His hands make an exploding firework gesture. 'Then a great big flash goes off in that small space.'

He's very calm. He even takes a sip of his tea. 'Because you're the commander, standing near the hatch, you have more time to get out. The others don't. You see them burn. You smell them burn. And you leave them to it. You hear them scream as you scrabble out. We're like family in that tank, all looking out for each other. But you leave them to it.'

He sits there, head down, fingering a puddle of tea on the dirty table top, drawing it out into a muddy river. Then he says – slowly, matter-of-factly – 'They give you another tank. And another crew. After a bit, they're not your family any more. They're just another crew.'

I look across the room to another tall-framed window with a petalled top and vertical bars. A guffaw of laughter comes from one of the groups sitting at the card table under it.

'So your brother was here, Freddie?' I could kick myself, the way it sounds, as if I'm making polite conversation – *well, well, there's a funny coincidence, the two of you both end up here, and brothers too, Freddie, isn't life strange?*

My insensitivity makes me feel sick. Or maybe it's Freddie talking about burning bodies. I know that smell. I remember that smell.

'When he got here,' says Freddie – still matter-of-fact, though I notice there's a disconnectedness about him, as if the voice doesn't belong to the body – 'they put him in a darkened room for three days, with one hour of daylight and one hour of electric light, and fed him on just bread and water. One of the psychiatrists said it would be good for him. He said it was a special treatment for tank commanders. He said our Alan had to mourn for the lads in the tanks and that he had to cry. He said he was numb with grief and felt guilty about leaving the lads and this was a way of letting it out. Once he'd done that, he'd be ready to go back.'

I don't get what he's saying at first. Here? Does he mean Northfield?

John's face mottles red. 'You mean they did that to your brother here, Freddie? In this hospital, you mean? The trick cyclists did it?'

Freddie nods. 'My brother told me to watch out for Dr Main; it was his treatment. "Kick up a stink," our Alan said, "tell them you'll try anything, but not 'compulsory mourning' – that's what they call it, Freddie, you steer clear of it." But Dr Main's not here any more. The sister told me. So that's alright. Our Alan will be pleased.'

He stands up. 'Anyone want another cuppa?'

We shake our heads and he sets off for the hatch. But he doesn't get there. He gets to the middle of the room and he stops dead and stares at a spot on the end wall. He stares like he did the first day we saw him in Charles Ward. John catches on that something's wrong and gets up to go to him but Freddie deviates off track and heads for the door.

His soft plimsolls patter down the corridor like a dog on a purposeful mission. John goes after him and I follow. Freddie doesn't get far, the length of the corridor must have bewildered him. He slows then stops, turns to the wall and sinks to his knees, his palms flat against the wall surface, so they squeak on the way down.

John reaches him first, then me, and we get him to sit down with his back against the wall. We sit either side of him, keeping him upright. He moans, then sobs, wiping his nose on the back of his hand. John goes for help and I stay with Freddie. He huddles next to me, sniffling.

Mary, the sister from Dr Hunter's ward, comes back with John and a muscular orderly. Freddie shows no resistance as the orderly helps him up. The last I see of him, he's shuffling down the corridor with the orderly, towards the vanishing point.

'Poor lamb.' Mary looks after them as they walk away.

'Where's he taking him?' John asks her.

'Back to Dr Hunter. He's a specialist for the kind of treatment Freddie needs.' She looks at John's stricken face. 'Don't worry, he's in good hands.'

'I hope they're not going to put him through bloody compulsory mourning,' he says.

She looks surprised. 'Fancy you knowing about that! No, that was just an experiment of Dr Main's. He stopped it after a while when he didn't get the results he was expecting. He's long gone. He was a good doctor, though. He respected the tank crews, thought they were the salt of the earth.'

John spits the words out. 'That's all we are to these doctors – bloody guinea pigs.'

'They know what they're doing,' she says, looking flustered, as though she isn't used to hearing the doctors being criticised and doesn't know how to respond. 'They've been doing it for a long time.'

He opens his mouth to reply but I grab him by the arm. 'Let's get some fresh air.'

I nod at Mary and she nods back and carries on past us to the day room.

I lead John away, touching him cautiously on the shoulder. He feels like a teak sculpture, the tension in him. Outside, we both stand still next to the door at the back of the hospital. It's another warm day, but it's overcast and the air presses in on us. John is still breathing heavily.

'Come on.' I set off walking slowly along a rough track, not touching him again, not pushing my luck. 'We'll head across to the oaks.'

The track is part of the short cut to the village pub Chalky showed John on the first day here. It leads past the walled rose garden and on past the Art Hut, then through a field with three large oaks in it, finally ending up at the hospital boundary stone wall. Up and over, and the Crown is a hundred yards down the road. To beat the curfew at nine thirty, the late route home is back over the wall and in through the kitchen window. The hospital is closed up by then, but you could get someone to let you in, as long as you gave them a time and you kept to it. Sometimes they'd climb in your bed and take your place if there was a bed check, then scuttle back to their own beds in different wards to get checked all over again.

The night duty officers knew about it and played along, most of the time. But one or two of them used to hide, then jump out and nab the latecomers, give them a talking to for breaking curfew, and send them off with a caution. It was all a bit like *Tom and Jerry*. A few latecomers got caught, though, and just for appearances, had their leave passes confiscated.

Under the third oak along in the field there's one of those benches that encircles the tree trunk and John and I often sit there after a junk room session to cool off. That's where I think we're heading, but we only get as far as the Art Hut, and John suddenly stops. The door to the Hut is open. Music drifts from it, a wistful clarinet, leading a delicate melody through a slow movement over muted strings.

There's another small bench under a copper beech at the side of the Hut and John heads for it, me trotting after him like some obedient spaniel. He sits down and leans back, his eyes closed. I sit down next to him, keeping a space between us. I can sense the tension in his body slowly drain away. The music comes to a gentle halt.

His eyes are still closed but a tear escapes down his cheek.

I keep quiet.

He opens his eyes and turns to me. 'Mozart's Clarinet Quintet.' I've never seen his face so soft. He's looking at me, but he's seeing someone else.

'My brother bought it. We'd listen to it when the old man was well out of the way.'

A shadow flits across his face and he stands up. 'I need a drink.' He sets off towards the oaks and the short cut to the pub. I follow him, but he turns and says, 'Sorry, my old lad. Not this time. I need to do some thinking on my own.'

I watch him until he vanishes behind the last oak, then I head back to the hospital, thinking about this mercurial man I've latched on to. You never know where you are with him, what he's going to do next, what pleases him, what infuriates him. A man who's reduced to tears by a piece of music, who's soft and tender with Freddie, who's likely to throw a punch at anyone. Me included, come to think of it, and I'm the closest thing he's got to a friend in here. Or I thought I was. It hits me then. There are no friends in here. It might be crowded, but you're on your own. There's no point getting close to anyone because they leave you behind. Or you leave them. It's all the same. You end up on your own.

12

He got back from his late duty and flopped down fully clothed on his bed. He knew he should get changed, go for a walk in the hospital grounds, anything to wash off the coalface, but he was too physically exhausted. His mind flitted back and forth from patients he'd seen on the wards, to his session with Bain, his memories of Spence, the conversation with Hunter and then inevitably to McKissock and the leucotomy. His head was full of secrets. That's what this job was about, holding secrets, your own and everyone else's. He closed his eyes, trying to let the day go. His thoughts gradually began to lose their shape, become less focused.

We know so little about the brain, Daniel. His father's voice came from nowhere.

The two of them in the study at home, examining a plaster model of a skull. His father, so pleased that Daniel, only twelve then, was already showing interest in following him into medicine. Daniel cupping his hands round the cranium, and his father running his finger along the coronal suture, saying: *Amazing piece of design, the human skull. Simple yet functional. It's fragile – it doesn't take much to shatter it – but the miracle is, it's strong enough to last most people a lifetime, keeping the brain safe without mishap.*

Then McKissock took over, drowning his father out. *Good morning, gentlemen. I'm here to acquaint you with the surgical procedure of leucotomy.*

Daniel lay there, too tired to fight the Barnwood memories.

*

He was one of six invited observers, all with white coats over their suits, standing in the corner of a small operating room usually allocated to minor procedures. The room was almost bare. A large theatre light hung in the centre of the ceiling, casting a brilliant white circle on the floor. A man was standing half in shadow at the edge of the circle checking instruments on a trolley. Dr Fleming, the Hospital Superintendent, had introduced him as Dr Mason, McKissock's assistant.

McKissock himself cut an extraordinary figure. He was dressed head to foot in white – white trousers and wrap-around shirt, in the style favoured by American surgeons, not fastened with ties in the ordinary way but with long strips of white tape. There was a leonine quality to the way he loped up and down in front of the group, marking the territory out as his own with every stride.

'I'm not going to give a lecture,' he said. 'I would much rather perform the surgery and explain what I'm doing as I do it.'

There were some appreciative nods in anticipation of the demonstration to come.

'One important thing, gentlemen,' McKissock continued. 'I insist on absolute silence while I work. No comments, no questions, please.'

He arced round the group. 'I'm assuming you're familiar with the basic procedure, in theory at least. Just to refresh your memories, the object is to sever the fibres connecting the frontal lobes to the thalamus. To gain access to this white matter, we drill burr holes through the skull.'

He paused, then said, slowly and deliberately, 'I must emphasise, however, that a key consideration of the procedure is to destroy the minimum of brain tissue possible to produce the desired clinical result.'

He swept around the group again. 'As you can appreciate, the operation is blind; we can't see exactly where we're going, although we know the architecture of the brain and can feel our way.' He turned to Mason and nodded. 'Bearing all that in mind, before we begin, I'd like to show you various instruments for the procedure, used by some of our colleagues.'

Mason reached down to the second shelf of the trolley and brought out a steel syringe-like tube and handed it to McKissock.

It was well rehearsed, this demonstration, Daniel thought.

'For example, our American friends use a "leucotome" similar to this.'

Daniel picked up a tone of disdain in McKissock's voice as he mentioned the Americans. He wondered if it was symptomatic of the frustration felt by many towards America because of their reluctance to enter the war, or merely professional chagrin that Freeman and Watts were so far ahead of their British counterparts. Probably a bit of both, he decided.

McKissock held the instrument up for them to see. 'You insert it, then release the loop mechanism' – he pressed one end with his thumb, and a thin wire loop appeared at the other end – 'which then engages with the brain tissue and slices a core out of it.' He retracted the wire into the shaft and handed it to Mason who put it back out of sight.

He breezed on. 'I believe Mr Willway, here at Barnwood, uses this.' Mason passed him another steel implement, this time flat and tapered. 'It is, in fact, a stiletto paper knife.' McKissock raised one contemptuous eyebrow as he held the knife up by its hilt, then returned it to Mason.

'And another of your colleagues, not with us today, has also developed this.' McKissock took from Mason a clumsy-looking contraption, similar in design to the leucotome, but with a blade fixed on one end. With a flick of his finger, he showed how the blade rotated.

'As you can see, it rather resembles a mechanical egg whisk.' He paused for a moment, then handed it back to Mason, saying, in a scathing tone: 'I consider the leucotome barbarous. In fact, all of these devices are problematic. They encourage a lack of control, and more importantly, a lack of precision.'

Physicians don't criticise other physicians, and there was a buzz of surprise at his directness. Fleming looked decidedly uncomfortable and examined his shoes.

McKissock seemed oblivious to the reaction and held out his hand to Mason, who placed a slim needle-like instrument in it, about nine centimetres long.

'However,' McKissock said, holding it up between two index fingers, 'I find this simple brain needle here does the least damage and is the most controllable. As you can see, it has a side eyelet just short of its blunt point, and a close-fitting stilette.'

He showed the needle round, then passed it back to Mason. 'One other key factor,' he said, looking directly out at the group: 'it is not a time-consuming operation – it can be done under local anaesthetic, as I'll demonstrate this morning with our first two cases.'

My God, thought Daniel. Local anaesthetic. For brain surgery.

McKissock continued: 'The whole procedure could take as little as six minutes – I have managed this myself – and it should seldom take more than ten.'

There was another collective hum of surprise at this.

McKissock quietened them with a look. 'I must stress, however – the operation is dangerous and should be carried out only by properly trained neurosurgeons.'

Fleming took to examining his shoes again.

'The aftercare of the patient is also paramount,' McKissock said. 'Close observation and detailed nursing care are both crucial.'

There were nods all round the group at this and murmurs of agreement.

He has the group in the palm of his hand, thought Daniel.

'I believe our first patient is now ready?' McKissock addressed himself to Fleming, who signalled across the room to an orderly standing just inside the door. He nodded through the window and another orderly wheeled in the patient, a woman, on an operating table.

The men positioned the table under the light, locked the wheels then made their way out.

The two surgeons took up their positions, McKissock on the woman's right side, nearest the group, Mason at the top of her head. The group shuffled closer, so that they were in a semi-circle on McKissock's side of the bed. Daniel found himself standing nearest to McKissock and roughly in line with the woman's eyes.

She was awake, although her movements were sluggish and she was restricted by straps holding down her arms and legs and also by thinner restraints at her wrists. Her head was shaved and held steady in a metal rest.

'Our first case of the day, gentlemen.' McKissock stroked the woman's shoulder soothingly. 'Housewife. Aged fifty. Melancholia. I believe she was a little resistant to the idea of the operation, so she's been given mild electro-convulsion therapy to calm her down.'

While he was speaking to the group, Mason cleaned the exposed scalp, then daubed gentian violet over both sides of her skull around the temple area.

Daniel found himself distracted by the woman's feet under the green sheet covering her lower body, the tips of the toes rippling like caterpillars on a leaf. As he watched, both feet jerked, the uneven row of green bumps disappearing as the feet flexed forward and went rigid. He glanced back up at the woman's face. Mason had just administered shots of local anaesthetic into her shaved head.

They all waited in silence while the anaesthetic took effect. The woman's eyes stayed open, the lids blinking slowly from time to time. Mason and McKissock checked through the instruments, not speaking, moving in easy rhythm, looking comfortable with each other.

McKissock turned to the woman and traced a line with his finger, about three centimetres inwards from the top edge of her eye socket and then upwards by about six centimetres. He tapped the centre of the gentian violet stain. 'I'll make an initial incision here . . . two to three centimetres in diameter, down to the bone.'

He took the scalpel Mason offered him and began to work on the shaved area. As he cut through to the bone, the woman made little waving gestures with her hands, bending them back as far as the restraints at her wrists would allow, each finger waving in the air like a baby exploring the world in front of it. He passed the scalpel back to Mason who placed it in a kidney dish and handed him a retractor.

'Now, I'll insert this to allow a wide exposure and a bloodless field.' McKissock seemed to have forgotten about the group. It was as if he were talking to himself.

He finished inserting the retractor and held out his hand. 'And now, I'll drill a one centimetre burr hole in the line of the coronal suture.' Mason handed him a small hand drill.

The burr hole was drilled in a few seconds.

The woman's eyes flickered open, then swivelled to the right slowly, in the direction of the drilling. Daniel had to remind himself she wouldn't be feeling pain; it would be the noise of the drilling that would be agitating her. He wanted to look anywhere but at her, but he was transfixed. The eyes were wide open now and full of terror. It seemed to him she had picked him out from the group and was staring straight at him. He was horrified and fascinated at the same time. But he forced himself to break away from her gaze and focus again on McKissock.

Mason passed across another scalpel. McKissock took it without looking. 'I'm now going to make a cruciform incision in the dura.' He made two firm strokes, one vertical, one horizontal, as he worked in the burr hole to cut through the membrane that lay between the skull and the brain. Mason took the scalpel from McKissock, set it next to the other one in the kidney dish, and placed the brain needle in McKissock's open palm.

'I'll introduce the needle, now, and position it on a certain line and to a certain depth, to access the targeted white matter of the frontal lobes.' He stopped talking and concentrated on manoeuvring the needle.

The whole of Daniel's body tensed. It was as if he were bracing himself for the intrusion of the needle into his own brain.

McKissock's strong, delicate fingers were sure and deft, inserting the needle into the burr hole with great care. The woman closed her eyes again, her hands and feet flexing then tensing, each movement weaker than the last, her will to resist ebbing away. There was a profound silence in the room, as though everyone had collectively breathed in, punctuated only by a soft pop-popping sound of air forced through the woman's tightly closed lips as she breathed out.

Daniel felt a kind of starburst explosion inside his head as he watched – he knew it was fanciful, but it felt like countless pinpoints of sharp sensations, as if he'd received a sudden shock. It *was* shock, he realised – he'd seen countless operations in his own medical training, ranging from minor procedures to several operations on brain tumours, but his own brain couldn't process what he was seeing now.

McKissock broke the silence. 'I'm withdrawing the needle' – he slipped it out as far as the entrance point, and then pivoted it upwards – 'and now I can push it . . . more deeply into the brain.' He fell into silence again while he worked, then nodded. 'I sense it has reached sufficiently close to the upper surface . . . so I'll withdraw it . . . and then reintroduce it along the original line, in order to deal with those fibres running from the lower part.'

He withdrew the needle, again back to the entrance point, then reintroduced it. 'During this final part . . . I withdraw it very carefully . . . for fear of damaging the grey matter . . .'

He spoke with some hesitancy, again concentrating hard on what he was doing, withdrawing the needle slowly. The woman was perfectly quiet now, hands and feet motionless under the green cotton. Her eyes were open, but half lidded. McKissock withdrew the needle and handed it back to Mason. It landed with a clattering metallic ring into another kidney dish.

Daniel stared at the white-ish brain matter clinging to the haft and clogging up the eye of the needle. Can it really be as easy as that – to scrape out someone's depression, their melancholy, their anxiety? To scrape out someone's emotions?

McKissock patted the woman's shoulder and said softly, 'Nearly done.'

He moved around to the left side of the woman and began the procedure again. He didn't talk this time, focusing all his attention on cutting, drilling, extracting brain tissue, the movements so precise, like a musician fingering a delicate part of the score. When he finished, he nodded to Mason who began dressing the burr holes with wet gauze pads.

'There we are. All done, my dear,' said McKissock, as Mason began to sew up the wounds with black silk sutures.

There was a collective sigh from the group as though everyone had suddenly remembered how to breathe again. They'd all been caught up in the action, mesmerised by what they were seeing. They'd lost all sense of time. Watching McKissock operate gave no impression of haste. When he'd stopped and spoken to the woman, Daniel checked his watch. From the time Mason had handed him the first scalpel, it had taken McKissock ten minutes to perform the surgery.

'A half-hour break, I think,' McKissock said, looking at Fleming.

'There's tea out on the terrace, gentlemen, if you'd like to follow me,' Fleming said and he ushered them out. The group was silent as they made their way to the library. McKissock, Mason and Fleming went in the opposite direction, to the committee room, to take their tea in private. McKissock was regaling them with the antics of a pair of long-tailed tits that had taken up summer residence in the fork of a tree at the bottom of his garden.

The French windows overlooking the well-groomed lawns were open. Daniel made his way out to the terrace and leaned against the stone balustrade. His whole body felt like it was at the crisis point of a fever, his skin paper thin, as if it would hurt if someone touched it.

All of his senses were heightened. The grass seemed an impossible green; the garrulous call of a far-off crow seemed up close and deafening. As he rubbed his finger along the balustrade top, he thought he could smell and taste the dust he disturbed, that he could feel the grittiness irritating his throat.

It was hard to process what he'd just seen. He should be able to be rational about it, but he couldn't. The brain needle in the kidney dish swam into his head, the sharp sound of it rattling against metal, clogged up with healthy brain tissue.

'Interesting morning.'

Daniel turned to find Jessop, the colleague who'd invited him to Barnwood, offering him tea.

'Indeed.' Daniel shook his head, and Jessop put the cup down on the balustrade.

'He's every bit as skilled as they say he is. And quick with it.' Jessop sounded cautious.

'Very deft.' He was all those things, Daniel thought. Skilled and quick and deft. That's what made it so confusing – to see a brilliant surgeon who you couldn't help but admire, then realise what he was using all those talents for. 'But it's healthy tissue. And the procedure is irreversible. That's the problem.' He realised he'd spoken this last thought out loud.

'You mean the *first, do no harm* thing?' Jessop said, and nodded his head slightly. Daniel was surprised; it sounded as if Jessop had his doubts too.

'Yes, the *first, do no harm* thing.'

'The question is, is it better to damage the brain a little and relieve the patient's suffering, or do nothing?' said Jessop.

Is that the question? thought Daniel. But he was suddenly weary, unable to think. He needed time to sort out his own arguments and counter arguments.

Fleming appeared at the doorway. It was time to go back for

the second patient. The observers were expected to stay for lunch but Daniel made his excuses and left.

He'd had to stop the car on the way back home. He got out and took in great gulps of air and blasted them out again, trying to blow it all away.

He lay there, trying to get his father's voice back. He needed the steadying words, the gentleness. But the voice had gone and he was left feeling bereft. He knew the onset of war had forced his grief to one side. His usual memories were quiet ones of the three of them doing things together, his father, Ian and himself. Like watching the Ashes and marvelling at Donald Bradman, or going out for a celebration meal when Daniel got to Medical School.

But this childhood memory he was left with now, of the skull in the study, was so vivid. So direct. Its connections with the earlier conversation with Hunter about McKissock were obvious. But there was more to it than simple interpretations of what doctors should or should not do to the brain. The memory of his father had taken him back to a time that seemed safe. Innocent. The memory of observing McKissock perform the leucotomy had left him with a tangle of unsettling feelings he couldn't quite identify. Unfinished business.

He decided then that he'd go to Sargant's lecture. Not to hear Sargant – if he really wanted to be irritated again by the man's self-importance, he could grit his teeth and re-read his book. But McKissock? He was a different proposition altogether. Daniel needed to face McKissock again, although he wasn't sure why.

What was it Reece had said about being ambushed? And what had been his answer? Face the memories. Ask yourself why they're so important. Cut them down to size.

Physician, heal thyself. Another commandment. If his patients ever started to talk in commandments or imperatives, he'd be wondering about their anxiety over losing control.

13

Another five thirty wake-up in sweat-soaked sheets. I can hear the spatter of rain on glass.

I need to get up and get away from snuffling bodies and the rank odour of the dorm.

I put my clothes on over my pyjamas and creep past John's empty bed. He's been AWOL three days so far since Freddie was carted off. I make my way to the outside door near the kitchens, picking up one of the old army capes left on the pegs there on my way out. The rubbery smell of it reminds me of slogging through the sucking mud of jungle tracks, head down, my cape weighing a ton from the monsoons. I step outside and this rain is soft and light and I lift my face up to it.

I'm not sure where to go. Someone has left an old metal chair outside the door so I decide to sit and watch the house martins. They're already on the hunt for insects to feed their new brood. Acrobatic as Spitfires, beeping and burbling, they hurtle in and out of the eaves and I feel my mood lift as I lose myself following their flight.

The kitchens are being extended and a trench has been dug for drainage. My memory reaches back again, to Louie and me, under a tarpaulin stretched between a triangle of jungle trees, and rigged just high enough off the ground to let the hot, damp air through. It's calming to think of him, so I stay there with him, hearing his voice. We've been stuck there for days, not moving, waiting for orders, the rains belting down. Louie passes the time telling me how to build a house, as enthusiastic as if he were there on the site back in Manchester with his men from Mayo. 'They're the best. Strong. Hard workers. Decent lads.'

Whether I want to listen to it or not, he builds the house brick by brick under that bloody tarpaulin. 'It's the most difficult part,' he says, launching into a description of something he calls 'bottoming off', knifing his hand through the air at a slight angle. 'You have to finish off the bottom of the trench so the pipes lie at the correct gradient when you connect them to the main sewer.' I would doze off at times but he never noticed.

We all hung on to the minutiae of the lives we'd left behind, the family routines, the day-in, day-out work. It was a way of keeping home alive. It got Louie through, remembering the men he'd worked with, the digging and the building – 'it's doing something constructive, not destroying things, like we're doing here,' he said.

He didn't see himself as a brickie; he was a builder. 'There's nothing I like better,' he'd say, 'than to take an empty space and see a well-made, well-shaped building rise up in it, something you can reach out and touch and say, "I built that, and I'm bloody proud of it."' When we finally emerged from under the tarpaulin, ready for yet another big push, I said to him, 'I could probably build a bloody house myself, now, after this.'

I wonder what he'd think of this trench. Not much, I shouldn't think. There doesn't seem to me to be anything remotely like a slight angle. Most of the men here join up for some detail or another to pass the time – gardening, general maintenance, or a bit of building work, then sink back into lethargy and fall away.

An image comes to me. Louie looking into the trench, shaking his head. And I wish it was real. I wish he was here to talk to. He sent me a letter a few weeks ago postmarked London. It's the first I'd heard from him since I arrived, but then I hadn't written to him. I haven't written back yet. Haven't written to anyone, not even Beth. Writing to those outside is too painful.

'It's all worked out OK,' he wrote. 'It's like a new lease of life down here. New job. New start. You get yourself right. Do the same.'

Same old Louie. Ever the optimist.

Cheery whistling and the clatter of pans from the kitchens remind me where I am and signal it'll soon be breakfast time. I have the rest of the day to get through. Including a session with Dr Carter. I need to do what John said. Keep schtum.

I go back inside to the morning racket of men on the move – doors banging and disembodied shouting echoing along the corridors. I take the cape off and shiver. It's like shedding a carapace. I feel exposed. Isolated.

'I beat up a young boy.'

Five minutes with Carter and I'm leaking memories all over the place. All he'd had to say was 'How have things been?' and I was off.

'I beat up a young boy. Back in Manchester. I smashed his face in and left him. He was nothing but a little runt – a young spiv called Vinny who thought he was James Cagney.'

Carter waits.

'I dreamt about it last night.'

He waits again then says, 'Is that the incident the doctor was referring to in the notes?'

'Yes.'

'Tell me a bit more about it.'

'There's not much more to tell. I was in a pub with a friend of mine. The young spiv insulted him – well, he insulted both of us. So I waited outside in the dark on the corner, and I went after him when he came out and I beat him up. Beat him to within an inch of his life by the look of him.'

Not just with my fists. Kicked his face in, I want to say, but don't. I stare back at Carter, wondering if the shame shows on my face.

He leans his elbows on the desk and steeples his hands, resting his chin on the tips of his two forefingers. I remember him doing this last time, when he seemed to be thinking through what I'd said, almost like he was testing it out, testing out the truthfulness of it.

'I've never done anything like that before. Beat someone up, I mean. And he was a total stranger. I'd only spoken half a dozen words to him.'

'What did it feel like as you were doing it?'

'Good,' I say. 'It felt good.'

'And afterwards? Did it still feel good when you remembered it?'

'No.'

'What did it feel like?'

'I felt ashamed. He was only a boy. And I couldn't stop thinking about what I'd done.'

'Do you think it has any connection to your breakdown?'

'Maybe. But I'd been having dreams or nightmares before that. About Burma. Like I said last time, I'd be ambushed by bits of memory. Then I started to dream about Vinny.'

He sits back in his chair. 'But you would have seen lots more violence as a soldier? I don't just mean the violence of war, I mean the violence that goes on among soldiers themselves. The way they tend to settle petty arguments with their fists. It happens in here sometimes – you must have seen it among the men.'

'There's a difference seeing others do it. You think you're not like them, but you are.'

'It's upsetting, yes, to find out some of the things we're all capable of.'

He waits.

I stay silent. *We're all capable of.* Is he doing that *I'm on your side* thing John was so scathing about?

'Perhaps you can tell me more about the dream last night.'

'It's not a dream exactly. Vinny just comes back to me. His face does.'

It's always along with the Japanese boy's face, I want to say. But I stay schtum.

John would be proud of me.

He nods again. 'It might be worth trying to note it down.

Details like when you dream it, what happens in it, how you feel when you wake up. Like we talked about.'

Here we go again with his 'catch them, write them down, control them' game. But I nod, as if I'm giving it due consideration.

'It's surprising how the memory works. The layers of it – you disturb one layer, only to find another underneath. And it's the one underneath that's the really significant one. The incident with Vinny – it may well be linked to something else. Something your mind thinks is best kept hidden.'

His voice is measured, neutral, his look thoughtful. He knows I'm holding something back.

'Yes,' I say, 'I'll try that. I'll try writing it down.'

The dormitory is deserted. I sit on the bed, staring at the far wall like Freddie on that first day. After my stint with Carter, my head is beginning to feel like it did back in Manchester. I don't want to remember. I don't want to think.

The package George gave me is on the locker shelf, still wrapped. *Something to keep you company.* I tear the paper off. Art books. Two of them. Paperbacks. Henry Moore and Paul Nash. *Penguin Modern Painters.* 2s 6d each. Bringing art to the people – typical George.

The books are beautiful in their own right – slim, thirty pages at most, with understated covers banded in subtle tones of cream and bleached sand. Kenneth Clark from the National Gallery has edited them. His influence probably explains the good quality plates of paintings and drawings, some in colour. The penguin on the front is dancing a jig. I choke up, thinking of George.

I select the Moore, flip it from the back, run my fingers over the silky pages. I'd forgotten how sensuous paper could feel after years of wartime flimsy.

Tube Shelter Perspective, 1941, falls open. Moore has drawn the figures lying down in two rows either side of the shelter in the Underground tunnel. They are tightly packed, stripped down, more angular than his usual rounded forms. There's an air of exhaustion about them, most of them lying on their backs, their knees and arms awkwardly bent in the cramped space, a few face down, their arms covering their faces. One or two sit up against the tunnel wall, not caring about the filth of it.

He's used a touch of earthy yellow on some of the bony figures in the foreground – it gives them an eerie kind of elemental life, links them with the London clay the tunnel is carved out of. I run my fingers along the lines of bodies, following them as they recede into the darkening distance, down the throat of the tunnel, becoming little more than rows of bones wrapped round nothing but air.

I see myself then, like Freddie, like all of us, heading towards the vanishing point.

The self-pity in that thought disgusts me. I can feel myself sinking down, but this time there's no John to hide behind, nothing and no-one to stop me looking at what I've become.

I open my sketchbook. Begin to draw. Make notes. Give in to thinking. Force myself to remember.

What was it Carter asked? *How did you get here?*

Part Two

Manchester

November 1946 – May 1947

My Mother

7.30 a.m. Railway station, Manchester. Two Lowryesque children and a pigeon.

'Christ!' I say to myself. 'Starving kids. We've come home to starving kids.' Two small boys, soaked to the skin, are sitting on the low station wall, stick legs dangling inches off the ground. Bird-sharp faces. They don't have any coats or socks on and their shoulder blades show like hangers through the thin material of their shirts. Maybe they've got used to going hungry, because they're giggling, throwing pebbles at a scruffy pigeon.

Louie has taken off down the station approach saying he'll be back, leaving me with the kitbags. I wait for what seems like an age. The November cold numbs my nose and the damp, sooty air of Manchester settles on my tongue. Uneven dips in the cobbles hold the rain like oily rock pools. A bike and sidecar rumble into view and stop in front of me. The bike is obviously ex-army issue, khaki still showing through the badly sprayed black top coat.

Louie pushes up his goggles on to his forehead and blinks at me, blue eyes in a face still tanned to the colour of stewed tea. The demob jacket and hat have gone. He's wearing a navy blue American-style windbreaker, new by the sheen of it.

'Stash the gear under that.' He points to the tattered canvas top of the sidecar.

'Where did this come from?' How many times in how many places have I asked that?

He thumbs over his shoulder in the direction of the ramshackle workshops under the railway arches. 'Charlie. He's been home a year. Owed me a favour.' He sits back. 'Hop on.'

The kids stop tormenting the pigeon and edge closer to take a look at the bike. I roll back the top of the sidecar to stow our kit and climb onto the pillion seat. Louie revs up the engine, eases it down to a steady chug and we move off, juddering over the cobbles.

The boys stand legs astride in the attack position, elbows bent to steady the machine guns slung at their hips, and rat-a-tat-tat a stretch of bullets along the sidecar bodywork.

The monkey puzzle.

I keep my eyes closed against the rain until Louie shouts, 'Tell me which road to turn down,' and I open them to huge beech trees and horse chestnuts, winter stark but standing solid, lining either side of the road through Didsbury. Seeing them again, still there, after five years, looking no different, lifts my spirits.

'Next turn on the left,' I shout, and he revs up as we turn into Oak Road.

'Which one?' he shouts again.

'Head for the monkey puzzle, over to the right.'

We coast past a row of Edwardian three-storey terraces, the sort South Manchester prides itself on. Plain bay windows, no Victorian frills. Patches of red brick showing through the grime. Pocket-sized front gardens, most dug over for vegetables, with low walls and gaps where wrought-iron gates used to be.

We stop outside the house with the monkey puzzle and Louie switches off. For a moment, we sit in silence. I make the first move. 'Thank Christ for that.' I lever myself gingerly off the bike and stand legs akimbo, arching my body back to iron out the kinks.

'Better than the bus. It would have been no joke, carrying this lot from the bus stop.' He lifts my kitbag out from the sidecar, exaggerating the weight, plonking it down on the pavement. 'You and your bloody books,' he says, not unkindly. He straightens up and mirrors my bending and stretching.

There are no books in the bag, at least none that I remember, but I let his comment pass. For an instant, I'm back at HQ in Chittagong, sitting on my camp bed reading, stripped to the waist. The sweat is streaming down my body from every possible pore, soaking the waistband of my shorts, dripping off the tip of my nose on to the page. *You and your bloody books*, Louie says, coming in with the post from home, handing over a brown paper package.

He'd had to walk an extra half-mile in the heat to pick it up from the parcel depot. Those little kindnesses. I'll miss them.

We stand facing each other, suddenly awkward.

'Come in for a cup of tea, meet my mother.' It sounds stiff, even to me.

He fiddles with the strap of his goggles. 'I'll get on, if it's all the same. Need to get back to the wife.' He pauses. 'If she remembers it's today I'm coming.'

'She'll remember.' I pat his shoulder. 'Keep in touch. You've still got the telephone number I gave you? It's next door's. Ring them, they'll get a message to me.'

He shakes my hand and climbs back on the bike. 'I'll say cheerio, then, old boy,' he says, in a mock far-back officer's voice, then zig-zags his goggles down. 'Don't let the bastards grind you down, mate.' The engine kicks in. He manoeuvres round in a tight semi-circle and stutters off. He doesn't look back.

I stare after him until the bike rattles round the corner, then pick up my belongings and start up the path past the monkey puzzle. It stands there, as dark and undemonstrative as ever, motionless in the rainy breeze. I've never liked this freak of a tree. There's something reptilian about its scaly, bristling branches. My father never liked it either. 'Interesting to sketch, but not a tree you can dream under,' he once said. When I was a small boy, in bed on light summer nights, I'd try not to look at the monstrous shadows it cast on the drawn curtains.

It holds no fears for me now, but I still don't like it.

The door opens. My mother comes rushing down the path and we meet in the middle. There's a great fumble of arms as I try to hug her and she tries to hug me.

'Welcome home, son, welcome home.' She steps back and looks at me, the beginnings of a frown on her face, quickly converted into raised eyebrows and a wide smile.

Home. I hear the word, and panic flutters against my ribs like an imprisoned bird.

Still life with bacon.

I potter into the morning room. My mother always called it 'the morning room' and my father used to tease her. It's a cosy room between the hallway and the back kitchen with a small fireplace and a single French window overlooking the garden. We used to do everything in here, the three of us. Then just the two of us. Ate our meals, read the papers or books, listened to the wireless. It's where the memories are. My father's paint-brushes are still on the top shelf of the Welsh dresser near the window, traces of ten-year-old paint on the wooden handles from the last time he used them. The fire's lit to take the chill off the room for breakfast, then it's allowed to go out to save coal. The clock says half past seven and the reluctant morning light creeps through the gap in the chenille curtains, rationing itself like everything else.

My mother pops her head round the corner of the kitchen doorway. She glances at me and purses her lips − dressing gowns downstairs in daylight hours are for when you're sick, as far as my mother is concerned. But the lips bend into a smile. She must be taking into consideration it's only my second day back.

'Knew the smell of bacon would do the trick. Be with you in a jiffy.'

The table is set with cheery yellow and orange china and a small loaf sits in the centre of a large breadboard. Two postage stamps of butter look lost on a side plate. My mother returns with two plates, two thin slices of bacon on one for me, one slice on the other for her, and cuts the bread for us both.

'I thought we'd celebrate your first morning back,' she says.

She cuts her rasher into thin strips, savouring each one slowly.

'Any more bacon?' I saw a doorstopper off the loaf, scrape butter on, take a huge bite.

'That's your lot. It's rationed, remember. And the bread and butter, so go easy.'

I put the slice down on my plate. 'I still can't believe it. Bread rationing.'

She laughs. 'It's not as bad as it sounds. You learn to cut it thin. But you have to queue for it. I'm good at queuing.' There's a hint of mock pride in her voice. 'Well, as good as I'll get.' She wrinkles her nose. We both know patience has never been her strong suit.

'Eat it up.' She nods at my plate.

'Bread rationing. In peacetime. It's ridiculous.' I can't let it go. I toy with a few crumbs on the breadboard, rolling them into small, sticky balls.

'We weren't expecting it, that's for sure,' she says. 'Some daft beggars emptied the shops on the first day, stockpiling stuff. What was the point? It wouldn't keep for long, would it?' Then she launches into a story about some girl, nineteen years old, who'd burned herself to death, back in July, the first week the rationing came in. She'd thrown six slices of stale bread away, then panicked, thinking the authorities would fine her if they found out, so she poured paraffin in the dustbin, set it alight and her clothes caught fire.

'It made all the papers.' She shakes her head. 'Poor little thing.'

A spurt of anger surges up and I stab the crumb balls into flat buttons.

'It's all politics,' she carries on. 'They think if we can show the Americans we're suffering shortages, they'll help us feed Germany.'

'What about feeding ourselves first?' I cut my slice in two.

She hesitates, then says, 'The war's over. It's been over for more than a year.' There's a note of wariness in her voice, as if she's not sure whether to carry on talking to me. 'But they're starving in Germany. Women and children. Living on boiled oats and dried milk, one meal a day. We're just suffering shortages, they're still starving.'

'We're starving, too. I saw two kids at the station yesterday, thin as rakes.'

'That's not starvation. That's neglect. There's enough food for everyone if you get yourself organised. And what were they doing, hanging round the station at that time in the morning, I'd like to know? Too long without their fathers, that's their trouble.'

I put the half slice of bread on her plate.

She puts it back on mine. 'There's plenty. All I have to do is queue.'

She changes the subject, chatting about the neighbours, and I'm conscious she's filtering the details. We lapse into silence. She pulls at the top button of her cardigan. It's a gesture I don't remember from before. The cardigan is ill-fitting, baggy around the shoulders.

She sees me looking. 'If I'd known I was going to lose weight, this past five years, I could have knitted it two sizes smaller and saved on the wool.' She shrugs and smiles and pulls at the button again.

We sit slowly sipping our tea.

She sighs, reaches across to my plate and cuts off the bit with the bite mark then takes the remainder of my slice and the loaf back into the kitchen. She comes back, breaks up the bite mark and the crumb buttons and heads for the French window with the breadboard.

'All God's creatures,' she says, drawing the curtains back, 'deserve their daily bread,' and she opens the door and leans out to brush off the crumbs into the grey morning.

*

A wisp of calligraphy on a scroll of white paper.

I lie rigid on the edge of the bed, trying to work out what kind of silence it is. It seems as if I've spent the whole war listening, like a wild animal, sizing up the threat.

'Breakfast! Get a move on.' My mother's voice drifts up, rise-and-shine cheerful.

I fight the urge to shout down at her to leave me alone.

Muffled, that's it, that's the kind of silence it is. Deadened down, but safe enough. I breathe out long and slow, watching the grey wisps hold their shape then fade away. Forcing myself out of bed, I dress quickly, gasping at the cold air. As I draw the curtains, the sudden brightness hurts my eyes. The first snow of the winter. Trees, houses, cars – next door's Austin lies lightly blanketed, its boxy black lines softened white.

In Burma, I'd fantasise about winter mornings like this. On sleepless nights, suffocating in the pre-monsoon heat, I'd try to remember what it felt like to scoop up handfuls of snow. Or get a snowball smack in the face, or even better, stuffed down the back of my neck. I'd swear I could conjure up the physical sensation of it, the shock of the cold, before finding myself back in my camp bed in the basha, or huddled in a slit trench, bathed in puddles of warm, salty sweat.

Frost has formed on the inside of the window. Delicate. Beautiful. I trace my fingertips along the edge of the filigree, feel it give and melt to water. My eyes fill with tears. I wipe them away with my cold hand. This wasn't how it was meant to be. The plan was to rest up for a few days, then go into the city to see Wadsworth at the *Manchester Guardian*. I know there's no chance of my old job back. A twenty-three-year-old messenger boy would be ridiculous. But Wadsworth is the Editor of the *MG* now, making a post-war name for himself. He'd taken a shine to me back in 1939, said I'd got potential.

If only I could get my energy back. The few days' rest has stretched into weeks and what had felt like plain tiredness at first has changed into heavy-limbed helplessness.

'For goodness' sake, David!' There's a brittle edge to the brightness in her voice now.

She's chirpy all through breakfast. I'd promised to go with her to the shops – our first time out together. She's looking forward to being seen with me in the village. I'm dreading it.

'The first snow of the year,' she chatters, 'make sure you wrap up warm.' She fusses like she's getting me ready for school. I half expect her to bend down and tie my shoelaces.

Finally, she leaves me alone while she warms a pair of socks that go on over her stockinged feet and then zips up her old ankle boots. She stands up, looking in the mirror as she knots her faded silk headscarf under her chin. The smoky blue of the cabbage rose pattern highlights her blue eyes and I think of the pretty woman she once must have been.

'That's a lovely scarf, Mother.' I smile at her.

She smiles back, then says, 'Wear your tweed cap, it'll keep the heat in,' and I breathe in silently to disguise my annoyance.

She keeps up a commentary the half-mile to the village: the gaps where the iron railings were taken for the war effort, the different properties damaged in one of the air raids. The pavements are treacherous and she clings on to me, both of us laughing out loud when we skid to a halt as we reach the High Street. She spots a woman in the distance – 'Mrs Philips, her son was killed at Monte Cassino' – and she steers me to the other side of the road.

Queues. Endless queues. Butcher. Grocer. We stand for ages in the bread queue, the woman in front prattling on about the four inches of snow at Ringway Airport and the electricity cuts this morning. Then the woman behind starts up about not having enough coupons for a decent dress for her daughter's wedding. I clench my jaw so hard, my teeth ache. I have to get away. I whisper to my mother, 'I'm tired, I'm going home.'

I pick my way along the glassy pavement, head down, intent on keeping my footing.

I look up to get my bearings and see the war memorial, its ornate cross on top of the tapered shaft set against the grey snow-laden sky, its stone plinth surrounded by wreaths and little crosses. Thank God I got home after Remembrance Day, I think, then feel a tug of guilt. The red poppies are more red than ever against the white of the fresh snow still on them.

Red poppies. White snow. Red ink. White paper.

Red ink on white paper. In a clearing, off the road to Imphal, with Louie, both of us staring at a grave – one single grave, the mound of earth covered with leaves, still green, delicately feathered. And set in the earth near the grave, a fat stem of bamboo, two feet high, split lengthways down the middle, and in the curve of its creamy fibrous inside: a wisp of calligraphy, drifting from top to bottom, written in red ink on white paper, ragged-edged, rough paper, hanging from a length of wire, and Louie whispering, 'Where the hell did they get red ink?'

Red ink. White paper. White snow. Red poppies. The inside of my head is chaotic.

I hold on to the frame of a shop doorway to steady myself, then I'm away, almost running, slithering and sliding, not stopping until I get back to the house.

The back door slams shut and I lean against it, giving a little groan, my shirt soaked with sweat. I go over to the sink, get a drink of water, hold it to my cheek, feel the ice-cold glass burn through my flesh then numb the skin. The sweat cools on my back and I begin to shake. I sit at the kitchen table, sipping the water slowly, then place the glass down with needless precision, noticing all the extra marks on the deal surface. Five years of life I know nothing about, mapped out in food stains and knife cuts and cup rings.

I don't know what happened at the memorial but it's left me drained. It was as if there'd been a slippage inside my head. Like watching a faulty film that jumped backwards, then righted itself, jumping back to the present, leaving me not knowing how long I'd been away, not even knowing where I was. Not knowing where you were or how you got there – that was a sign of madness. I begin to shake again. It would be safer in my bedroom. But I can't trust my legs to get me there.

The dead. What do you do with the dead? Precious little, there's no time. No time to bury them. No time to find bodies, parts of bodies, put them back together. Or you do find them, but they might be booby-trapped, so you can't even touch them to get the dog tags. No time, no place for funeral games. And yet, we'd found this green and gentle clearing, this single grave. This thing of grace.

Captain Evans had followed us into the clearing where the grave was. 'They call it a *sotoba*,' he said, pointing at the bamboo cradling its red ink calligraphy on the makeshift scroll of paper. 'It's their marker for the dead.'

My mother's hands.

My mother comes home and finds me at the kitchen table. She makes a cup of tea and we sit and drink it, not speaking. I stare out through the window at a blackbird standing on the frozen snow covering the tiny vegetable patch, its neck stretched upwards, as if reaching for the sun's weak rays. It reminds me of sitting in the kitchen when I was small, watching my mother baking. She'd pass me the pie funnel and I'd push the shiny, ceramic blackbird down through the apples piled on the pie dish, then she'd drape the pastry over the rolling pin and lay it across the filling, gently forcing the bird's yellow-painted open beak through the top.

The bird takes off from its snow crust and flies away over the hedge.

Black bird. White snow. Red poppies. White snow. Red ink. White paper.

I stir my tea, chanting the words in my head, clinking the spoon on the inside of my cup to the rhythm of the chant, trying to get some control over what's happening.

'I was thinking,' my mother says, 'maybe it would do you

good to go into town – do what you said, the day you came home. Look up some of the people at the *Guardian*. Get your old job back.' The brittleness is back in her voice.

'I was only a messenger, Mother' – I sound sharp, but I carry on – 'and I'm not a boy any more.' As I say it, I glance at her, see the tension round her mouth, notice the weariness in her drooping shoulders. I wish it could be different, wish I could be different.

'It wouldn't do any harm just to go and see them.' She inches her hand across the table, as if she's anticipating another snap back. Her fingertips stop just short of mine. My father always used to say that when you draw people's hands, you're drawing what people are thinking, what mood they're in.

My thoughts begin to scramble again, but I manage a weak smile. 'You're right, Mother, it wouldn't do any harm.' But I leave my hand where it is, just out of reach.

We rub along for those first few weeks. I tell myself it's not easy for either of us.

She's had five years of the house to herself, I've had five years living amidst the clamour of other men. We meet in the kitchen or on the stairs, and there's an awkwardness, amusing at first then annoying, at least for me, as we manoeuvre round each other. Slowly, we settle into an uneasy way of using the same space, but not at the same time. Like Mrs Fine and Mr Wet.

George Collingwood

A jolly company of books.

I finally get round to unpacking my kitbag. It's been propped up against the bedroom wall since I came home. I come across the book, musty and water-stained, stuck to the canvas at the bottom. On the fly leaf in George's careful copperplate: *August 1946 – a companion for the voyage home.* He always did have a sense of occasion, old George. It was the last book he'd sent out and it arrived just before we boarded the troop ship from Bombay. I'd riffled through the pages, then stuffed it down the side of the bag, knowing I'd never read it.

His paperbacks kept me going during the war. They'd fetch up like weary homing pigeons, wherever we happened to be. The first two years, they were mostly about adventure in the skies, or military escapades – *The Flying Dutchman*, *Night Flight*, *The Gun*. I devoured them all, reading them in bashas, monsoon rain rattling the bamboo walls, or in slit trenches under tarpaulins – anywhere we'd been told to hole up and wait for orders. I'd imagine myself back in George's second-hand bookshop, at the back of the shelves, sneaking a quick read when I should have been tidying the books, earning my pocket money after school. But it was like seeing a stranger, imagining myself as a fifteen-year-old schoolboy.

Round about the time of the D-Day landings in 1944, there'd been a subtle change in theme in the books he sent. A gentle Englishness crept in – *The Warden* arrived, closely followed by *The Compleat Angler* with its wood engravings by Gertrude Hermes. The beauty of her work saddened me. I found myself thinking how much my father would have liked it.

Then, finally, it was over – the Americans dropped the bomb, the Japanese surrendered, we thought we could all go home. But they kept us out there another year, the rumours that we'd be off to fight someone else slowly wearing us down. Our nerves were shot. I swung from high anxiety to deep melancholy and stopped reading altogether.

Captain Evans understood. 'Comics are just about my limit,' he said. We were in hospital together the New Year of 1945, both of us getting over a bout of malaria. We'd pass the time on the verandah, sharing abandoned copies of *Superman*. He struck a mock Romantic poet pose, fingertips on forehead, reciting: '"Books; what a jolly company they are" – Christ! How does it go? I've forgotten . . . de-dah-de-dah-de-fucking-dah . . . "Which will you read? Come on; O *do* read something; they're so wise . . . all the wisdom of the world is waiting for you on those shelves . . .".'

His face was uncharacteristically sad. 'Never realised the irony of Sassoon's words before. I'm supposed to be going back to Cambridge after this lot. Quite fancied myself as a warrior poet – can't imagine ever opening a wretched book again, now.'

It was the only time I'd ever seen him downbeat. He got us through, Captain Evans, kept us going. We all owed him a lot. I owed him a lot. He *was* a warrior poet. A tough, instinctive fighter, but also the one who would know things like what a *sotoba* was.

His words come back to me as I chuck the book into the waste-paper basket. Then, remembering George too and his past kindness, guilt prompts me to fish the book out and drop it on top of the other paperbacks fanned out on my desk under the window. It lies there among their oranges and reds and blues, dishevelling their little pool of vitality like a small brown trout.

'George came round a few weeks ago with them; he thought you'd enjoy a good read when you got back,' my mother said, when I'd asked where the other books had come from. 'You should go into the city to thank him. It would do you good to get out.'

He never spoke of his time in the Great War, but now he might think there's an understanding we can share. The last thing I want to talk about is his war, or the misery of mine. But my mother's right, I need to get out. A day away from each other would do us both good. The bookshop in the centre of the city would be somewhere definite to aim for.

A row of capering Penguins.

The two old wing-back chairs are where they've always been, cramped in a tiny alcove off the kitchen. We sit facing each other, a low table between us piled high with paperbacks. Old. He's grown old. I take in the way his eyelids slide down and up in a slow blink, more owlish than ever. He tamps down the tobacco in his pipe, going through the ritual of lighting and puffing and pausing and puffing again, then leans back and rests his head against the chair. The first release of sweet smoke mingles with the familiar bookshop smells of old leather and dust and a definite hint of long-gone mouse from the overstuffed upholstery.

'So what did you think of the *Odyssey*?' he says.

I think back to the book lying with all the other unread paperbacks on my desk.

He reaches across the low table and takes a copy of it off the top of the pile, placing it between us. 'The very first of the Penguin Classics, out January this year, very timely.' He takes a few puffs of his pipe, then leans back in the chair again. 'I liked the idea of you reading it on your way home – a bit corny, I know, but still. So, what do you think of it?'

My thoughts race, trying to invent plausible details of a struggle to read the book against all the odds. 'It was awkward to read on the go,' I say. 'We travelled in trucks, trains, ships – the ship was the worst – it's hard to keep your eyes on the page when you're swinging in a hammock, trying to read by torchlight and the man below you is being sick in a bucket and the man above is either farting or snoring or both.' I hope I've made it sound amusing.

He nods. 'Maybe you need to read it when you've got where you're going.'

'Maybe.' I'm drifting away. I know he wants to get into conversations about books, like the old times, but I can't concentrate. *Books; what a jolly company they are . . . Christ, I've forgotten how it goes . . . de-dah-de-dah-de-fucking-dah . . .* I'd once believed what George had told me, that books were a civilising force. That they could lead us to some sort of truth.

I feel a sudden sense of loss.

He waits patiently, like a kindly professor trying to encourage a shy student.

I dredge up a vague memory of skimming the first page. 'It's a straightforward translation, sounds like everyday English, not too highbrow.'

He puffs on his pipe again, three little pops of pleasure, then says, 'He's good, old Professor Rieu. Sound choice for the job, I think. Penguin wanted someone erudite, which he is, of course, but also someone who'd make Homer come alive for ordinary folk.'

He sounds as if he's addressing his night school class at the Workers' Educational Association. I can sense him getting ready to give a lecture, probably on how Penguin are planning to bring the Classics to the masses. I stare past his head at the two shelves of paperbacks, blue and orange and green and yellow and pink, the little penguin logo standing plump and firm on the spines of books published in 1935, a much skinnier version dancing a jig by 1945.

The penguins begin to caper round in my head and I drop my gaze, closing my eyes. Give in to the drifting again.

My twelve-year-old voice, still unbroken. 'Why is there a penguin on the front?' We're in the same chairs at the back of the bookshop.

George doesn't answer my question. He's busy running his finger down the front cover of a soft-backed book banded in startling jewel-like colour, cobalt blue at the top, white in the middle, cobalt blue again at the bottom.

He waves it in the air. 'This little book will change the world, my boy, you wait and see!' He opens it and reads out loud: '*Ariel*, by André Maurois. Published July, 1935.' He nods at me. 'Remember that date.' He points to the number 1, printed in bold type under the penguin's feet. 'The very first Penguin paperback. Published this month. Just think of the people who'll be able to buy books now,' he carries on. 'People who couldn't afford them before. They're selling them in Woolworths, for sixpence, for goodness' sake! Less than a packet of cigarettes, not that you'd be interested in that, I hope.'

I begin to think of all the other things I could buy for sixpence at Woolworths.

He reaches over the table and stuffs the book into the breast pocket of my school blazer. 'Jolly useful. Fits in your pocket too. See?'

'I like the penguin,' I say. 'It's like having a friend on the front.'

George's voice drifts in. 'Did you notice the mistake on the front?'

'Sorry?' It takes a moment to sort out where I am. 'The what?'

'Did you spot the mistake on the front?' He taps the *Odyssey* with the stem of his pipe. 'Look.' He points to the roundel about the size of a penny piece, centred under the title block. Inside it is a sketch of an ancient Greek ship under full sail in choppy waters, gusting along against the backdrop of a busy-looking cloud.

'It's beautiful.' I've not really studied the actual cover before, beyond noticing its dullness. Now I see that the colours aren't drab at all, but done in subtle hues, the soft sea-green of the ship washing across the acorn brown of the cover, the Greek border of wave scrolls giving it the look of a classical pamphlet.

'It certainly is finely done, like a detail on an Attic vase.' The puffs on his pipe are almost toots now. 'But look at these.' His finger follows the single row of oars slanted back along the side of the ship, ready to pull forwards.

I trace my finger where his had been, down the fine lines depicting each oar. 'They look like perfectly ordinary oars to me.' I'm beginning to find this game childish.

'The boat's under full sail. You never have your oars out under full sail. You certainly don't see that in Greek Art, not to my knowledge anyway. Looks very odd.'

I study the roundel again, taking in more of the detail. The boat *was* under full sail. The oars *were* out. So? I want to say. So?

'There's been quite a fuss about it.' He puffs, then smiles, then puffs. It's just the sort of thing he'd spend hours deliberating over.

'I see what you mean.' I'm beginning to drift again.

'It's so important to get these details right, don't you think?'

'Very,' I say, sighing. 'The most important thing in the world.' The sarcasm hangs heavy in the air.

His face falls a little. He does his slow blink then puts his pipe down on the beaten copper ashtray on the table and heaves himself slowly out of the chair. 'Best put these back, tidy the old place up a bit.' He gathers up the paperbacks, leaving Homer on the table, and turns to put the rest on the shelf behind him.

I find myself getting more and more irritated watching him sorting out the books, lining them up, first in colour order, then rearranging them by author. Fat penguins, thin penguins, shuffling across the bookshelf.

I go back to staring at the Greek ship in the roundel, feeling as though I've just failed some little test, but not quite sure what it was.

Finally, he seems satisfied with what he's done and turns towards me.

'I'd better be off,' I say, not giving him time to sit down.

He pats me on the back as I go out into the street. 'Call back and see me next time you come into the city.' Such decency after my pettiness. I can't bring myself to apologise. All I feel as I walk away is a rising resentment, as if it's his fault I've behaved so badly.

I walk back towards the bus stop. The rain has turned to sleet. As I turn the corner into Mount Street near the Art Gallery, a shower of icy pinpricks needles my face and I'm almost lifted off my feet by a gust of freezing wind at my back.

An ancient Greek ship in full sail.

The warm fug of a café. The quiet hum of conversation around me. A woman's face wavers into focus, staring down at me, pencil poised, eyebrows raised, professional smile. She repeats the question, speaking loudly, as though I'm deaf. 'Would you like to order, sir?'

A fist of anxiety flexes in my chest. I clear my throat. 'Could you tell me where I am, please?'

She stiffens a little and takes a slight step back. 'Where you are, sir?'

I realise I've unnerved her, so I try to recover, smiling and settling my face into what I hope is an 'aren't I a duffer?' expression. 'Sorry – I mean the street we're on. I'm new to Manchester – seem to have lost my bearings.' I wonder if she gets many loonies in here.

Her body relaxes and she smiles a prim smile back. 'Albert Square, sir. You're in Albert Square.' She sweeps the pencil round over the neat tables, most of them occupied by women in smart hats, probably on their way home from an afternoon matinee. 'This is the Kardomah.'

I nod, hoping I look as if I'm finding out something new.

'The best café in Manchester,' she nods back. 'Now what would you like?'

I mumble tea would be good. I look around, slowly recognising the familiar décor. The cosy Kardomah, my father called it. He'd bring me here for Welsh rarebit after our visits to the Art Gallery. The sensation of melted cheese and hot toast suddenly fills my mouth and the sharpness of mustard prickles my nose.

The waitress comes back with tea and dubious rock cakes.

I watch her weave her way back through the tables to the kitchen. I'm still struggling to get my head right. The last thing I remember is passing the Art Gallery and feeling the sleet on my face and the wind at my back. The Kardomah is in the opposite direction to where I was heading. I check my watch. It's a quarter past three. Five minutes of the fifteen since leaving the bookshop are a blank. A rush of nerves skitters up the back of my neck into my scalp and I think I'm going to keel over on to the floor. It passes, leaving my whole body weak, my hands cold and clammy. Five minutes. And I have no idea what I've done in that time. No idea at all. This slippage is even worse than the *sotoba* slippage. I signal the waitress to bring the bill. She comes over, looks at the uneaten cakes on the tray and purses her lips.

I walk out into the Square, the sleet slicing almost horizontally on to my face, and make my way past the Albert Memorial. For a moment, I think I feel my father's hand ruffle my hair. I hurry back towards the bus stop. I need to get home, I must get home. The wind is at my back again, funnelling straight down between the buildings. Blowing me along like a ship in full sail, battling through sea-green choppy waters, a line of oars out where there really shouldn't have been any.

I can't face visiting George in the shop any more but he organises little jaunts out to rare book auctions and a few literary lunches at the Liberal Club. At one of these lunches, we bump into Wadsworth from the *Guardian*. He's one of George's guest lecturers for the WEA. 'The role of the *Manchester Guardian* newspaper in the history of great British newspapers' goes down well with the students. He's a self-educated man himself, unusual in the *MG* higher echelons, with their Oxbridge degrees, and a fact George always used to our advantage when tackling my mother about my not going to university. We'd mounted a joint campaign back in 1939 to persuade her to let me leave school at sixteen and work for the *MG* as a messenger boy. 'It didn't do Wadsworth any harm to work his way up, did it?' he'd say, winking at me.

Wadsworth shakes me by the hand, says it's good to see me back safe and sound. In the New Year, I should come and see him, there may be something with the paper for me.

George nods at him and beams at me. Subterfuge has never been one of his strong points. He never stops trying, in his own way, to get me right.

Beth

Still life with four eggs.

'You remember Beth.' My mother ushers the woman into the morning room.

Slim. Shoulder-length auburn hair. 'David,' the woman says. The smile is slightly reserved but the look is direct.

I can't place her at first then as I shake hands and mumble hello, it clicks. George's niece. A girl in school uniform, hair held back by a green ribbon. She would call into the bookshop after school and say hello, then sit at the back and lose herself in her sketching. There was an air of self-containment, even back then. That same composure is still with her.

She hands my mother a biscuit tin, then takes off her coat and hat. 'A present for you, Ginny. Uncle George was visiting Leo Marwick at his farm in Wilmslow yesterday. He brought these back.'

'Dear Leo, how thoughtful,' my mother says and I remember our last visit to the Art Gallery before I went away, and Leo's attempt to please her by damning Lowry with faint praise. Leo had obviously lost out to George. My mother smiles a lot when George is around. They go away for a few days, sometimes, 'to visit churches of interest'.

My mother goes over to the table and takes the top off the tin. She gives a little squeal. 'My goodness! What a treat!' She's looking into the tin as though she's adoring the Magi. She tips it an angle so I can see inside. Nestling in newspaper are four brown eggs.

'Uncle George told me to tell you he swapped two Trollopes for them,' Beth says, laughing. We have the eggs for supper. Scrambled. Creamy yellow on slabs of buttered toast. Extra thick slices. My mother gives me a long look as she sets the plates down. Afterwards, Beth offers to help with the washing-up but my mother tells her to keep me company, and leaves us to ourselves by the fire.

Beth leans forward and spreads her hands towards the coals to warm them. 'It must be difficult, coming back after so long away.' She turns to me. 'So much has changed.'

'I'm slowly finding that out.'

'Still, it's better than the alternative.' She gives me that direct look again.

'The alternative?'

'Not coming back at all.'

It's the first thing I learn to love about her. That directness. There's no playing games with Beth.

Demoiselle cranes.

She says she can get tickets for a lunchtime piano concert in Manchester. Chopin. Nocturnes.

I sit there, lost in the music. I can't believe my luck that this woman beside me has walked into my life.

We find a little place that serves a passable shepherd's pie. The ordinariness of it all, the simple everydayness of being in a café with an attractive woman. Four months ago, I was on a troop ship, stifled by the unbearable stink of too many male bodies in too small a space. Now there is just the two of us in our own corner and the faint jasmine of her perfume.

I look across at the planes and angles of her not quite beautiful face, a face I can't stop going back to and taking pleasure in, and those hazel eyes, sometimes greenish brown, sometimes brownish green, depending on where the light falls.

I smile at the memory of a skinny girl sitting in one of the wing-backs in George's shop, bent over a sketch pad.

She tilts her head to one side. 'Penny for them.'

'I was thinking of the times you'd come to George's shop and sit at the back and draw.'

'Long time ago.'

'I thought you'd be living the bohemian life by now, away at Art School.'

'It didn't work out. Most things didn't work out for everyone, thanks to the war. You just end up making the best of it. At least I'm alive. And I've got a good job I'm interested in – not many women can say that, can they?'

'What do you do?'

'I'm personal secretary to Leo Marwick at the Manchester Art Gallery.'

My face must show surprise, because she goes on: 'I ended up at Miss Wilkinson's Secretarial College for Young Gentlewomen. Uncle George paid my fees.'

We burst out laughing. Wilkies was well known as a very select establishment with a reputation for taking posh County girls who went on to find jobs where they landed husbands with prospects. *Guardian* messenger boys wouldn't have dared try their luck back then.

'It was Uncle George's way of making it up to me, I suppose,' she says, 'for not being able to go to Art School in London. Mind you, I think he was heartily relieved when London became too dangerous – he and my mother were worried about me going down south. As it turned out, with my mother's illness, I was better off staying in Manchester. And then when she passed away last year, the house was mine and I suddenly had a degree of independence.'

'I'm sorry about your mother,' I say. 'It must have hit you hard. The last parent to pass away.' I suddenly wonder what it would feel like if anything happened to my mother.

She draws herself in a little. 'People said it was a blessing. She suffered so much towards the end.' Her face clouds over. 'It didn't feel like a blessing to me. I guess I was selfish but I didn't want to be without her.' She gives me that direct look again. 'It was as if she hung on until the war was over, as if she didn't want to leave me until I was safe.'

I try and break through the air of sadness that suddenly stretches out between us.

'George would make me sit outside your house in the car, when he dropped us both home from the shop. I remember it as a big, rambling sort of place.'

'I rent out rooms – two doctors on the first floor and a student at the top.'

'Can't imagine you as a landlady.'

'I've turned the back room into a studio. That's where I paint, when I can.'

'So you still paint?'

'I try. Not up to much, I don't think.'

'I'd like to see your work.'

She has kept the whole of the ground floor for herself. The entrance hall and the front room are dreary, old-fashioned, wood panelled. But the studio at the back comes as a complete surprise – the room is both a bedroom and a studio, cleverly divided off from each other by a full wall partition of frosted glass doors etched with bladed leaves. The real joy is the roof over the studio section – large panels of clear glass, so the light floods in to both the studio and the bed space.

'The studio was once a large conservatory,' she says. 'My mother had the glass walls bricked in, but left the roof. She knew how disappointed I was that I wouldn't be going to Art School so she spoiled me a little. She let me design the whole floor. I had the glass partition put in. It lets the light into the bedroom.' She gestures at the heavy red drapes, patterned in Indian crewel work, at either end of the partition. 'I can always draw the curtains at night, but I love the night skies. I was lucky, all this glass survived the war without a scratch.'

We have to walk through the bedroom to get to the studio. Brass bedstead. Dressing table piled high with books, spilling over with jewellery and scarves. An angular Chanel No 5 perfume bottle. A silk kimono draped over an Oriental fretwork screen.

The studio has a small fireplace, now closed off, the hearth stacked with canvases. On the wall above it is an oil painting of three demoiselle cranes around an ornamental pond.

'Yours?' I lean forward for a closer look.

'Nothing like as good as the original. I copied a painting I adore in the gallery. It's by Janet Kirk. Only she painted four cranes.' She stands back with her arms folded and studies the painting. 'This looks like a child's colouring page compared to the subtlety of her work.'

'It looks good to me.' I can pick out vermilions for the bright irises of the birds' eyes, flake-white for the elegant plumes stark against the black faces, blue-greys and ivory for the velvety feathered bodies, rose madder at the tips of the bills. Each crane with its own distinctive neck movement, stretching upwards or dipping or coiling into its elegant body. They are graceful, contained, observant creatures. Calming to look at. Soothing.

Kimono.

I can't take my eyes off her as she moves naked round the room. She bends to pick up the kimono from the floor and the flesh of her thighs pulls taut as she reaches down, then softens again as she stands. The grey silk clings against her breasts when she slips on the robe.

As she walks across to the partition, the pattern on the back of the kimono shapes and reshapes itself, geometric slivers of ochre cutting into scarlet circles, rippling over the dips and swells of her body. She folds back one of the doors and goes through. The afternoon light of a rare blue December sky floods through the roof of the studio, turning the frosted glass wall into a pale wash of blue-green. She flits around on the other side of it, a smudge of glimmering colour, airing her wings as she reaches up to shelves for cups and saucers.

The light diffuses into the bed space, brightening the faded turquoises of the Indian shawl that serves as a coverlet. The mattress is a little dipped in the middle. I can still feel the weight of her flesh against my side, the rise and fall of her breasts lifting my arm slightly with each intake of her breath.

I move over to her edge of the dip, breathing in the lingering scent of her. Jasmine and sweat and salt. And sex. The sex with Beth is surprising – she is surprising. We'd sat around in the studio, she stretched out on the battered sofa, me opposite her in a small leather armchair. We spend a little time talking about the concert, about her job at the Art Gallery, about Art, until we both realise it's not what we really want to be spending our time doing. The conversation dries up and we look at each other, aware we've drifted into the space where one of us has to make the first move.

'Would you like to go to bed?' she says. I nod and she leads me through the glass partition to this big brass raft of a bed.

The physical presence of her – skin and flesh and bone, the warm smoothness of her, the hard edges. I'm nervous, awkward, fumbling. It's been such a long time. She takes my hand and kisses it and rests it on her breasts, then leads me to the softness between her thighs, tensing around my fingertips, the hazel eyes wide open, darkening now. A blush spreads down her neck across the curve of her breasts.

There's a freedom about the way she moves, the way her body asks for what she likes. It makes me feel free too and I take her hand and guide her to me. I know I should take my time, stroke her, touch her. It's too soon, I know it's too soon, but I pull her to me and lay my body over hers. Little gasps of her breath puff against my cheek as she raises herself to me, drawing me in. I barely move, I try to hold back, but I can't help but lose myself in her, in the rhythm and ache and pleasure and release. No present, no past. No memories.

We lie there, perfectly still, as if we are fused together, then I gently lift myself away, stroking back her hair, kissing her forehead. She smiles, but there's a sadness about the mouth. I put my arm round her, anxiety taking hold and squeezing my chest. I'm sure I've disappointed her with my fumbling and awkwardness and inconsiderate haste.

She wriggles out from under my arm so she can turn and look at me. She kisses the pad of her index finger, then presses it gently to my lips. She smiles at me and slips out of bed and heads over to pick up the kimono on the floor.

I watch her move about behind the glass, and think about what's just happened. The anxiety eases but I'm left feeling unsure. I try and explain away the haste to myself. It's the first sex I've had for nearly a year. Not only that, I'm twenty-three years old, and I've only had sex twice in my life, before this. As my body quietens, of all the things I could be thinking about, this is the thought I'm left with.

I don't know whether to laugh or feel depressed, detailing this sorry record. A nurse back in Chittagong last year after a farewell party for Captain Evans. And before that, a secretary in Durban on the way out to the Far East in 1942. I can't remember much about the sex itself, except that in Durban we were both eighteen and neither of us wanted to die a virgin, and that it was clumsy, but with a deal of goodwill on both sides. Mainly, I can only recall the places. Durban, humid and sweaty and the hum of a useless ceiling fan. Chittagong, in a downtown hotel bedroom, the smell of spices drifting in from the street stalls outside.

Sex in foreign places with women I hardly knew and whose faces I'm already struggling to remember. For some men in our battalion, that would be something to boast about. That and the brothels. Another rite of passage for the serving soldier that I opted out of.

I'd not really thought about it until now, this lack of sexual encounters. Another loss I could put down to the war – four years of sexual discovery, of sexual experience, taken away from me. Since I've been back, I could have remedied all that. But it's been as if everything has switched off. It's pathetic. I'm pathetic.

Now Beth. To feel her body as part of mine, not knowing where I end and she begins, the sheer physical pleasure of abandoning myself to sensations I'd forgotten existed. To feel that alive. And to feel that alive with someone like her.

She comes back with a papier mâché tray, sprays of painted cherry blossom painted under its black lacquer, two cups of coffee and a plate of plain biscuits on it. I sit up as she hands me my cup. 'Chicory, I'm afraid. Leo Marwick gets me the real stuff sometimes, but you're out of luck.'

'I wouldn't say that.' I pat the bed.

She sits on the edge, puts the tray between us. 'No, I'm the lucky one.' She hesitates, her eyes holding mine in a steady gaze. 'I want you to know. I've had one lover.' She picks at a loose thread in one of the embroidered birds on the coverlet. 'He was the first man I slept with. He was killed two years ago in France. There's been no-one since. I shut down, I think. Couldn't bear to get close to anyone else and then lose them too.' She strokes my hand. 'So I'm lucky this time it was with you.'

I kiss her fingers. 'I'm a little out of practice,' I say ruefully. She looks down, shaking her head.

Why did I say that? It meant there'd been others. No matter how few, it's not something women want to be reminded of, even I know that. It's not just the sex I'm inexperienced at, it's being with women at all. I feel like a gauche sixteen-year-old.

She lifts up her face to me and she's smiling. 'What a pair we are,' she says, shaking her head again. She leans forward and kisses me, the taste of Camp coffee sweet and sticky on our lips. 'What a perfectly pathetic, insecure pair this war has made us,' she says. We kiss again, longer this time. 'But we're still here. We stumbled through. And we've the rest of our lives to make up for it. We *are* lucky.'

She pushes the tray out of the way and lays her head on my chest and I breathe in the jasmine, stroking her soft body through the silk. I believe her. At that moment I believe what she says. I believe in her. In us. In the future.

*

The sex gets better. Or I get better at it. Probably both. It begins to feel less like just sex, which would be enough, if that's all it was; it feels more like an act of love, for which I have no words. We spend whole afternoons adrift in the brass bed, watching the blues and gunmetal greys of the winter skies through the glass roof.

Sometimes, I stay overnight at the studio, telling my mother I'm meeting up with old army pals. She usually nods and doesn't look up from her knitting.

I have no more slippages when I'm with Beth. No *sotoba* moments, no ancient Greek ship problems. Nightmares, sometimes. I wake up sweating, she calms me down. Once, she finds me in the studio lying on the floor in the dark, my pyjama top off, giggling, my mouth open, rubbing my arms and my body as if I'm sluicing myself down. The rain is spattering down hard on the glass roof. She leads me back to bed and is caring and loving. She never asks questions.

Beth and George spend Christmas with us. He gets a turkey from Leo Marwick's farm. Says he traded a complete set of Dickens for it. Leo is another of George's guest lecturers for the WEA students, on Art. He will eventually donate the Dickens to the WEA, together with the Trollopes bartered for the eggs.

We see the New Year in quietly, with glasses of good sherry, also courtesy of Leo. On the stroke of twelve by the mantelpiece clock, we stand by the fire and raise a toast to Peace.

I begin to tremble and hope no-one sees it. Beth slides her hand into mine. We exchange chaste New Year kisses and she whispers in my ear: 'We'll be alright.'

The Guardians

The Manchester Guardian. *Top floor. A row of wood-panelled editorial offices, known to all as The Corridor, home to the editors, correspondents and reporters. At the end, a small, windowless room. A chair and three large box files stacked on a table.*

'These papers are in a mess, truth be told.' Wadsworth talks rapidly and has a habit of pausing while he pushes his tortoise-shell glasses along the bridge of his nose, as if he's changing gear before starting off again. 'We were a trifle lackadaisical during the war – so many other things going on.' He allows himself a wry smile. 'There must be all sorts in here. Mostly Mr Crozier's stuff.'

Funny, how everyone still talks about the late editor as *Mr Crozier*. He was the only one who the other senior men referred to as Mr Crozier, never by just his surname or his initials, like they did everyone else.

The job he has just offered me involves sorting through documents from the war period. It's a clerk's job, although he doesn't call it that. He assures me it needs to be done.

'Things might get lost.' He takes a puff of his pipe, nodding, as if agreeing with himself. 'That would be regrettable. They may come in useful for reference when we get round to revisiting the war years and what went on here. A sort of archive.'

He looked at me. 'Do you think you can do it?'

'I'm sure I can, Mr Wadsworth, sir. It might take some time, but . . .'

'Time we have. Or rather, you have. Mrs Tipton will be here to help you when you come to indexing and what not.'

He heads for the door then stops and gestures at the files with his pipe. 'All this – it will be a good way of you working your way back into the paper.'

Sunt meliora.

It's difficult to tell, but Mrs Tipton looks to be in her early forties. Slim. Discreet make-up. Grey two-piece costume. She's been with the paper ever since leaving school, and has worked her way up to assistant secretary to all those on The Corridor. My room next to her office is no bigger than a storeroom.

'It *was* a storeroom – mine, as a matter of fact,' she says archly, when I joke about this, 'and you're extremely lucky to have it.'

Wadsworth is right. The files are a mess. Copies of letters from 1936 onwards between Mr Crozier and various special correspondents; memoranda; scraps of notes on paper; staff lists. Shoved into the three files, not in date order, so you don't know what will turn up where. They'd obviously been used to store random papers after his death in 1944.

It's hard to hold Mr Crozier and a sense of chaos in the same thought. An image comes to mind of him, glimpsed through the door of his room. Bent over his desk, writing, horn-rimmed glasses on the edge of his nose. A brown study of concentration, surrounded by order, not a thing out of place.

'Mr Crozier reminded me of my Classics master at school,' I say to Mrs Tipton. She's taken to sharing her tea break with me. I get the feeling she's more interested in the files than she's letting on.

'He was a great scholar,' she nods. 'All sorts of Latin and Greek books in his room – together with the Bible, of course. He wrote a book on Pontius Pilate, you know. Not my sort of book, mind you, too highbrow for the likes of me.'

She pauses as if deciding whether to carry on, then says, 'I took over temporarily as his secretary in September 1941. He used to write things in Latin in his diary. It threw me into a tizzy at first. I thought it was a sort of secret code, it was the war, after all. Then again, I thought, if he put them in his office diary, they couldn't be that secret, could they?'

She smiles as she remembers. 'There was one phrase in particular: *sunt meliora*. I really liked that. It sounded like a soft fruit. I plucked up my courage and asked him what it meant. He said, "It means 'things are looking up', Mrs Tipton," and he gave me a sort of shy smile, then said, "We haven't been bombed for a good while, the worst of the Blitz seems to have left us, so it seemed appropriate."'

She pats the file. '*Sunt meliora*. I still say it to myself some-times.' She raises her eyebrows in a self-deprecating fashion. 'It's the only Latin I'll ever know.'

'It's not a bad thing to know in any language,' I say.

She busies herself with putting the cups back on the tray, as if she's suddenly embarrassed at mentioning something personal. 'Yes, well, must get on.'

I spend the rest of that week sorting out box one, numbering each document, writing the details under the headings Mrs Tipton has suggested. *Item. Date. Subject.* I don't bother much with anyone else. Just me and the files and tea with Mrs Tipton. I lose all track of time, of days. It feels like reading a history book. Another time. Another life. I'm not a clerk. I'm a chron-icler. And I'm back where I belong on The Corridor.

For the first time since I've got back, I feel as though I'm home. First Beth. Now this. *Sunt meliora.*

Staff List. Miscellaneous.

In the middle of box one, I find the first faded staff list, September 1939. All the *MG* staff in the Manchester office are listed there. Names, ages, duties. All the staff, from the manage-ment and the office workers, to the men on The Corridor. The Greats. Men who'd worked here since the time of C.P. Scott. Men who'd covered the Great War, the Russian Revolution, the Irish Civil War, the Spanish Civil War, the abdication of Edward VIII, the rise of Mussolini and Hitler.

I scan down and find my name, scribbled on the typed list in pen. I'm the last one in, as I started in August 1939.

I'm under Miscellaneous, after Secretarial, Librarian, Cartographers, Indexing. There I am – *Messenger Boy: David Reece. Age:16.* Even now, nearly eight years on, reading my name listed on the same page as these great men makes me tingle with excitement.

And that's when it starts. That's when the sediment of memory begins to stir itself. Each grain separating, rising up, colliding with each other. Places. Faces. Voices.

March 1933. I am ten. It's early evening in the morning room. I'm reading a book.

My mother is darning socks. My father is reading bits out of the MG to her.

'First-class stuff from Voigt,' he says to her. Voigt is a special correspondent for the *MG*, based in Berlin. Hitler has just seized power. I don't understand the significance, but I sense my father's indignation and my mother's agitation about what is happening.

My father reads slowly and gravely, like Alvar Lidell on the wireless: '"The period of the Legal Terror has begun . . . not mob rule or random disorder . . . Systematic terror."'

He puts the newspaper down on his lap and takes his horn rims off. 'He's right, random disorder might not be so worrying. But systematic terror? Hitler means business.'

A few days later, my father comes home from lunch at the Liberal Club to say he's heard that the *MG* has been banned in Germany and that Voigt has left Berlin for his own safety and is now based in Paris. The rumour is that he ran a network of well-placed sources in Berlin. My father says he has now come to the attention of the Gestapo who have also set up in Paris.

As I listen, I make up my mind then and there – I want to be like Frederick Voigt. No, I want to *be* Frederick Voigt. Special Correspondent for the *Manchester Guardian*. Searching for the truth. Running a network of informants. Scourge of the Nazi Gestapo.

August 1939. I am sixteen. I'm drinking ginger beer and standing in a corner of a large, elegant room with a baby grand piano at one end.

The end of my first week at work at the *MG*. I'm invited to Arthur Wallace's Saturday Open House. Wallace, always known as AW, has had a spell at most things on the paper – literary editorship, theatre critic, literary sketches called 'back-pagers'. His Open House is legendary, diverse people who seem to mix and mingle. This week, most of the reporters and correspondents are here, plus a harpist from the Hallé Orchestra and a Labour MP for Salford.

Hitler invaded Czechoslovakia in March, Poland will be next. Our government has given a guarantee to support Poland if that happens. Most people now think it will, whatever Hitler says to the contrary. So there is definitely going to be a war. And I'm delirious with excitement about it. It'll be a short war, and I'll be here, at the centre of the paper that's gained a reputation for telling the truth about Hitler's Germany since the early 1930s.

The guests at the Open House talk of everything but the war. The paper this week has been full of it. Air raid shelters to be provided in the basements of major buildings in central Manchester. Anti-aircraft guns to be stationed north and south of the city. Imminent petrol rationing. Writing about it is one thing, talking about it off duty is another. It would come up, then someone would change the subject.

Mrs Wallace wafts in from time to time with sandwiches and cake. She sits with me and we talk a bit about my mother – they know each other from the Friends of the Art Gallery Society. We both drink ginger beer. AW comes across and helps himself to cake. 'Come and meet the others,' he says, taking my arm, and I try not to look too thrilled and fail.

AW turns to me. 'How are you settling in, young Reece?'

'Very well, sir.' I'm almost dumbstruck. It's the first time any of the major correspondents has said anything to me other than 'take this to . . . pick this up from'.

'My scouts tell me Mr Crozier has taken quite a shine to you,' Wallace beams.

This is news to me. I feel myself blush. 'That's good to know, sir.'

There is a lull in the conversation and the Labour MP's voice booms out. 'I believe Hammond said to Mr Crozier, "I think you'll be losing your young men." Typical Hammond.' He pauses. 'He's right, of course. We'll be losing them all too soon, if you ask me.'

AW frowns at him then turns to me, gesturing around. 'There's none better, young man, than these old sages who surround you – learn all you can while you can, there's none better.' He moves off to join the crowd round the piano. Mrs Wallace is arranging her music and is about to play. She begins and everyone goes quiet. Chopin, I think. Chopin is everywhere, these days.

I stand at the back, running my gaze round the semi-circle. There's a quietness about them now, faces flushed to varying degrees of redness, but anxiety is creeping in, round the eyes, round the mouth, in the tightness of their fingers clutching their glasses of sherry.

There's much clapping after Mrs Wallace finishes. We all leave shortly after. That's the last Open House for some time. A month later we're at war with Germany.

I show Mrs Tipton the staff list. 'I remember typing that,' she says. She strokes the paper gently, running her fingers down the names column. 'I was told to keep quiet about it. They didn't say, but I knew what it would be used for – making decisions about who wasn't essential to the paper so they'd be eligible for call-up or war work. It felt strange, typing all our names, especially my own.' She hesitates, then says, 'No, not strange. Frightening. I was frightened. We were all a kind of family here, and it felt as though the war had suddenly come right into our front room and someone somewhere was choosing who to snatch away from us.' She looks at me over her teacup. 'Still, we didn't lose as many people as we could have. Mr Crozier and then Mr Wadsworth fought to keep everyone they could.'

Spotters on the roof.

I come across a note at the bottom of box file two from Mr Crozier to various members of staff, dated September 1940 and headed: *Arrangements for Air Raids.* All of us were to be put on a rota as spotters on the roof for incendiary bombs. All of us together – journalists, printers, management and miscellaneous.

December 1940.

Nothing prepares us for the bombings of 22nd and 23rd December. I'm on duty up on the roof when it starts. Mr Crozier is up there too, and Mr Wadsworth. It's exciting at first, the roofs all round our buildings lit up with incendiaries, like Christmas lights scattered down from on high. Then the Royal Exchange is bombed, no more than a hundred yards away, and collapses in the street, slowly, gracefully, like a grand old Victorian lady, sighing on her way down.

Eleven incendiaries in all fall on our roof. We put them all out but it's a close-run thing. It's the first time I've been face to face with fire – the power of it, the speed of it, licking up everything before it. The explosions and the flames. It isn't exciting any more, it's terrifying.

I walk out of the city at about nine in the morning. Buildings are still burning. I can feel the heat on my face, taste the smoke. A curious body of brackish water ripples between two burning buildings, joined by skinnier tributaries as it purls along. I squint at it and realise it's a river of rats, hundreds of them scuttling, trying to escape.

A wind is getting up. We don't know it then, but that is to be the worst day – the wind will blow sparks and set more of the big warehouses on fire.

It's a six-mile walk home and I don't remember any of it.

My mother takes one look at me and sends me up to bed, smoke-blackened face and all. It is beginning to dawn on me what the war really means. It's already become more real this past year, with the casualties of Dunkirk, and what Churchill now calls the Battle of Britain. We're supposed to have got the upper hand against the Luftwaffe. But now it seems the Luftwaffe have just turned their attention elsewhere. To our cities. Terror bombing of civilians. Systematic Terror, as Voigt would say. It has come right here to our doorsteps.

'They're picking up where they left off in the Great War,' says my mother. But it's a world away from Zeppelins and a few Gotha bombers over London.

I'll be eighteen in four months' time and eligible for call-up. I'll be fighting in the war, not just flapping around on a roof putting out fires with a stirrup pump. War in Europe. That's what I'll be going to. I'll have to postpone my plan to learn my craft as a journalist.

The Valette.

At the bottom of box file two, I find a letter from Mr Crozier to Voigt, dated 31st March 1936.

Voigt is still in heroic mode. He wants to visit Berlin, but Mr Crozier says it's too risky.

The SS know that you are the most serious opponent of Nazi Germany in the English Press . . . as soon as you set foot in Germany, they would run you in for high treason . . . One has only to consider your stuff about the concentration camps which is going in the paper tomorrow (1st April).

My heart lurches when I read 1st April. I hear my father's voice. See him sitting at the breakfast table, newspaper in hand, shaking his head.

1st April 1936.

I am thirteen. 'Voigt's done it again.' My father reads out loud: '"Treatment of Prisoners in Concentration Camps. No improvement in Germany. From our Special Correspondent."'

Then he just reads out names. Sachsenburg. Mohringen. Dachau. 'So many camps,' he says, 'for so many different kinds of people.' He reads on silently, then says, 'Good God!' He looks across at my mother and they both look across at me. My father goes back to silent reading.

While my mother is upstairs making the beds and my father is getting ready to go out to the Art Gallery, I retrieve the *MG* from the pile of papers in the back kitchen and read the details. Sachsenburg: prisoners strapped down on a kind of trestle called a *Prügelbock* and flogged till they are unconscious. Dachau: prisoners flogged when they arrive. Fuhlsbüttel, a camp for political prisoners: two Trades Union leaders, sentenced to death and beheaded.

Voigt not only has the facts, he has the names of those responsible. 'The names of the camp officials and guards who order, superintend and carry out the floggings in the Sachsenburg are in the possession of your correspondent,' he writes. Voigt the fearless, the fact finder. Your Correspondent. And more than ever, I want to be Voigt. My secret ambition to leave school at sixteen and join the *MG* grows even stronger. I've not mentioned it to my parents yet, but I sense my father would approve.

I stare at Mr Crozier's letter, willing my memory to stop at the point where I'm sneaking a read of Voigt's article. It's painful enough, hearing my father's voice reading it again. But the memory slips on, to later in the day, and I can't pull it back.

I'm at the Art Gallery. My father is on the selection committee for the spring exhibitions and is at a meeting in the back office. I wander round the Gallery, then sit on the half-moon bench in front of Valette's *Albert Square 1910*, and wait for my father. We always meet up here. It's his favourite painting and he would often sit gazing at it. He'd been Valette's pupil at the Manchester School of Art and my mother said he'd always wanted to be an artist, until he came back from the Great War. He still painted, but settled for a job in the family textile firm.

I've tried hard to like the painting. My father would always do his best to describe it to me like an artist would. He would point to the foreground, to the working man, hobnail-booted and with a featureless face, and tell me to observe how he hunches his body, straining to push a handcart over the cobbles. And then he'd describe how the skinny nag, harnessed to an overladen delivery cart, steals a meal from its feed bag, and how the hopelessness in the slope of its back mirrors the man's. Then he'd move on to the background, where a couple of men wearing Homburgs, and with what my father would call that 'Manchester self-made air' about them, make their way from the Town Hall entrance across Albert Square, past the Albert Memorial. With a final flourish, he'd wave his hand over the whole painting, telling me how much he admired the Impressionist-style blue-grey fog – Valette's trademark, so he said – and how it shrouds the scene, blurring the figures, rendering them ghost-like.

I try again now, looking hard at it, wanting to see what he sees, but there just isn't enough excitement in it to keep my interest for long. I find myself drifting off, thinking more about going for tea and Welsh rarebit at the Kardomah Café. My father comes up behind me and ruffles my hair. 'Time to hunt the Welsh Rabbit, don't you think?' His little joke.

It's a bright spring day, no Valette moody blues. My father's step is sprightly; he's always in a good mood when he's been to the Gallery. A nag clops into the Square, head down, lugging a coal cart, a workman walking beside it, holding its halter, his hobnail boots sparking off the cobbles.

'What does that remind you of?' My father points at the horse and the workman. I look up at him and say it's like the Valette and he beams at me. 'Well done, David, well done.'

He walks with his hand on my shoulder, the tap of the stick in his other hand light and rhythmic. Two men are making their way towards us across the Square to the Town Hall, well-dressed important types, and I hear my father mutter, 'Blast! No time to take evasive action, prepare to be bored to death,' and I giggle as he raises his hand off my shoulder to return, half-heartedly, the wave they give him. His hand comes down again, too quickly, and grips me so hard, I cry out. His fingers dig into the soft flesh below my collarbone, his thumb presses against my shoulder blade. I can't turn to look, but I sense him falling, his grip loosening, his hand sliding down my back. I hear the stick clattering down. He's lying on the floor clutching his arm, his face ashen, his lips turning blue, drawn back in a rictus of pain.

The two men run up to him and one gets down on his knees, saying something about *don't worry, old chap*. The second one shouts over to the workman to go into the Town Hall, tell them Alderman Webster says to fetch a doctor, his friend has collapsed. He tells me to go with him, they'll look after things here.

I look down at my father. His eyes are staring at me, but they're not seeing me. I do as I'm told and walk towards the workman, who is busy tying the old nag to a bench seat. The horse begins to forage in its nose bag, enjoying the unexpected rest, and then lifts its head out of the sack.

It has the long ears and flat nose of a mule. It's free of all shackles, but it's pinned to the ground by two of the muleteers, one of them sitting across its upturned flank, the other sitting on its head. Rapid snorts of breath escape through its nose as it panics, realising it is trapped. The Doc severs the vocal cords, his movements quick and practised.

The poor creatures, I think. De-brayed. Rendered dumb. But it has to be done. It will certainly help now all the mules are silent; the Japanese won't hear us coming. They won't hear us in this room, this airless, poky room, next to Mrs Tipton's office. They won't hear me.

I'm dizzy. Unfocused. Ungrounded. Floundering in a swirl of memories. The world that was. The boy I was. That foolish, naive boy. The future I thought I had. Hitler means business. Voigt. My father ruffling my hair. My father falling, falling away from me. Welsh Rabbit.

142

Ginger beer. Open House with the Greats. *Well done, David, well done.*

There are no boundaries. I can't control what grain of memory will float by next or how long it will linger or where it will settle.

Miss Tipton rattles the tray. She's come in, unnoticed.

I grab on to the present moment as she comes fuzzily into view. 'I've nearly finished box file two. There's just this to do.' I wave the letter at her and manage a vague smile.

'I'll log that for you, if you like.' She takes the letter from me gently and passes me a cup. 'Only so much sorting out of the past you can do in one day,' she says, patting my shoulder. 'Drink your tea and catch an early bus home. They say more snow is on the way.'

I have a quiet Saturday with Beth. I don't tell her the slippages are back. I wake up in the night slick with sweat, tasting the sickening mix of chloroform, blood and disinfectant.

A jolly bonfire.

Monday, I drag myself into work. One more week on the files should see the job done. Wadsworth will find something else for me. I need to see this job done.

At the bottom of box file three I find another staff list, September 1940. The usual names, ages, duties and a new column added: *Reasons for deferment from military service.*

A considerable number of people are listed in the reasons column as being over military age. Then there's Miss Taunton, aged 18, noted as having a deformed leg, and one of the reporters listed as a conscientious objector. My name is still at the bottom. But now I'm permanent, it's typed. Aged 17 and 'under age' in the deferment column.

Muddled up with routine memoranda, I find a copy of a letter from Mr Crozier to Mr Haley, who handles the deferment appeals against call-up on behalf of the Newspaper Society. Mr Crozier writes that the two he's most afraid of losing are Miss

B, one of the secretaries, who can write shorthand and type at any speed; and Mr T, because of his work with maps. Both would be severe losses. Someone else has scribbled at the bottom: *Our messenger boy, young Reece, is 17 at the moment, so technically still under age. But he will be 18 in just over six months. I fear there is nothing we can do for him when that time comes.*

It hits me so hard to read this. It shouldn't, I suppose, but it does. Even when I was up on the roof, sweating it out alongside them, putting the incendiaries out, they must have known they would be letting me go. *You will be losing your young men.* I was the least needed. *There is nothing we can do for him.* I don't know why I'm so shocked to see it there in black and white. It was the way of things for all eighteen-year-olds.

The Guardians. I felt safe with them. I'd joined the paper three years after my father's death. I was Owen Reece's boy. They'd look after me. They'd help me achieve my greatest ambition to become one of them. To be like Voigt. My head reasons they were right, there was nothing they could do. But the reality of it hits me in the chest, making it difficult to breathe. I need to get out.

I find myself walking down The Corridor, past the quiet hum of the Reporters' Room, down the stairs, out past the reception office, on to Cross Street. George's shop is only ten minutes away so I make my way there, stumbling over the heaps of dirty snow shovelled to the edges of the pavements. But the shop is shut – it's his booksellers' lunch day when they all get together and talk books and business. I see the 'Closed' sign, the shop in darkness and a flush of rage takes over. The one day I need you, George, and you're not here.

I decide to let myself in, make a cup of tea, calm down before I go home. I go round the back to the shed where he keeps odds and ends. A few broken shelves, a couple of paraffin heaters. His old bike with the basket. Before the war, he'd ride round the centre of Manchester on it, the basket full of books, bringing great literature to the workers. A regular Mr Chips. The key to the shop is where it usually is, under the tiny plant pot on the shed window ledge.

I don't bother with the tea. I stride straight through to the shop. Up and down between the rows, pulling out fine leather volumes, part of this or that set, first editions, tipping them over, enjoying the flap and the splat and the thunk of the books as they hit the floor.

The shelves are soon looking like rows of bombed out terraces, the odd old volume left leaning at the end, or wobbling defiantly in the gaps. His treasured paperbacks are next. I think of him fussing about, placing them in order, shuffling them again. I grab armfuls and take them outside near the shed. Make a funeral pyre, criss-crossing the broken shelves on top of the snow. Heap the books up, orange and blue and green and pink, Homer clothed in his acorn brown on top. Soak them with paraffin from the heaters. Set them all alight – *a jolly bonfire of jolly books, de-dah, de-dah, de-fucking-dah*. They're capering now alright, his precious Penguins, flippers semaphoring like crazy as the flames tickle their flat little feet. Pages curling up nicely, burning a treat and all their bloody wisdom with them. Fire against snow. Red ink. White paper. *Sotoba*. A marker for the dead.

I check the bike. Its tyres are pumped up so I take it and ride it all the way home.

The wind is at my back again, funnelling straight down between the city buildings. The wind, gusting me along like an ancient Greek ship in full sail, battling through sea-green choppy waters, a line of oars out where there really shouldn't have been any.

I follow the route Louie and I took on our first day back. Turn into Oak Road, get to the monkey puzzle, waiting for me, as undemonstrative as ever. My mother is at her Women's Voluntary Service meeting, so I go round the side of the house, get the axe from our potting shed, come back and lay into those ugly, reptilian branches. Chopping and swinging on the splintered limbs until they break off. It's tough going, it's solid and unyielding and it's not an ornamental tree in an English garden any more, it's a stand of bamboo higher than two men and thicker than organ pipes, and I'm hacking through, fearful the Japanese are creeping up in their silent soft shoes, picking off the stragglers at the back one by one.

'You look busy,' my mother says. I turn and see her making her way across the frozen earth of the vegetable patch. 'Mrs Roberts rang the WVS to tell me you were home.'

She nods her head at next door, where the net curtain twitches. She comes up close and puts her arm around my shoulder. 'Time for a rest now, son.' Her tone is calm and even and she gently takes the axe from me and drops it on the ground.

'I never liked this bloody tree,' I say.

'Neither did I.' She gathers me into her as I begin to weep.

My mother never mentions the monkey puzzle. But one day, I notice it's gone. Someone has finished what I started. The earth is freshly dug over where once it stood.

Mr Wadsworth sends a message. I can take as much time as I like before I come back.

George comes round. He pats me on the shoulder, says it's OK, the bookshop was tidied up in a jiffy. And books are replaceable, especially paperbacks, there's no real harm done.

But there is, George. There is so much harm done.

I go back to the MG after a couple of weeks. The job still needs to be done. Everybody says so. Mrs Tipton keeps a close eye on me and keeps the tea coming. I have a suspicion the last box file has already been sorted through. Sanitised. It doesn't matter. I get on with the clerking, indexing the documents. The memories seem to have settled themselves down, still shifting underfoot, but less turbulent. Easier to handle than the chaos.

Beth, my mother, George, even Wadsworth and Mrs Tipton, all of them in their way, they all get me back on track. They can't get me right, but they get me back on track. Enough to keep going, at least.

I drift through February. The winter is one of the worst on record. I hardly notice it.

Then Louie rings.

Louie

On the telephone, he said he'd be here by six. I'm early. It's not a part of town I know well. The pub is down a backstreet near the railway arches in central Manchester. Three grimy, single-storey terraces knocked into one, with two steps up to the splintered front door. The sign says 'Tommy Ducks'. There's a rumour it should have said 'Tommy Duckworth', after the owner, but the signwriter ran out of space.

Inside, a foetid smell hangs about the place – male sweat, stale tobacco, over-ripe lavatories. A spiv glances over his shoulder at me as I stand beside him at the bar. I get a sense of a feral face and dark, insolent eyes. I order a pint and the spiv turns his back to continue his conversation in low tones with the barman.

I take my drink over to the corner furthest away.

I'd been surprised to hear from Louie, then pleased. I'd been so wrapped up in myself, I'd forgotten how much I missed him. He hadn't said much, just that things were OK. I had the feeling he was holding something back, but then I'd often had that feeling with Louie.

The door swings open and in he comes. He spots me and waves. 'You found it, then?' he says, coming across to the corner, grinning.

'With some difficulty.' I grin back. We shake hands and I can feel the callouses on his palm. The backs of his hands are a criss-cross of weathered cracks.

'That's the idea. The regulars here aren't too keen on being found.' He jinks his head in the spiv's direction. 'It's one of Charlie's haunts. I'm staying with him at the moment, so unfortunately it's my local, not that I use it much.'

I'd forgotten about Charlie from the railway arches and the motorbike. I laugh.

He grins again. 'I'll get them in.' The spiv gives him the once-over, then ignores him.

We drink slowly, checking each other out over the rims of our glasses.

'You look bloody terrible,' he says, frowning.

'You don't look too chipper, yourself.' His face is even thinner, the sharp cheekbones and dark shadows underlining and emphasising the blue eyes. He's wearing a navy donkey jacket, clean but worn, over a neat collared shirt and tie. His rough trousers are streaked with dust and spotted with dried mortar.

'I've just come from work.' He shakes his head. 'This bloody winter. The site's been closed more than it's been open. Christmas bonuses all went up the swannee.'

'At least you've got a job. I told you there'd be work for you.'

'Aye,' he says. 'I count myself lucky. I got a job right away, back with my old boss. But I've got another one. In London. That's partly why I rang you, just to let you know.'

'London? Why London?'

'This job I have here is OK. The builder I work for did well in the war with his contracting business – he didn't build much, but an awful lot had to be torn down, what with the bomb damage, and now the building is starting again. But it's small stuff – a few houses here, a few there. The really big stuff is happening down south. Do you remember that major I told you about, in Chittagong last year? The one in charge of that mathematics course I did?'

'You did so many bloody courses.'

'They were free,' he grins at me, 'and it passed the time while we were waiting for the boat home. Anyway, the major worked for Taylor Woodrow – Contracts Manager or something quite high up. We got to talking about building and the construction industry and he said if I ever wanted work after the war, I should contact him in London. So I did.'

He drained his glass. 'I start in a couple of months' time, soon as I've finished up here.'

'I bet Annie is pleased.'

He hesitates as if he's working out how to say something. 'Annie's gone.' He shrugged. 'She'd gone by the time I got home. Not exactly a surprise.'

'I'm sorry. That's such bad luck, Louie.' It sounds hollow, but it's all I can think to say. He'd never talked much about his wife. He'd got a letter just before we caught the boat back from Bombay which seemed to make him angry, then quiet, but he didn't say what was in it.

'It was never right, not really. It wasn't right before the war, and four years of me being away finished us off. She wrote to say she might not be here when I got back.'

I remembered our first day home when he dropped me off, the hesitancy when he said he wasn't sure she'd be there when he got home.

Louie shrugs again. 'It's not all bad. I meant it – I do count myself lucky. I've got the chance of another good job and there are digs to go with it so I've got somewhere to live. It's more than some poor buggers came home to.'

I nod at him as I take a sip of my beer. I can't help but feel glad for him, but underneath it, there's a pull of sadness. It feels like he's ready to move on with his life, and I'm not.

'What about you?' he says, as if he's read my thoughts. 'What have you been up to?'

I talk about being back at the paper. About being back on The Corridor, with Wadsworth the Editor, and the top men in the Reporters' Room. I don't say I'm a filing clerk. I don't tell him a direct lie exactly, but I let him think I'm doing reporter-type work. And I don't tell him about the problems I've been having. Or the 'slippages'. Or the bonfire of books. Or the monkey puzzle.

I do tell him a little about Beth.

'About bloody time you got yourself a sweetheart,' he says.

I smile to myself, wondering what Beth would think about being described as anyone's sweetheart. 'I'll drink to that,' I say.

'We'll both drink to that. Let's move over to the bar. We'll have a quick whisky, then I've really got to go, mate. I'm dog-tired. I need an early night.'

We move over to the bar.

'Same again, Vinny?' The spiv nods and the barman pours a large whisky. Close up, I realise the spiv is just a youth. Good quality woollen overcoat. Loud tie. Slicked back Brylcreemed hair. A gold signet ring, the size of a gobstopper, bulges on his little finger.

The barman serves us our drinks. 'How long you been back?' He looks at Louie. He has the barman's knack of sizing up his customers from the moment they walk in.

'Four months,' says Louie.

'The war's been over more than eighteen,' Vinny chips in. 'Couldn't tear yourselves away?' He smirks at us. His voice is surprisingly whiny, at odds with the tough guy image.

'Something like that,' says Louie, amiable enough.

'Not surprised. Free beer, free bed and board, free French letters – I should be so bloody lucky.' He winks at the barman who is paying close attention to wiping down the pumps.

'You missed out the sun tan and foreign travel,' Louie says, a little wearily.

Vinny looks round the bar to check out his audience and raises his voice. He seems well practised at this kind of taunt. 'Then you get back and they give you demob money and a free suit – not that I'd be seen dead in one of those.' He fingers the thick lapels of his overcoat.

The barman moves on to wiping down the bar top. I get the impression if he's forced to take sides it will be with Vinny; he probably depends on black-marketeering to boost his sales.

The rage wells up from somewhere near the pit of my stomach.

Louie finishes the whisky and puts it down on the bar.

His silence seems to annoy Vinny, who picks up where he left off, the voice squeaky now. 'And then jump the queue for jobs. Or say your nerves aren't right enough to work yet, after all you've been through – meanwhile we just get on with it, like we did in the war while you lot were swanning around.'

I look at his soft white hands with the gold dobber of a ring on the little finger and think of Louie's hands, cracked and calloused.

'As if you'd know what an honest day's work is,' I say and take a step towards him.

He balls up his fists.

Louie takes hold of my arm. 'Let's go,' he says, 'and leave this young gentleman to it.'

His voice is quiet but his grip on my arm is like a vice. I resist him for a moment, but he pulls at me and we both back away then turn and go through the door. As it swings back, I hear a snort of laughter. I'm all for going back in again, but Louie shakes his head.

He stands there, breathing deeply. 'Just breathe in,' he says, 'breathe in that fresh air.'

'It makes you wonder what we fought for.' The sharpness of the air sears my nose.

'Not for that little bastard, that's for sure. But it's not worth rising to the bait. You could have a fight on your hands every bloody day if you did. There's plenty around think like him.' He turns to me. 'I must be off. Early start in the morning. Up the workers, eh?' He holds out his hand. 'I'll let you know when I'm moving to London.'

'We'll meet up again before you go.' I feel the rough callouses again.

'Better not make it Tommy Duck's,' he says, with his old grin.

And at that moment, I almost ask him about the Japanese boy. If he dreams about the Japanese boy like I do. If he relives what happened like I do. Because from the moment he came in the pub door, that's what I've wanted to ask him about. And now he's going away, I might never be able to speak to him again about it. I almost call out to him as he walks away. Call him back. But I don't, and he turns the corner.

I cross the road and wait in the shadows for Vinny to come out. I'm not sure what I'm going to do.

As I wait in the cold, I stamp my feet, trying to keep the circulation flowing, and my mind begins to wander. But it always comes back to that face, that young Japanese face, surrounded by the green jungle fronds of camouflage he'd stuck in his helmet, like some pagan halo.

I wait about half an hour, then the pub door opens and a man comes down the three steps. It's Vinny and he's on his own. There's a gap between the pub wall and the wall of the building next door, a narrow alleyway used as somewhere on the way out for those who couldn't be bothered waiting for the lavatories inside. Vinny turns down it. A dirty yellow light shines from a small window high up in the next-door building, just enough to outline his skinny frame as he turns towards the wall.

I follow him in, the stench stinging my throat, and before he turns, I kick him in the back of his legs and he falls forwards. He's too drunk to catch on to what's happening to him and I turn him over and sit astride him. He flails at me, catching me in the eye, shouting, and I can feel his runty body between my legs, wriggling and writhing.

He gasps. 'Get off me, yer fucker!' I look down at his bony face. At his bony Japanese face. And I began to beat it. Punch his nose. Stud into an eye socket with my knuckles.

He's not moving much now and begins to moan. I slide my hands down to his throat. 'Kill me, would you? Kill me?' I say, over and over. He makes little gurgling noises as I tighten my grip.

I look down at the face above my hands. It's Vinny's face.

I climb off him and back away. He moans and turns his face towards me. His bones take on a mosaic of light and shadow in the glow of the sickly light. His eyes are half-lidded, struggling to open. I was wrong. It's not Vinny. It's the Japanese boy. I walk towards him again and this time, I kick. Kick until those shadows lose their sharpness and the toe of my shoe feels a softness where there'd been bone. I stand over him, exhausted, watching his legs and arms kicking feebly, like some upended insect trying to right itself. Then I stagger away.

My fists hurt. My eye is tender. He must have landed a punch in my ribs; it's painful to breathe. How will I get home? One foot in front of the other, just like bloody Burma, that's how I'll get home.

Nambu.

Louie saved my life in Burma. He'd get annoyed when I said that to people.

'It wasn't your time to go, simple as that,' he'd say. 'Nothing to do with me. After nearly four years going through this lot, the one thing I've learned is when your number's up, it's up. When it isn't, it isn't. Nothing you or me can do about it.'

He might be right. But if he hadn't been there, I'd be dead.

They never gave up, the Japanese. They dug themselves in, built bunkers and hunkered down, defending a lost cause. We threw everything we had at them, and they still stuck there. When the lads finally blasted them out on Kuki Piquet, they found an underground camp, tunnelled into the hillside, complete with an HQ, a repair shop, even a hospital.

They were starving towards the end. God knows, our rations were bad enough, but theirs were non-existent. Their supplies had long been cut off. Some of the bodies in the bunkers didn't have a mark on them and were little more than skeletons.

We once found a dead Japanese in a bunker with his thighs wrapped round a mortar – the flesh had thinned away to nothing, the hip bones so pronounced they reminded me of a wing nut round a bolt. He must have known he was dying from starvation and decided he'd take a few of us with him, if we came into his bunker firing at random, as we often did.

'Watch it,' Captain Evans would always say, before we moved in, 'they're dangerous even when they're bloody dead.'

The stench. Like nothing I'd ever come across before – not just dead or burning bodies, we'd got used to that. It was some stinking midden of maggot-ridden, rotting flesh, cordite, excrement, burning rubber – the putrid detritus of human bodies mixed in with the metallic, acrid fumes of the mechanical waste of war.

We came out of one bunker-checking job, and Louie stopped behind me to be sick.

I walked back to the two dead bodies I'd just passed. The greenery was attached to one of them, the body sprawled over a long rifle with a fixed bayonet. A haze of flies rose and then fell as I passed them. I was reeling, trying to draw breath to get the stink out of my nose and mouth. I heard a sort of yelp from Louie – 'Fuckin' little fucker!' – and I turned round.

He was standing there, his rifle raised, but there was something not quite right with what I was seeing. It was no more than a split second but it felt a lot longer before I worked it out. The undergrowth I'd just walked past was on the move. I froze on the spot as a giant serrated frond rose up like a droopy green hand, then I heard a rifle shot and the hand flopped down again. Louie was staring down at the bundle of leaves spread-eagled on the ground.

I walked back. The greenery was attached to a body, sprawled over a long rifle with a fixed bayonet. There was a pistol lying on the ground near the right hand. Louie turned the body over with his foot. The torso was emaciated, stick arms and legs protruding from ragged remnants of uniform, the head oversized in its field helmet. It looked like a praying mantis, fallen from its branch, lying prone on a bed of leafy camouflage.

Maybe it was the thinness of it, but the face looked very young to me. A boy's face. I stared at this face, thinking what was he doing on his own, this boy? How long had he waited beside that other dead body? The action had finished the day before; he must have waited all night. They never surrendered, but why didn't he try to run away? He must have known we'd be coming through with grenades and bayonets, clearing out the remnants from the bunkers.

He'd hidden there and waited. Others must have walked past him. But he chose me. It was me he decided to kill.

And the urge took over then, to do that body harm. I wanted to plunge my bayonet in, like he would have done to me. I didn't care if he was already dead.

I'd never killed anyone up close, but I wanted to rip into him, rattle his bony ribs.

'What the fuck's going on here?' Captain Evans came up behind us.

'Louie shot him, sir. He was going to kill me, and Louie shot him.' I was gabbling.

Captain Evans stared down at the body. He bent down to pick up the pistol, saying, 'He probably meant to commit suicide, Corporal, after finishing you off. Here's a souvenir to show your grandchildren. If I'm not mistaken, it's a Nambu. Service issue.' Then he frowned and bent closer. 'He's still breathing,' he said flatly. He straightened up. 'How many times do I have to tell you? Never trust a fucking corpse.' He handed me the pistol and walked off.

I bent down close to check the breathing for myself. His eyes were half opened.

A flicker of eyelids, then a full, unfocused gaze woozily finding mine, locking on.

I shot him through the temple with his own gun. I felt nothing.

'He was dying anyway,' Louie said. 'You just put him out of his misery.'

Later, I gave the Nambu back to Captain Evans.

Cracks.

After that night at Tommy Ducks and the incident with Vinny, I think my mother will winkle away, try and get the story out of me, but she doesn't. She asks me once what happened and when I say I don't remember, she leaves it. But she insists I go to see Dr Jenkins. He checks out my ribs, says they're bruised but not broken, says there's nothing he can do for the shiner, asks a bit about Burma, says it was a bad show.

'Come back and see me if you're still having problems – any kind of problems,' he says, looking straight at me.

I go back to work. I've been away almost more than I've been there. They still welcome me back. Mrs Tipton makes me tea. Mr Wadsworth says I'm doing a job that needs doing, he's found more boxes of files, but I mustn't overdo it. I notice I'm not left alone for very long.

I have a major slippage when I'm with Beth. We go to a Hallé concert at the King's Hall, Belle Vue. It's Tchaikovsky and we're in for a romantic evening. Sir John Barbarolli is back from touring Austria and he gets a standing ovation when he walks on the stage. The clatter of clapping hands, those thousand little cracking explosions, each one a pistol shot, get right into my head and I find myself fighting along the row of seats, then sprinting up the aisle out into the open, my heart fit to burst.

Beth follows me out and cradles my head against her shoulder, not saying anything, just holding me. But even Beth, my hope, my love, my future, even she can't get me right.

The Japanese boy's face – I keep seeing it, on passers-by in the street, on a poster advertising Brylcreem. Split-second changes – their ordinary faces – flash, then Vinny – flash, then the Japanese boy – flash. It always stops me in my tracks.

The nightmares and dreams come. Bodies – barefoot, burning, emaciated – but mostly, camouflaged and rearing up, about to do me harm. A praying mantis. The haft of a pistol.

Vinny's face, caved in and bleeding. The boy with a hole in his temple. I cry out, and fight my way up to consciousness again. And Beth is there. Or my mother.

I begin to fight sleep because if I sleep, I'll dream and the dreams will be of Vinny and the boy. But I eventually fall into a fitful sleep anyway. So, I start doubling up on the sleeping powders, making sure I knock myself out so there's no time or space for dreams. I'm groggy the whole of the next day, which is a blessing.

I slowly slip down. I'm so weak to be giving in like this. So ashamed of being so weak. Feel weaker because I'm so ashamed.

One day, I try to get out of bed to go to work. But it's so much safer to stay where I am. So that's what I do. I stay there, under the bedclothes. And the day after. And the day after that.

No amount of cajoling from my mother will make me budge. So she doesn't cajole.

Beth comes round and sits with me. Kind and loving and tender. But I feel a chasm grow between us and there's nothing I can do about it.

Dr Jenkins comes to see me. Prescribes medicine to calm me down. It fogs me up.

I don't feel any better. In fact, I don't feel anything much at all. He recommends a private clinic in Manchester. He also suggests a spell in hospital might help. He gets things in motion. More medicine from the consultant at the private clinic to calm me down and tide me over.

I begin to function. Get up in the mornings. Sleep-walk through the day. Go to bed.

The chasm between Beth and me grows even wider. She says she understands. I say she can't possibly understand, can't know what's going on in my head; I don't know even know what's going on in my head.

Other cracks appear – between me and my mother, between me and the rest of the world, between me and myself.

We've all been through the war. Those I left behind have been through theirs. I've been through mine. It feels like they were different wars. I brought my war back with me. It doesn't match theirs. Nothing fits any more.

How did I ever think I could pick up where I left off? How stupid could I be?

I don't notice the spring. The worst floods ever follow the worst winter ever.

I drift through May.

The end of the month, the letter comes from Northfield.

Part Three

Northfield

August – September 1947

I

I scribble a title on the first page of my sketches and notes. *On Not Recalling War*. It reminds me of John. He's still AWOL. It's been four days now. He's been absent overnight before, on one of his benders, but he's always crept back in the morning. I've begun to breathe easier without him. I'm surprised about that.

I almost throw the notes on Vinny and the Japanese boy away. It feels so risky, writing it down. But in the end, I keep it in. Maybe, deep down, I want someone to know. It may as well be Dr Carter. I deliberately bump into him near his room as he's heading for the wards.

'It feels a bit like handing in homework.' I shove the papers into his hands, knowing he won't have time to talk. 'You asked me how I got here. Well, here it is, as much as I know.'

'*On Not Recalling War.*' He reads out loud, his eyebrows raised. He sounds weary.

'It's a sort of joke. Before I came here, I did nothing else but recall war in one way or another, although I didn't realise it at the time. Everyone at home was telling me not to. Then I get here, and I still do it – everybody does it. Well, nearly everybody. And then you tell me it's not a bad thing.' I hear myself mumbling.

'We'll maybe talk about that in our next session,' he says.

After meeting up with him, I wander across to the Art Hut. The music playing today is Victor Sylvester, 'You're Dancing on My Heart'. Not John's cup of tea, I shouldn't think, but I find its steady tempo reassuring. Sylvester's trademark two pianos are tinkling away, one sticking with the melody in the solo, the other deftly improvising in the background, sounding like the bubbles in lemonade. Two men are dancing together at one end of the Hut, the one taking the lead breathing 'slow, slow, quick-quick-slow', and cursing mildly as the other stumbles. There's some sort of hospital dance on tonight, although they're not as well attended by the village women as they were during the war, now their menfolk are back.

I've been coming here since the day after John took off. I drift in, then drift out again. I've still not painted or drawn anything. We're all drifting, it seems to me, patients, staff, the whole hospital. Then today – I don't know if it's anything to do with the work I've been doing for Dr Carter, maybe I've loosened up – I decide I'll take a turn to paint on *The Island*.

I choose a cheap hogshair from a chipped vase crammed with brushes, dried-up rainbow colours crusting their wooden handles. Someone has already mixed the paints in jam jars, primary school fashion, and lined them up on a side table. An image flashes in, of my father's brushes and oil paints stuffed into two earthenware jugs on the Welsh dresser at home. They stand untouched, except for my mother dusting them in some daily ritual of remembrance.

We're on the last twenty feet of paper. Every day the men roll up the work they've done, leaving a fresh stretch of white along the trestle table for the next group. The fat end of the roll has a month's work wrapped up in it: Errol Flynn-style action – tanks, guns, parachutes; the London Blitz with more than a nod to *Guernica* – angular figures, angry colour, a bomber circling St Paul's; versions of Home Sweet Home – grass, sun, sky, in heightened hallucinatory green, yellow, blue.

Sergeant Bradbury makes a point of telling newcomers to the Art Hut how *The Island* got its name. He'd had this idea of doing a painting on one continuous roll, 'a Bayeux Tapestry effect, but more random, more free expression,' he says, 'and I told the first group about it and said it was up to them to decide what we called it.'

Someone in the group had said he didn't think he could paint on a continuous roll alongside other people, he'd find it too inhibiting, then someone else said no man is an island, and anyway, according to the doctors, it's good for us to work together, so the first man said OK, man might not be an island, but he would dearly like to be on one, instead of here in this loony bin, all of us going quietly mad, if we weren't mad before, and the second man said let's call the painting on the roll *The Island* then, if that'll make you happy.

The first group has long gone, but the name stuck.

'That's how it works in here,' says Sergeant Bradbury, 'we argue, sometimes we even agree, but don't count on it.' He gestures expansively round the hut. 'Paint anything you like. Paint on *The Island*, or at one of the easels, or don't do anything at all, just watch the others.'

Where he got the paper from, given the shortages, who knows, but he was an artist before the war and has posh connections in London. He conjures up powder paints, brushes, even charcoal, though he's choosy about who gets to use that. The paper comes in three-hundred-feet lengths, three feet wide. The sergeant stands the finished rolls round the walls, like giant scrolls in a Medieval library. Says it makes the place look less like a Nissen hut.

I suck the end of the brush and try and look as though I'm pondering.

'Get a move on, son, the paint'll have dried up by the time you've started.'

A voice from behind me. Joe, I think. It's a large group today and he's raring to go.

'I don't know what I want to do.' I hear myself whining like a ten-year-old.

'Don't think about it. The more you think about it, the more you'll freeze up.' Joe again.

'You could say that about a lot of things.' This from Steve, prompting a few sniggers.

'Don't paint anything if you don't want to,' says Sergeant Bradbury.

I haven't painted anything since my father was alive. In summer, when I was a boy, he'd set up a small easel next to his on the back lawn. We'd paint, but he'd forget I was there. I'd get bored and wander off to the wild patch at the bottom of the garden to catch butterflies in jam jars, mesmerised by the tawny reds, creamy whites, dusty blacks of their wings, oblivious to their distress as they fluttered and weakened. Beating bands of colour in jam jars.

On today's section, there are two straight rows of muddy brown daubs, cocoon shaped – that's Michael's contribution. There's a desperate precision about them, all the same size, near as dammit, and the same number, two rows of eight, lined up like pawns on a chessboard. Next to the daubs is Steve's effort – a pencil drawing of a woman, cartoonish, a look of *Jane* from the *Daily Mirror* about her. Long-limbed, pert breasts, the *Jane* of the early war years when her perky modesty was always more or less preserved by her lacy underwear.

After *Jane* is a stretch of virgin white paper, staring at me.

Panic. 'I can't think of anything.' I hand the brush to Joe, who's already mixed some red and yellow in a saucer and immediately starts to paint a Christian cross in darkish orange.

'Maybe you'd like to work over here.' Sergeant Bradbury steers me by the elbow to the easel corner. 'Try this.' He hands me a stick of charcoal, the first I've held for over five years.

I balance it on the tips of my first two fingers, circle my thumb along it, enjoying the textures, the smooth and slightly rough pitted patches, then hold it up and twist it to catch the dull sheen of black satin.

I begin to draw. I don't think much about what I'm drawing, it just comes.

Vertical strokes – flat black trees, splintered and scorched. Horizontal sweeps – fierce black bunkers sunk into the outline of a hillside. Thumb-smudges – hazy black clouds, hovering at ground level.

Fractured images. No refinement, no perspective, no cohesion. Quick and dirty.

That'll do. I turn to look for Sergeant Bradbury and see him watching me.

I hand him the charcoal and go over to the sink to wash the black off my fingers. My hands shake under the running water. A stocky man, with greasy blond hair, sits on a high stool, resting an elbow on the wooden draining board. He hasn't painted anything since I've been coming to the sessions. He watches what other people are doing and smiles when you go near him, a curled-lip, knowing sort of smile like the one he's sharing with me now. He's in charge of brewing up today so he gets down off the stool and potters over to the primus on the corner work bench. By the time he's made the tea, I'm calm enough to stand with the others.

There's one final flourish from Victor Sylvester, then the music stops.

'So, what have we got?' says Sergeant Bradbury, in that thoughtful way he has, conducting us round as if we're the judging committee for the Royal Academy Summer Exhibition. Only, he doesn't want us to judge, he wants us to talk. At the beginning of each session, he reminds us we can speak our minds freely about the paintings or about any general thoughts or feelings they bring up. He puffs on his pipe and reminds me of George. I'm surprised by a twinge of guilt, as I remember that time in his bookshop – *so what did you think of the* Odyssey? – and the hurt in his eyes when I was so sarcastic. Then I remember the burning, capering Penguins and the twinge of guilt becomes an ache.

We start on *The Island*.

'Michael's still on his dead bodies,' says Steve, pointing to the daubs.

'They're the unresurrected dead,' Michael explains, to nobody in particular. He explains this every day. According to the others, he's painted nothing but the unresurrected dead since he started coming weeks ago. No-one comments on it much any more. I think of asking him who the unresurrected dead are, but I lose my nerve.

'Cheerful as ever,' murmurs Steve, standing next to me.

We move on to Joe's crosses – there's five of them now. He's painted them in a line, along a jungle path overhung with serrated leaves and elephant grass. His older brother had been captured at the fall of Singapore and died on the Burma death railway. My stomach flips. Here we go, this will be about what the Japanese did to prisoners.

Even before he says a word, I'm already back there at Kohima, sleeping – no, dozing at best, one ear cocked, leaning upright in the pitch dark, against a bank in a gully. Listening to them creeping around, then calling out *Hey Johnny* in English, hoping we'd call back and give our positions away.

I don't want to be reminded of what it felt like, listening, having to keep schtum, fearful all the time. Fearful of falling asleep, of falling into oblivion. But most of all, fearful of getting caught.

I hear my heart pounding.

If I can ease myself out of the group and escape outside, I'll be OK. But Sergeant Bradbury asks Joe if he'd like to say something about his crosses.

I have to stay put. Listen. Keep schtum.

The crosses, Joe says, should be crucifixes with the body of Christ on them, but he says he's not good at doing bodies. 'I told the Padre, I'm not good at doing bodies.' Then he tells us how the Padre brought him a crucifix made of cheap white metal, belonging to one of the Gurkhas. The loop in the top, for the chain to go through, had broken. Joe was a wireless operator and had a reputation for being a whiz at repairing delicate equipment and the Padre wondered if he could mend the crucifix – maybe solder the loop together again?

Joe shakes his head as if he's right back there with the Padre. 'I told him, you can't solder white metal, Padre, it just dissolves. He looked that disappointed. Then I had a bit of a brainwave.' He's warming to the tale now, and he smiles and the smile makes his old-young face look young. 'The shells had a big brass

168

container for the cordite. It was expensive, being brass, so we had to send them back to be reused, but we had a damaged one, a tank had run over it, and I got permission to use it.

'I flattened it, cut it and made a small cross with a loop. Beaten brass, it was lovely, even if I do say so myself. The Padre was so pleased, he had a little blessing ceremony, there and then, at the work bench. Then he says could I make him some more? I say how many, and he says there's another four Gurkhas who are Christians. So I made four more.'

He pauses, then says, 'It cheered me up no end, thinking about those crosses, maybe keeping them safe.' He touches one of the crosses on the painting with his fingertips as if he's checking to see whether it's dry.

We sink into a respectful silence, verging on the sombre.

'Didn't keep enough of us safe, though, did he, God?' says Steve.

That breaks through the melancholy. And off we go, on familiar territory: cursing God, praising God, denying God, questioning God's motives – where was God in the Blitz – always a hot topic in the Art Hut. This leads on to stories about padres – good ones, bad ones, ones who lost their faith or went off their rockers, in the desert, in the jungle, up a mountain in Sicily, in the country lanes in Normandy.

I've got a padre story too, about the one who offered Holy Communion at Kohima to a group behind us as we mounted a bombardment on the bunkers – *the body of our Lord Jesus Christ, which was given for you, preserve your body and soul to everlasting life* – punctuated by the whump of the shells finding their target.

Half of me wants to tell the group this, join in, but the other half says keep it tamped down, you never know what will bubble up once you take the lid off, so I stay quiet.

Sergeant Bradbury says maybe we should take a look at Steve's *Jane*.

'Is that supposed to be the wife?' says a voice from the back.

169

'Not married, mate,' says Steve. 'It's the lovely *Jane*. She kept me going in the war.'

'I liked her better with her scanties on,' says Joe. 'Later on, when she started to take all her clothes off, I thought that was a bit much. She was British, after all.'

'She looks like a lot of men's wives – no better than she should be,' says the same voice from the back, a sharp edge to it.

And that triggers off the most popular hot topic of all in the Art Hut. The women, our women, sleeping around with the Poles, the French, and worst of all, with the bloody Yanks.

—What some of the wives did to their men – it was worse than any German.

—You're being unfair to our girls.

—It got me through, knowing my wife was waiting for me.

—Not all of them gave it away for a pair of nylons from the Yanks.

—Enough of them did.

'The women weren't like that in Italy,' Steve chips in. 'They behaved themselves when their men were away. It's their religion. High moral behaviour, that's what it is, it's drummed into them.'

'Didn't see much of that when I was there – we managed to fuck and fight our way across Italy very nicely, thank you very much.' It's the same voice that started the whole thing off.

The group shuffles, opens up a little. I turn round to check. It's the stocky man with the knowing smile who brewed up for us. There's a definite space round him now and he fills all of it, standing legs akimbo, arms folded across his chest.

'I'm talking about ordinary decent women, not whores.' Steve sounds rattled.

'So am I,' says the man, raw anger in his tone now. 'One of my mates got back, catches VD from his wife. It's not supposed to be that way round, is it?'

There's a lot of *it didn't happen to me, it happened to a mate of mine*, in here.

It feels like we're back in an army barrack-room. But it's just talk. That's all we do in the Art Hut. We're usually so wrapped up in our own misery, it's hard to break out of it, but somehow, it's different in here. We talk. Or shout. Or stare out of the small window at the patch of sky and listen.

Sergeant Bradbury keep a steady eye on proceedings but doesn't intervene.

The group sinks back into an uneasy silence.

'My wife isn't in the best of health,' Michael says suddenly, in that vague manner of his. 'Her nerves aren't good. All I really want to do is get well enough to go home. Make sure she's alright.' It's the first time he's spoken about anything other than the unresurrected dead. But what he says seems to hang in the air.

Getting well. It seems so remote. What would it feel like to get well? One last surge of frustration arcs round the group:

—It's the army, they should have looked after our families better when we were away.

—It's the bloody war, we wouldn't be in the army, would we, if it weren't for the war?

—It's buggered up everything, the war.

We always seem to end up here. We always end up blaming the war. As if it's made us into something else, something less.

Sergeant Bradbury says we've run out of time. We can take our work from the easels with us or he'll put it away for next time. We've finished the tenth roll of paper and he says he'll make sure the paint has dried, then store it with the rest around the walls.

A thousand-yard memory. Stranded on *The Island*. And us with it.

I grab my sketch and make my way out. The afternoon has grown overcast and muggy. There's a thunderstorm coming; oily clouds are massing over the hills in the distance. I sit on the bench under the beech tree outside the Art Hut door, my head throbbing. The others wander past, not saying much to each other, as if they've left the confessional, and it's time to close down, close off again. The stocky man walks a little way behind them, head up, a hint of a swagger, each swing of the body shouldering the world away.

I lean forward, resting my forehead in my clammy hands. I'm suddenly aware of the sweet smell of Sergeant Bradbury's tobacco and glance up to find him about to sit next to me.

'Lively session,' he says, puffing on his pipe and looking towards the clouds.

I'm not sure if it's a question aimed at me or a statement meant for himself. 'They always are, the ones I've been to, anyway.' I try to keep it light.

'Every group's different. This lot – they're a rumbustious bunch.' He glances across at me. 'You haven't said anything in the group, yet.'

'It's not compulsory, is it? You said we didn't have to.' I sound defensive.

'Indeed not. No compulsion to speak at all.' He smiles. 'It's just that I couldn't help noticing after you'd finished, you were somewhat shaken up.'

He directs his gaze back into the distance. 'You might feel the need to say something, but if the group is a little . . . muscular . . . it can put you off.'

'No, I would have spoken up if I'd wanted.' It rings false, even to me.

He looks at me again and nods, then points the stem of his pipe at my sketch, now folded up and stuffed in my breast pocket. 'You handle charcoal well. Done a lot of art?'

'Not really. Not since before the war. My father was the artist in the family.'

'Professional?' He looked interested.

'He could have been. The Great War got in the way.'

'Ah, yes,' he said, nodding slowly, 'it still has a lot to answer for.'

We both look off into the distance at the clouds rolling in.

He tries again. 'The sketch – it was something you'd actually experienced, perhaps?'

'I'd no idea what I was going to draw,' I say. 'It seemed to surge up from somewhere on to the page. Doesn't mean much.' I'm sidestepping and I know he knows it.

'Often the way it works,' he says. 'I wouldn't struggle trying to make sense of it.'

He stands up and glances at his watch. 'Nearly teatime. Are you coming in?'

'I'll stay here a little longer.' I watch him make his way along the path, his shoulders slightly hunched, until he disappears through the arch in the wall leading to the main building. I take the sketch out and study it, a faint tremor in my hand making the images shake.

I'm lying on my back in a slit trench, once one of theirs, dug out at the bottom of the ridge. Six inches of rain has just pelted down, lightning fast, and I'm giggling like a schoolboy, almost choking, my mouth wide open, the cooling water falling straight in, stinging my parched throat. I'll pay for it when the monsoon cloudburst stops, I'll be plagued by insect stings and bites, I'll probably get malaria, but right now, after the smothering heat, this is bloody glorious.

I sit up, thinking I'll take my shirt off, sluice myself down. The space in front of me is a paddling pool of scummy water. Then the surface of it breaks and scraps of uniform float up. It takes me a moment to realise what it is – a lower leg, wearing a puttee, held in place by cotton tapes, criss-crossed Japanese style; a cap with an Imperial Star in the centre, the filthy neck flap cradling a ragged-edged face with no jaw. The body, what's left of it, slowly surfaces. It must have been there since we pushed them back up the hill, weeks ago, covered by a slab of earth blown over it.

I scrabble to my feet. I don't feel any horror or compassion or even hatred – resentment is what I feel; I resent this stinking mess for spoiling my moment of pure joy. I turn my back on the puddle of water, edge up the trench, take my shirt off, let the rain course down my chest. Wash the filth away. Get a tin of bully beef out of my pack. Eat it half-crouched.

The rain stops as suddenly as it started and I can see up the hill again. Our guns have blasted their bunkers and everything else to bits. The trees are stripped and blackened, not one left whole. At the bottom of the hill, sodden parachutes from yesterday's supply-drop slump like popped blisters over splintered branches.

The bodies strewn around are mainly theirs, but there are some of ours too. The flies are non-partisan, clouding low over the living and the dead and busying themselves in the heat that's already built up after the rain. They drone down the hill to investigate the bully beef and the putrefying thing behind me, then fly back, a smudge of hazy black again, over the bodies.

There must still be a trace of charcoal on my hands. I've made a grey thumbprint where I've been gripping the top corner of the sketch.

I thought the memories were done. Where's this one been lurking? It didn't come up when I did the work for Dr Carter. Will they never let go of me? It must be Joe, reminding me of the Japs and their jitter raids, and the whole bloody nightmare of Kohima.

This work we've been doing on *The Island*. This memory work. It'll all be just the same tomorrow. Someone will lay out the first length from the new roll, someone else mix the paints in jam jars. Michael will bring back his unresurrected dead, Joe fashion his crucifixes with no bodies at all, Steve draw the women he's lost out on. Sergeant Bradbury will hand out the charcoal, possibly to me, maybe to someone else he thinks needs a nudge. Others might drift in, take our place, join in or not, say nothing or say too much. And off we'll all go, on the next thousand yards.

The storm finally breaks. Fat drops splat on to the sketch, blurring the charcoal lines, dissolving the images. I let it fall to the ground. The rain begins to pound down and as the paper at my feet disintegrates, I grind it with the toe of my shoe until the pulp dissolves into the earth.

2

It was nine o'clock when Daniel finished his evening duty. For once he didn't head for his room, but took himself off to the tea room. He knew it would be deserted. Hunter was away in London so there was no chance of meeting him, thank the Lord. He'd been insufferably smug since Daniel said he'd be going to Sargant's lecture.

He heated up some milk and sipped it slowly at the table. It had been a miserable day. There'd been an attempted suicide. Mondays were always a danger time, after weekend visitors. The man had tried to hang himself from a beech tree in a secluded part of the grounds. That particular beech was getting a reputation as the hanging tree. Back in May, one of the secretaries had found a body there when she'd come into work early and taken a short cut. The security patrol had found this latest one. They'd been early doing their midnight round, otherwise he would have succeeded. He'd wrapped sheets round his middle to knot together, and had already hidden a stool in the bushes earlier, so he could stand on it and then kick it away.

He wasn't Daniel's patient, not that that mattered. Suicides and attempted suicides affected them all, medical staff, patients, administration. We all get drawn into the what-ifs, thought Daniel. What if there were more doctors so they could have more sessions with the most vulnerable patients? What if someone had spotted the signs? But then, suicides often don't give any sign. Or they give false signs. Those who spoke to him said he'd been fine at teatime and had seemed bucked up by seeing his fiancée.

His case had been flagged up early in his treatment at one of the doctors' meetings.

He'd gone through Normandy, first as a tank crew member then as tank commander. He and his crew had all escaped from their burning tank, only to be machine-gunned as they fled, and he was the only one to survive. 'Why me?' he kept saying. 'Why me?' The burden of surviving seemed to be just too much for some of the men. Daniel remembered the Chindits, and the struggles they'd had with the randomness of their survival.

The room was stuffy. He went over to open a side window in the bay and spotted Hunter down below, getting out of a taxi. Time to make a quick escape. He used the back stairs to the office, to pick up a few more new assessments. He checked his pigeonhole and found a note from his duty nurse, informing him that John Bain was still AWOL, so he wouldn't be attending his appointment scheduled for tomorrow. Damn it. All Bain had needed to do was to keep his head down for a few weeks more. But he couldn't even do that. He'd been away for some time too, he'd absconded over a week ago. He'd be absconding all his life, one way or another, thought Daniel. From authority, from relationships, but from himself mostly. He was another survivor, guilty about surviving. Daniel couldn't help thinking about him with a mixture of both concern and irritation. The man seemed set on his own destruction.

He got to his room and noticed a journal shoved halfway under the door. He let himself in and picked it up. It was an old copy of the *Lancet*. A note was clipped to the cover. It was from Hunter. He must have nipped in quickly on his way to his room to leave it for Daniel. Thank God they'd missed each other. He could feel the irritation begin to rise as he read Hunter's scrawl:

Went for a drink this weekend with Prof. Sargant,
– toadying bastard, Daniel thought, noting the cosy equality of the encounter Hunter had painted – and he reminded me of McKissock's seminal work back in 1943. I'm sure you'll remember this article

that ruffled all your collective psychotherapists'
feathers? Anyway, wasn't sure you'd have kept
a copy, so I fished one out for you. Bit of
homework before the lecture? So you can dazzle
people at the drinks reception afterwards?

He remembered the article alright. As he sat down at his desk, the heaviness triggered off by the attempted suicide began to press down on him.

He riffled through the dog-eared pages until he got to the article dated 20 March 1943. He ran his fingers over the heading, instinctively tracing over McKissock's name first, apprehension causing his vision to blur momentarily.

Prefrontal Leucotomy – A Further Contribution, by WYLIE McKISSOCK, Neurological Surgeon to the EMS, and G.W.T.H. FLEMING, Medical Superintendent, Barnwood House.

And underneath the heading, there she was. Case study number 1. *Housewife, fifty, Melancholia. Leucotomy. August 1941.* It had taken months for the memories of Barnwood to fade, but when the article had come out two years later, it had brought it all back. He remembered sitting in his old room, reading it through, his head swimming, the old feelings of guilt rising up. And there'd been anger too – seeing her written up as a case history somehow legitimised what had gone on, gave it a positive slant at odds with how Daniel felt about it. She wasn't a case study, he'd thought; she was a human being and she'd been put through hell in the name of experimental work. *Terror in the extreme.*

He recalled throwing the journal into the waste basket in disgust. Over the years since then, he'd been able to rationalise the experience under 'essential training'. Foulkes arriving a month later at Northfield had provided him with some necessary distraction until the memories had gone. Or so he had thought. Until Hunter had mentioned McKissock's name.

One good thing had come out of the article, Daniel had to admit. At least McKissock had publicly acknowledged the patient's distress under local anaesthetic and had recommended general anaesthetic should be standard practice. But there were many hospitals who still used local anaesthetic for leucotomies. It was quicker and cheaper. Ethics didn't seem to come into it. The Freeman and Watt anecdote had become something of a joke among leucotomists. In their book, *Psychosurgery*, they recounted a conversation they had with a patient as the leucotomy operation proceeded under local anaesthetic:

Surgeon: 'What is going through your mind now?'

Patient: 'A knife.'

When he'd first heard this, it had reminded Daniel of the terror he'd observed in the woman's eyes. The terror, then the resignation. Then the nothingness. Freeman and Watt had meant the anecdote to be amusing. It had made Daniel feel sick. He became slightly queasy, recalling it now.

He forced himself to read on and noticed that the other case histories were heavily annotated – *interesting! – fascinating! – so many potential applications!* scrawled here and there in the margins, in Hunter's spidery handwriting. It looked like they were recent scribbles. It seemed he was also doing his homework so he could dazzle the great men at the drinks reception afterwards. It helped to release some of his tension, thinking of Hunter's fawning idiocy.

He was struck, as he always was, by the seemingly random, wide-ranging nature of the selection criteria for the operation. Melancholia, of only five months' duration in one case. Manic depression. Schizophrenia. Obsessional behaviour of compulsive masturbation, with its implied sexual deviancy. Hunter had noted next to this case in the margin – *Interesting! potentially appropriate also for homosexuality?* – with a small asterisk over 'masturbation'. Leucotomies for homosexuals? Daniel thought of his brother and felt a pulse of anxiety.

According to the article, only two cases showed no improvement after the operation. Hunter had written next to these – *potential negative personality traits already present in patients before* operation? So, Daniel thought, according to him, it was the patients' fault, not the ineffectiveness of the operation itself, that resulted in no improvement? God help us all.

He'd had enough. He tossed the journal aside and switched off the desk lamp. The dark soothed him and he tried to lighten his mood by thinking about the trip to London. The Sargant lecture was still a week away. He'd swapped day shifts for the less popular evening ones so he could call in a few favours and have the whole weekend free to go up to London. They were so short-handed, it was a year since he'd had a break away from the hospital.

His brother was at Birkbeck, but was away on a field trip, so Daniel had the use of his flat in Bloomsbury. He was already looking forward to the comfy sofa, the books, the music, but most of all, to being nowhere near a damn hospital, at least not one where you were on duty.

3

'"Would you like to say more about Wadi Akarit? Prison in Alexandria? Absconding from Hamilton?"'

John mimes Dr Carter's habit of taking off his glasses and massaging behind his ears.

I laugh, but there's a cruelty in his mimicry that makes me feel uneasy. Another silence stretches between us. There have been quite a few of them so far. It's not the same when we're together now. He lost his place in our dormitory when he went AWOL so I don't see him as often. Or maybe we don't make the effort to see each other as often. I thought the junk room sessions were a thing of the past, but I bump into him today and he suggests we meet here rather than the day room – that's not been the same either, without Freddie.

He'd been ten days AWOL altogether. Then in he comes, over the wall. He looks awful, bloodshot eyes and the shakes. He's never said what he'd been up to out there. But he's different. Harder. Moodier, if that's possible. That edge he's always had is sharper, more dangerous. He seems to have got away with being AWOL for so long. Carpeted by the CO.

A note on his record. 'Bet they can't wait to get rid of me for good,' he says.

I'd told him about the attempted suicide, said he'd been right about the bed sheets, but it was a tree the man had tried it with, not a lavatory cistern. All he'd said was, 'What do you expect? We're in a loony bin.'

'Bloody Carter.' He's been rumbling on about Dr Carter since we got here. He hasn't had another session with the Doc since the one that tipped him over into a bad mood, just before Freddie was taken away. It's as if we're right back there. Whatever went on, it rattled him.

His present mood may be fuelled by the whisky he's been drinking at a steady pace for the past hour. I have a small glass to keep him company, but I sip it, wondering where he got it from. Mavis at the Crown wouldn't have such free access to spirits that she could sell them or give them away. He must have brought it in with him when he came back.

His body is taut as a bowstring, knees drawn up to his chin, arms wrapped round his legs. I sit with my legs outstretched, watching him from the corner of my eye. It's been a warm day and the late afternoon atmosphere in this small space is oppressive.

He suddenly breaks the silence. 'What was the worst thing about Burma for you?'

I'm surprised. It's an unwritten rule in here that we listen if someone wants to talk about their experiences, but we don't probe. And John in particular asking me that question – it's a step towards me, and I'm more used to him taking a step back, from me, from everyone. Then I surprise myself. I answer him with no hesitation. I don't even have to think about it.

'The fear of getting caught. You always fear dying, wherever you are, but out there, towards the end, the fear of getting caught was worse.' And for a moment, I can hear the bamboo shifting in the night breeze, and I'm listening out for the Japanese. Listening so hard, I think my eardrums will split. Snatching tiny, noiseless breaths.

The best answer to noise is silence, Captain Evans always said.

He's made the first step, so I take a risk. 'What was the worst thing for you?'

He shrugs.

Maybe it's the whisky that does it, but I risk it again. 'I'd really like to know.'

He rubs his bottom lip with the peach-stone knuckled finger.

Gives me a long look, then looks away. And begins to tell me about Wadi Akarit.

He never looks straight at me. All the time he's speaking, he's looking down at the whisky glass balanced on the top of his knees. He tells me about the Germans retreating to the Roumana Hills above Wadi Akarit on the way to Tunis. About the British Brigade, including the Gordons and the Seaforths, being assigned to attack the ridge – the Seaforths set to lead the assault, the Gordons to dig in as support, then follow on. He tells me about digging in for the night, close to the foot of the hills, with his mate. About coming under mortar attack, about taking turns, one trying to get some sleep, the other manning the Bren gun. He tells me about the Seaforths, on the move before first light on their way to attack the ridge, creeping through the Gordons in their support positions exchanging whispered words.

He stops at this point. Thinks for a while, then says, 'The Seaforths going first – I was glad it wasn't us. Then I felt guilty for feeling glad. Then I felt sorry for the poor buggers – it would be daylight when they got up there. Against the morning light, they'd be easy targets. Then I thought I hope they finish the job otherwise we'll have to clean up after them.'

He goes on to tell me about the machine-gun fire, the shouts and cries, about seeing specks moving on the hillside as it got lighter, about the noises stopping, about the specks becoming still. 'We were ordered to move up the hill, in single file. We reached the foothills, then began to climb towards the place where we'd seen them. Dead Seaforths, dead Germans, strewn around.' He stops speaking and closes his eyes.

It sounds so like the things I'd seen, the things I'd done in Burma. The randomness of who gets killed and who doesn't. You watch men become specks. You go past them. No time for funeral games. The bodies on the hillside. The bodies in the bunkers. The Japanese boy.

So, this is what drove him to desert. One forward move too many. One horrendous scene too many.

He remains silent for a long time and I am just about to say I've been through that too, when he opens his eyes again and says, 'The men in front of me stopped. They fell out of single file and some of them started to rove around the bodies. They looked at the dead, the dead Seaforths and the dead Germans. And they bent down' – he takes a sip of whisky – 'and they started to loot the bodies. They took watches and wallets and rings. From the Seaforths and the Germans.' His voice has grown husky and tight, so he has to force the words out. 'Our own men, looting our own.' He looks across at me now, anguish on his face.

I knew of men who stole from the Japanese dead. Seikosha watches and wrist compasses were especially prized, then wallets. I'd seen men pocket blood-soaked Imperial caps from shattered heads. I'd even seen men laugh and tear up photos of wives and children and scatter them over the dead bodies. But I'd never seen our own looting our own. I don't want to believe him.

'Are you sure they weren't searching their mates' bodies for things to send back home to their families?'

'Didn't look like that to me.' He shrugs. 'Anyway, I'd had enough. You say fear is the worst, fear of dying, of getting caught, of getting wounded. For me, it was the fear of not feeling any fucking fear at all. Of not fearing anything. I didn't care if I lived or died. I turned and I walked away and kept on walking and no-one stopped me, no-one even noticed me.'

He looks at me again, more defiance in his face now than despair. 'It was desertion. Whatever the others did that day, they all stayed. They went on fighting. I didn't. They stuck with it. I didn't. That's the real difference between them and me. Not that they looted and I didn't. I walked away. They didn't. I am a coward. They are not.'

I try and absorb what I'm hearing. His eyes are closed now, his body hunched forwards over his knees as if he's in great physical pain. 'So when Carter says you must try and remember in order to forget . . . it's so much baloney. I'll always remember and I'll never forget.'

He suddenly stands up, uncoiling like a spring. He grabs the empty whisky bottle by its neck, smashes it against the back wall and heads towards the door. I watch him go. He leaves a trail of anger and violence behind him that seems to thicken the air and I don't want to breathe it in. It's his anger and violence, not mine.

4

His brother's flat was in Marchmont Street near Russell Square Station. It was after eight o'clock when he got there. As he walked down to the end, the two pubs he passed were already spilling out Friday night noise and laughter. During the day, the street was always lively, bustling with butchers, grocers, bakeries, bookshops. Bloomsbury had escaped much of the serious bombing – there was a story still doing the rounds that Hitler had chosen the Senate House of London University as his post-war HQ, so the area around it wasn't targeted. Enough stray bombs had dropped there to scar it, though – and one of them had landed on Marchmont Street, damaging sewers and destroying three houses. So it could hold its head high; its bomb credentials were impeccable. It had suffered and survived.

Long past its heyday, when Virginia Woolf and the Bloomsbury set had done their shopping there, it was now decidedly scruffy, albeit bohemian. It was an enclave for writers, musicians, the odd actor or two, usually living in tiny rooms let out above the shops or in the side streets.

No tiny rooms for Ian, Daniel mused as he let himself into the Georgian terrace. Two spacious rooms on the ground floor – two rooms for one person – pure extravagance.

He never ceased to marvel at his brother's capacity to land on his feet. A combination of boyish charm and being in the right place at the right time had often blessed him with good fortune. This time, it had led to him taking over the sub-let of a wealthy would-be musician friend of his, a man he'd met in some jazz club who worked for a bank in the City. He'd been offered a spell of time in their New York office, so he'd gone, and asked Ian to look after the flat, paying a peppercorn rent.

The whole building had been done up in Victorian times, and odd alterations carried out since then, so it was a mishmash of styles. The Georgian windows on the ground floor let plenty of light into the living room, while the bedroom was private, over-looking the back.

A small kitchen off the living area held a hot water geyser and a doll's house stove. The shared bathroom at the end of the entrance hall was surprisingly clean.

Ian had been humble, saying that he couldn't believe his luck – he'd been in London for less than a year when he'd taken the flat over. He had his university studies and did some tutoring, rich kids around the Bloomsbury area, mostly. He seemed to spend the rest of his time playing jazz and dipping in and out of relationships. He was as carefree as Daniel felt constrained. And why shouldn't he be? Daniel thought now, looking round the room, with its clutter of books and records and a decidedly shabby Kelim rug covering dark painted floorboards. His brother had spent most of his young life going through the war not knowing if he had a future or not. He couldn't begrudge him his fun now. Christ, he thought, if he heard me say that, I'd get the avuncular speech again.

He dropped his suitcase near the small dining table pushed up under the window and collapsed on to the overstuffed sofa. The walk from Euston Station had been longer than he'd remem-bered, and hot, despite the relative cool of the early evening. The heatwave of the previous week had gone, the last hurrah of the summer, probably, but the buildings still radiated the heat of the day and there'd been no rain in London for most of August. Layers of dust swirled over stickier layers of filth. The streets stank with rotting vegetation, hidden from view but never very far away, mingled with blocked drains and acrid fumes from the traffic. The whole city needed a damn good wash down.

As I do, he thought, suddenly aware of his uniform, stiff with sweat under his armpits.

He headed for the sink in the kitchen and took off his jacket, shirt and vest. He hung the jacket on a hanger swinging behind the door, hoping the creases would have fallen out by morning. The water from the tap was running slightly warm and he splashed it under his arms then put his head under it. As he straightened up, he caught sight of himself in the cracked mirror above the sink. Hair plastered to his head, red-rimmed baggy eyes, a day's stubble.

I look like one of Hunter's deep narcosis patients in their twilight phase, he thought. Bed. An early night. That's what I need.

He went back to his suitcase near the table and sat down to take off his shoes. Then he noticed the brown paper bag in the middle of the chenille tablecloth, next to a record in its sleeve. A note propped up against the bag said, *Dinner with Django. Whisky in sideboard.*

He peered inside the bag and drew out a tin of salmon. He felt a spark of pure delight, like a child finding the sixpence in a Christmas pudding. For a moment, he'd thought it was the dreaded tinned snoek, the fish from South Africa the government was trying to persuade everyone to eat – oily, bony, stomach-retchingly disgusting in every respect. But tinned salmon! It was increasingly hard to get and the price of it had soared since March. Trust Ian to get hold of such a luxury.

The bag also yielded two potatoes, a carrot and a tomato, a little wrinkled, but still edible. Half a loaf was wrapped up in a tea cloth. He'd stoked up on a substantial stodgy hospital lunch before he'd begun his journey – you never quite knew when you'd get to where you were going these days when travelling round the country. The salmon and vegetables would keep for two days and do nicely for his Sunday lunch. God bless you, little brother, he thought, and felt himself choke up, realising how much he missed him. He took the food back into the kitchen and made himself a tomato sandwich and then went back to the living room, feeling slightly light-headed.

The damask curtains were threadbare enough to let light through when he drew them, so he didn't have to switch the corner lamp on. He took the record across to the record player on the sideboard and sure enough, there in the bottom cupboard next to a sizeable assortment of glasses, was a bottle of Black Label with about two inches of whisky left in it. He poured half the amount into a cut-glass whisky tumbler. The record slipped easily out of its sleeve. He put it on, and padded back and stretched out on the sofa, resting the whisky on his stomach.

The first bitter-sweet phrase from the clarinet flowed into the room and he felt himself slow down, the tiredness in his body ebbing away. Django's guitar took over, low, slow notes rippling gently up to the higher notes, taking Daniel with it, the fingering as light as the delicate passing clouds Django was painting with the music. The second clarinet came in and joined the first, the duet slow, dreamy and sad. The French had taken 'Nuages' to their hearts during the Occupation; it was played everywhere. No wonder, Daniel thought, floating along with the melody. There was so much longing there, so much mourning for a world long past and out of reach.

He sipped the whisky slowly, eking it out until the last gentle, echoing note drifted away. The room was in deep shadow, and he lay there, a disembodied presence, shapeless, formless, feeling curiously empty. He tasted salt, then realised his cheeks were wet.

Maybe it was just the release of tension. He'd almost worked himself to a standstill to get this weekend off and was exhausted. He found himself thinking of Northfield and of all the men he'd treated there. Men who'd seen their comrades whole one minute, then blown to so much undefinable meat the next. Men racked with guilt because they'd survived and the man standing next to them hadn't, or tortured by the knowledge that they'd had to leave their wounded comrades behind in the desert, in the jungle, in burning tanks. Men who'd lost their own families to the bombing at home while they were away, then came across other innocent casualties of war – women, children, in Normandy, North Africa, Burma, Italy, wherever the armies rumbled through. Men who were the first to enter the concentration camps. Men who had to live with unbearable secrets.

Sadness took the place of tiredness, but he wasn't sure who he felt so sad for.

He'd been locked away with these men at Northfield for the past five years or so. Years of absorbing all their experiences, their anxieties, their distress. Their anger. His job had been to put them together again, then send them back to the action. Tom Main's euphemism came back to him – 'helping them recover their poise' – at best, that's what he'd been doing. The ones who worked out why they'd broken down, why they were like they were, must have known that he was doing a patch-up job so they could go right back into the situation that had made them like that in the first place. He wondered if there were any of them out there who'd survived and hated him for sending them back for more. He could understand it if they did.

He found himself thinking of David Reece. He was the future, Reece, one of a growing number of newly classified civilians battling to keep their war experiences in check. Reece had shoved the bundle of papers into his hands as he was heading down the corridor for his first ward round, mumbling something like, *You asked me how I got here? Well, this is as much as I know.*

Daniel had spent the train journey to London reading *On Not Recalling War*. When he'd finished, he sat with it on his lap for some time, staring out of the window. So it was the Japanese boy soldier – he was the memory, the true source of his patient's torment.

What men like Reece had seen, what they'd done and how it had changed them, would leak out at some stage, Daniel was certain of that. They might find a way of dealing with their memories. But they'd struggle with it, they wouldn't be human if they didn't.

Our generation, he thought, were brought up by parents who were still coming to terms with the Great War. His father had been at the Somme and never spoke of it. Daniel had once surprised him in his study, sitting with a copy of Ivor Gurney's *Severn and Somme* on his lap, his face stricken.

And all the mothers too – a generation of women, going through it all twice. His mother had died in 1936, but by then, she must have had the same anxiety about her sons as Reece's mother had about him. We were all brought up on the warmongering of Hitler and Mussolini, Daniel thought. What they did to towns and cities like Guernica and Barcelona in the thirties, attacking them from the air. And what the Japanese did for that matter, bombing Shanghai. By 1938, we all knew that the terror of the next war would be from the air. But when it came, it was worse than we could have imagined. Reece, Ian, himself – we were all inter-war children, he realised, although we hadn't known it at the time. War was always with us, whether we looked behind us or looked ahead. We were primed for it throughout our childhood.

The other thing that struck a chord with him was the sense of Reece surrounded by father substitutes. George Collingwood and the men at the *Guardian*. Wadsworth could have been Reece's father, in age, the others his grandfather. The irony of the paper's name didn't escape him. Young Reece and his guardians. What must it have felt like to have lost your own father, to learn that the world was not a safe place, then be looked after by these men, to begin to feel safe again, to think you'd be looked after for ever?

And what must it have been like six years later, home from the war, to see yourself on those old staff lists, to think of all those guardians, fighting to keep you away from call-up? Then learn that they'd made a conscious decision not to keep you after all, when forced to make a choice on who might be the most useful to them?

Not much we can do about young Reece.

That's something else we have in common, Reece and I, thought Daniel. Both searching for the love of fathers. We'd both needed them but they weren't there. Reece compensated by finding father figures, and I compensate by becoming one. I know that's what I am to many of the patients I treat. And Ian is right – I've tried to become a father to him. Protect him.

Foulkes, of course, was his father figure and Foulkes knew it. *Watch out for this counter transference, Daniel – and don't collude with patients who may see you as a father figure. Make sure you recognise that's what is happening. Then you can work appropriately with it.*

Reece was maybe looking for brothers too. Louie, a big brother for an only child. Captain Evans, the warrior poet who quoted poetry at him and who understood him and looked the other way when he shot a boy who was no longer a danger to him. Even John Bain, perhaps. Daniel had noticed they went around together. Reece had said nothing in his work about Bain, but then it was about his time before Northfield, before Bain. *How I got here – as much as I know.* How we all got here, Daniel thought, as much as we know.

His head ached from remembering, and from nervous tension about the encounter tomorrow with Sargant and McKissock. He got up wearily and stumbled into the bedroom with the suitcase. It was pitch dark outside, but he didn't bother drawing the curtain. He got into his pyjamas, his whole body a leaden weight as he flopped down on top of the quilt. The bed was soft and wide and welcoming. His eyelids slowly closed over sore and scratchy eyes.

Men dressed in the Blues drifted in and out, identical in build and shape, like the cardboard cut-out base figures from a little girl's paper dress-up doll set. But their faces kept changing above the uniforms. D-Day tank commanders. The gunner with the burnt face from the Stage Group. The Chindits wrapped in their khaki blankets. Spence with those sad eyes. Bain sitting beside the bed in a chair, gripping the arms of it with those knotty, knuckled fingers of his. Reece showing him a sheet of paper covered with red Japanese ideograms.

His own father wandered in, his hands cradling a skull, followed by McKissock who took the skull from his father and turned it round so that Daniel could see the burr hole at the side of the right temple. Then the face turned towards him. It was Housewife, fifty, Melancholia, her eyes flitting slowly to the right so she could look directly at him. The skull turning and turning, burr holes and bone sockets and eyes.

He started awake, his head and shoulders jolting up from the pillow, then fell back. He switched the light on and looked at his watch. Four o'clock, and he knew he wouldn't sleep again so he got up. His throat was parched and he pottered into the kitchen, switching the lights on as he went, the standard lamp in the corner, the small lamp on the side table, the kitchen light. He boiled a kettle for some weak, black tea and took it back to the sofa.

He sipped slowly, fighting to keep the thoughts of the night at bay.

He forced himself to think more rationally about where the anxiety was coming from. That's what he was always trying to get his patients to do. He realised that much of it was really about his going to the lecture today, meeting up with Sargant and McKissock again and all they represented to him.

And what did they represent to him exactly? McKissock in particular. Their paths had never crossed again after Barnwood. Why was Wylie McKissock still such a bogey man?

Back in 1941, Daniel had acknowledged to himself that he had deliberately chosen to be at Barnwood. It was a medical opportunity to see McKissock at work and he'd taken it. He'd been complicit in what went on. But afterwards, he hadn't had time to address how he really felt about this. It had been during the darkest days of the war and there was no time for self-analysis and introspection. You just got on with the job of mending your patients sufficiently to send them back into action, and there was enough uncertainty about the morality of that to keep his conscience working overtime. McKissock's 1943 article in the *Lancet* had triggered the whole thing off again, but the war was still grim, and he'd managed to parcel the memories up once again. The arrival of Foulkes at Northfield and immersion in the new work had helped.

He reflected on Bain and his anger and guilt about witnessing something disturbing, whatever it was. Then he thought of his own anger and guilt. And shame. He'd never spoken out about what was going on in the name of psychiatry. He'd never told anyone he'd witnessed a leucotomy. Not even Foulkes.

That's why I've come here, he thought. It's not about McKissock himself. It's about what he represents. He represents my weakness. He has the courage of his convictions and acts on them, even if they're mistaken. Where has my courage been all this time? I'm here to face my own shortcomings, not his.

A sense of calm began to settle over him. It slowly became clear that he would not be alone at the lecture today. All the men he'd treated at Northfield would be there with him. And Housewife, fifty, Melancholia. They'd been silent in his dream. But he could give them all a voice. That's what he could do. Maybe that's all he could do. It would be no more than a pathetic little gesture, he knew that. But when the time came, he could give the powerless a voice.

5

We're in our usual spot on the corner bench outside the pub door, finishing off our first pints. John tries to catch the eye of two brawny-armed farm labourers who pass by us on their way in, but they don't look at us. 'It's worse than being a bloody leper,' he says, his voice edgy.

We'd been lucky. Mary from the hospital had been on the way out with her boyfriend when we arrived, and they'd gone back in and got us our drinks. Patients from Northfield aren't allowed in the pub. We're all on medication, so we're not supposed to drink alcohol. We occupy the unofficial territory outside, but we always persuade some sympathetic local to fetch us a drink. It suits the landlord – he still gets the business and we don't frighten the natives inside.

Today, there are six of us. We stick out like sore thumbs. John and I are brightening up our corner nicely, glowing in our delphinium Blues. The other four are standing a little way off, outside the open pub window, wearing their greatcoats, preferring to swelter in the warm August evening rather than be marked out in their Blues, as if everyone didn't know where they were from.

The heat from the whitewashed wall radiates through the back of my jacket. If you didn't know what the Blues signified, we must look so ordinary, John and me, friends sitting outside an English village pub on a fine summer's evening, enjoying a pint. So simple. So everyday. But he's been angry and agitated and drinking solidly all week. He'd thought he could sweet-talk Mary into letting him into the acute ward to see Freddie last week, but she told him Freddie wasn't there. He'd been discharged. He's back home in London.

'Dr Hunter says if he needs further special treatment, they're better set up down there,' said Mary.

It was all done quietly, no-one knew he'd left.

John drains the last of his beer, wipes his mouth with the back of his hand, and looks directly at me. I know that look. I've been expecting an explosion over Freddie. But when it comes, it's not about Freddie, and it's not an explosion, it's a low rumble. 'What I told you – about Wadi Akarit. I should never have told you. Bloody Carter. Stirring it all up again. I should have done what I told you to do – said nothing. I want you to keep schtum.'

I hide my surprise. 'Water under the bridge. We've all got things that are best locked away.'

His eyes are bullet hard. 'The lads I fought with were the best. They trusted me and I trusted them. That's what kept us alive, got us through. What happened, it could easily have been me too – you lose all sense of what's decent. The bloody army – they treat you like animals long enough, you end up behaving like animals. You end up debasing yourself.'

He loosens his tie a little, undoes the top shirt button, then stands up, saying, 'Bugger this,' and takes his jacket off. He walks over to the four greatcoats and asks them if they fancy another, then strolls past me into the pub, shoulders back, head up, a faint smile on his lips. Whatever his demons are around Wadi Akarit, they're well hidden again behind the bravado.

A little later, he comes back out, carrying four pints in a cluster. 'Mission accomplished,' he says to the greatcoats and they grin and take them off him. He goes back into the pub again and comes out with ours. He hands me mine and smiles.

'Are you staying?' His tone is casual, disinterested. It's obvious he doesn't want me to. I don't want to stay either. I sit back up again, the flannelette shirt wringing wet on my back. 'No, I want to be back on time.'

They let us out on a late pass on Fridays in summer. The clematis gates stay open from three in the afternoon, so we can go out on our own – at least those men who are well enough – or visitors can take us out. But the gates swing shut at eight on the dot and I want to be inside, not outside, when they do. Subverting the rules has lost its charm.

I stand up without finishing my pint. 'Right, I'm off.' I sound casually dismissive, like he does with me, these days.

He nods. 'See you at ten, kitchen window. If I'm not there bang on time, forget it.'

He gets up and heads across to the greatcoats. There's something in the way he walks, a determined sort of stride, that makes me think he's set for a long night.

Small groups of people are standing outside the clematis gates when I get back, saying their goodbyes. A few mothers – not many fathers, I notice – but mostly wives and sweethearts decked out in their weekend best, with their well-worn, slightly faded summer frocks, scuffed peep-toe shoes, their faces with a touch too much make-up to hide their tired mouths. The heat intensifies their perfumes, heady floral mingling with the sharp sweat of the men suffering in their Blues and khaki. The men stand slightly apart from the women, not touching, as if they are afraid to get too close.

I think of Beth – the way we would walk along with my arm tight around her waist, and hers round mine, her breasts brushing lightly against my chest in rhythm with our steps. She's coming on Sunday. I've been here long enough to have weekend visitors, so I've taken the plunge; I've written to Louie and Beth, telling them it's OK to visit.

I've arranged it so that Louie is coming tomorrow, then Beth on Sunday afternoon. Maybe my mother and George the week after, but I'm not sure I want them to see me at all in here. A surge of excitement, then a skitter of nerves, make my fingertips tingle. All of them – my mother, George, Wadsworth, Mrs Tipton, even Beth and Louie – they're becoming people from another world. I've noticed that most of the patients prefer to say their goodbyes outside the gates, then walk back through, as if to keep the two worlds apart.

The sergeant, keeper of the keys, coasts down the hill as usual and leans his bike against the wall. There is a sudden flurry of movement. The mothers hug their sons close to them, the 'I'll make it better' hugs that mothers give, the few fathers or brothers shake hands stiffly, then stand back. The wives lean forward and kiss the men, and they in turn move to stroke the women's hair, their faces, their skin, as if they realise they've left it too late for the touches that matter, the touches they'll store up and remember till next time. Then they pull away and walk back through the gates. The sergeant comes out to those left outside, saying firmly but gently, 'Look sharp, ladies and gentlemen, if you please, visiting hours over for today,' and ushers the stragglers through. The gates clang shut.

I tag on to the end of the line of Blues and khakis, trudging up the incline in silence.

I make my way round the back to Reception, my footsteps leaden. I think about John and about this gap that has opened up between us. He let his guard down. He let me in too close. Now his gloves are up again. I'm on the outside. But then, I always was. I was just a little slow in realising it.

I wait at the kitchen window until ten thirty. Then I leave him to come home with the sparrows.

6

He arrived at the National Hospital late and out of breath, covering the last hundred yards into Queen Square at a brisk trot.

He'd spent the morning indulging himself. He'd fallen asleep on the sofa at first light, even though he didn't think he would, and didn't wake up till ten. He couldn't remember the last time he'd slept for over four hours undisturbed. His tongue was almost stuck to the roof of his mouth and he stank. The cat lick from yesterday evening hadn't made a dent on the grime.

A long hot bath, a shave and a clean change of clothes did the trick.

Then heaven, drifting up and down Marchmont Street, finding a café and reading the morning newspaper over tea and toast. Out into the sunshine again. Greengrocers chatting to their customers in front of the vegetable displays. Women doing their Saturday shopping, still summery in their cardigans and cotton dresses. A man ambling down the street taking his Jack Russell for a walk. Into another café at lunchtime for a surprisingly good pie and mash.

It was all so bloody normal. What was it Bain had said? *Becoming human.* That's what it felt like. A clock somewhere struck three. He'd better get a move on. He hadn't looked at his watch for the past two hours. Foulkes would have a field day about all this subconscious procrastination – he'd say Daniel didn't want to go to the lecture, even after all the positive deliberations of the early morning.

And Foulkes would be right, he thought, as he found himself

almost going into reverse as he reached the door of the Old Board Room on the hospital ground floor. He steeled himself. Sargant would be preaching to the converted. Daniel would probably be the only army psychotherapist there. But he'd sit through the lecture, do what he needed to do, then beat a retreat.

The Old Board Room was like he imagined a gentlemen's club to be. Wood panelling, polished mahogany furniture and a pervasive sense of quiet power within its four walls. The biggest names in medicine and psychiatry had all met in here at one time or another. Daniel wondered how Sargant had managed to secure such a prestigious venue for his lecture. If the gossip was anything to go by, he'd crossed many of the powers that be in London's influential medical circles, and more than a few of them would be glad to see the back of him and not encourage him by allowing him to use the platform of one of the key London hospitals.

Most people were in their seats in front of an oval table at one end of the room. Daniel stood at the door and looked round, trying to spot someone he knew, feeling sweaty and conspicuous in his army uniform. Three of the VIPs were sitting at the table. Eliot Slater, with his unmistakable shock of blond hair falling over his forehead, was flanked on either side by William Sargant and Louis Minski.

Slater being there explained the Old Board Room venue. He was a physician in psychological medicine at the National, and a good friend of Sargant's. The two of them had been together at the Sutton Emergency Hospital during the war. Slater had been the clinical director, Sargant his assistant director. While Sargant was known as a maverick, Slater had built up an impeccable reputation, seen as a humane man who liked to run a happy ship.

Daniel reminded himself that Slater had co-authored the psychiatry textbook with Sargant while they were at Sutton back in 1944 – the one that had driven Foulkes to despair. Not for the first time, he wondered how much of the book was actually Slater's, and how much Sargant's.

Louis Minski cut an imposing figure with his broad rugby player's shoulders and his thick dark hair. He'd also gone through the war based at Sutton with Slater and Sargant, as the medical superintendent, and was still there. He was a genial sort, known as someone who got things done. So, it was the Sutton triumvirate, together again. Sargant certainly had powerful allies. Then Daniel spotted another army uniform on the front row. The nose was up as usual, on point. It was Hunter. He was sitting in the middle, as near to the table as he could get, without actually being one of the VIPs.

The rest of the audience filled up the three rows of chairs, and Daniel found himself on a back row seat at the end. As he'd anticipated, he didn't recognise any other psychiatrist specialising in non-physical treatments. It was why Hunter had goaded him to come. This is where the future lies, he was saying. I'm part of it. And you, old boy, are very definitely not.

The first two rows were taken up with a group of fresh-faced students, notebooks in hand, talking in hushed tones, as if acutely conscious they were in the presence of the Gods. These young people all had their choices before them, Daniel thought, as he once had until the war came along and squeezed them all out of shape. What must it feel like to be young, the war over, the rest of your life just beginning? Just thinking about it made him feel jaded.

Slater looked towards the back of the room and smiled. Daniel turned round to see who he was smiling at. Wylie McKissock had just entered the room.

An image came to Daniel of McKissock coming into the Barnwood operating theatre six years ago, in those extraordinary whites of his, fastened with white tape. But today he was immaculately dressed in a beautifully tailored three-piece pinstripe, complete with dark blue silk handkerchief peeping from the breast pocket.

He didn't look much different from the first time Daniel had seen him in 1941. A few extra lines on his face, perhaps, but no stoop or drooping gait which many people seemed to have developed as they'd battled their way through the interminable grind of the war and the miserable first years of the peace. He was still as charismatic as ever.

He could have sat alongside the other three, there was room, but after he shook hands with them all and apologised for being late, he placed himself on his own at the short end of the table, at right angles to the others. Interesting dynamics, Daniel thought. McKissock looked like a man who also didn't want to be here at all.

Slater remained seated and chinked his pen against his glass of water, signalling for the audience's attention, and then began his opening remarks. How heartening it was to see the third-year medical students on the front rows. How pleased he was to introduce his distinguished colleagues, Louis Minski, Wylie McKissock and Will Sargant.

Daniel was surprised at the use of Will rather than William. There was a sense of the solid, the hearty, the open, about the name Will. Daniel studied Sargant. Narrow-jawed. Tension in the lean face. Slightly hooded eyes constantly scanning the audience. There was a haunted look around those eyes. Nothing straightforward about Sargant, Daniel decided. Definitely not a Will. And yet Slater sounded genuine in his praise.

'As you are all aware, Will is leaving us for a year in America – which, I have to say, is a great loss to us all.' Slater paused, smiling at Sargant, while a slight buzz of agreement from the audience echoed his sentiments. McKissock looked up at Slater as he said this, then looked down. Daniel noticed he didn't join in with the rest.

'But before he goes, he's agreed to share his latest research with us.' Slater gestured to Sargant to take over. 'So without more ado . . .'

Sargant stood up, pushing his chair back slightly and re-arranging the typewritten papers in front of him. It would be important to him, Daniel sensed, to have the audience obliged to look up at him.

'As Eliot says,' he began, 'I'll be taking a sabbatical at Duke University in North Carolina – Visiting Professor of Psychiatry.' He pronounced the academic title slowly, as if allowing time for the importance of his elevation to Professor to sink in. 'I'm leaving with mixed emotions. It's been a privilege to be part of such a group of bold experimenters' – he gestured round the table – 'for that is what we were, indeed, what we still are.'

McKissock had begun to doodle on the sheets of paper in front of him. He didn't look up as Sargant was speaking.

'Of course,' continued Sargant, 'you sometimes have to pay the price for that – there is still great opposition to the kind of work we do – but, as the Good Book says, "no prophet is accepted in his own land".'

Daniel could see Hunter nodding his head as if he were all too familiar with the problem.

Sargant raised his sheaf of typewritten papers. 'My paper will be published in the *British Medical Journal* this November, but I'll be in America then, so I thought I'd present it to the group as a little valedictory present.' He adjusted his glasses, and then said: 'Before I introduce the paper, however, I'd like to take the opportunity to familiarise you with the exciting and ground-breaking work we've been doing at Sutton with regard to using physical methods of treatment.' He began to read in a low, monotonous voice directly from his notes.

Daniel sighed inwardly. Sargant's lecture was obviously going to be a regurgitation of his book. He'd have to sit through all that guff before McKissock got to talk about his leucotomies, which was what Daniel was really interested in. He wondered whether it was worth it. But he reminded himself of the promise he'd made and hunkered down in the chair, gritting his teeth.

7

I wait for Louie on the oak plank bench outside the gates and it reminds me of the day I arrived, Louie anxious and trying to cheer me up. It's overcast, not like that baking June day, but it's sticky. I begin to wonder if I've done the right thing, organising it so that Louie comes today and Beth tomorrow. It might be too much. Dr Carter would probably say I've set myself some sort of test – see how I fare with the people closest to me in the outside world, the normal people I've left behind. But it's done now, they're coming. I'll have to see how it goes.

I hear the sweet rumble of a bike engine before I see anything. It has to be him. He comes round the slight bend in the lane, the sidecar sporting a fresh coat of paint and a new canvas cover with clear plastic windows. He sees me and gives a cheery wave that turns into a salute, mimicking an AA patrol man.

I go to meet him as he turns off the engine. He sits there, his goggles up on his helmet, frog-like. 'You've been busy.' I gesture towards the bike.

'Paid for with a bit of moonlighting,' he says. 'Posh folk in London, nowhere to park their motors. Me and a mate of mine can do a garage in a weekend. Money for old rope.' He grins. 'Spent the extra cash on the bike, and a few other things.'

The few other things obviously include new clothes – he's wearing a leather flying jacket, smart trousers and newish-looking shoes.

'Very natty,' I say, eyeing the shoes and suddenly conscious of my canvas plimsolls.

'Charlie,' he says, by way of explanation.

'But you're in London – Charlie's in Manchester.'

'They're all called Charlie,' he grins again. He gets off the bike and takes off his helmet.

'How can you run it with the rationing?' I stroke the rim of the headlamp.

We look at each other. 'Charlie!' we say in unison, and laugh. Petrol coupons are one of London Charlie's specialities, it seems.

He hangs the goggles over the handlebar and turns to me, grinning.

'Good to see you, you old bugger.' It seems like years, not months, since I last saw him.

I think I spot a look of caution in those blue eyes, but he shakes my hand. 'You too.'

His hair is plastered down in a coating of Brylcreem and sweat. 'Christ, it's warm! Fancy a pint? I passed through a little village about five miles back, duck pond, village green, the lot, complete with Ye Olde Village Pub. The sort of thing we used to dream of in the middle of the bloody monsoons, remember?'

Five miles the other way is new territory for me. The Crown is the limit of my safety zone, between the real world and Northfield. 'We've got our own local,' I say, hoping I sound cheerful, pointing the opposite direction to the way he's come. 'Just a few hundred yards along the road, they know me there – they're used to us.'

He shrugs. 'Hop on,' he says, 'we'll arrive in style.'

And I do hop on, and for a moment I'm back at Piccadilly Station, and those skinny kids, and us juddering over the cobbles and riding out of the city to Didsbury, past the great sooty trees, round the bend past the grand houses and into Oak Road.

But then the picture changes to me on George's bicycle, arriving at the monkey puzzle, and I begin to shiver.

By the time we've gone the few hundred yards to the pub, my eyes have filled up. I blink the tears away quickly as I'm getting off the bike. I've got good at blinking tears away quickly. We all have at Northfield.

Louie pokes around in the sidecar and pulls out a wicker basket. We head up the pub path, Louie half tough guy in his John Wayne jacket, half milkmaid swinging his basket.

The corner bench outside the door is empty and we head for that. He puts the basket down in the space between us and takes off the jacket. He's wearing a neat blue shirt and tie and a patterned pullover, home knitted. He looks well looked after. Cared for.

'It'd be better if you go and get the pints for us,' I say, tapping my delphinium jacket. He looks puzzled, then cottons on and heads off for the bar. I realise how much I've got used to the Northfield inmate way of doing things – keeping close to the hospital, begging others to buy drinks for us, because we're so different. We scare people. I scare people. I scare myself thinking that.

I can feel myself dipping down again and suddenly I want Louie to come back. Just as I begin to think about walking away, out he comes, pints in hand.

'Mavis.' He grins. 'Lovely girl. Lovely smile.'

'Don't get your hopes up, she smiles like that at everybody.'

'Not interested. I've got a pretty smile waiting at home. Not just a pretty smile either.'

There is another moment of awkwardness. I wonder if he feels he can't say too much because he's obviously happy and thinks I don't want to hear about it because I'm so obviously not.

'I thought so,' I say, 'you've found yourself a sweetheart.' For a moment, I'm back in Tommy Ducks and hear him calling Beth my sweetheart.

He glances at me, a surprisingly sheepish look on his face. 'I certainly have. She's the best thing that ever happened to me. Her name's Nuala.' He sees me raise my eyebrows and nods. 'Yes, she's Irish. She's a nurse. I met her at Hammersmith Hospital when I had to take one of the lads from the site there.'

'I'm glad, Louie, I really am.' I think back to how it must have been for him, finding Annie gone, but never giving up, trying to work out what his next move would be.

He taps the basket. 'She thinks I need building up – I keep telling her I'm nothing but a long drink of water, but she's not having it. Anyway, she fixed us this.' He pulls out a pack of greaseproof paper containing two thick sandwiches, which turn out to be ox's tongue, a knife and a small jar of piccalilli, and proceeds to layer the pickle on to the tongue.

'And that's not all,' he says, and takes out a blue checked tea towel folded up and knotted over something large and round. He unwraps it with a flourish like a magician, to reveal a home-made pork pie, minus a slice, smelling delicious, the clear jelly layer in it making my mouth water.

'I tested it out on the way up,' he says breezily. 'I've been on the road since eight.' He cuts it in half and offers me a chunk.

It tastes as good as it looks.

'Nice bit of pork, that.' He wipes his mouth with his hanky.

'My compliments to the chef.'

'And to Charlie,' he says, grinning. London Charlie, purveyor of quality meats and provisions on top of everything else.

We start on the sandwiches, washing them down with beer. There's a burst of laughter from inside the pub. A couple of sparrows have already positioned themselves for crumbs near our feet. Louie chucks them a few.

'Do you remember those bloody hawks at HQ in Chittagong?' he says.

I nodded. We'd had to cover our mess tins, walking between the mess tent and our basha, or the birds swooped and stole the food.

'The flies were worse.' I wish I hadn't mentioned the flies. A thumb smudge hovering over dead bodies flits into my mind then out again. But I don't miss a chew, I keep on eating.

Louie laughs. 'And Captain Evans saying we had to catch our quota of flies and bring him the dead bodies before he'd let us into the mess tent, the crazy bastard.'

A comfortable silence settles as we eat.

'Just think,' he says, 'V-J Day, two years ago this month.

We were in Chittagong, celebrating with an extra rum ration.'
He shakes his head. 'That week, waiting for the Japs to
surrender, it was almost as bad as being in the thick of the
bloody fighting. I didn't think they'd surrender, not even after
the second bomb. I thought we'd have to fight them until the
last man standing.' He pauses, then says, 'Still, there'll be no
more wars like that, now we've got the bomb.'

'What if the others get it, though?'

'What others?'

'Anybody who isn't on our side. It stands to reason, we're
always going to have enemies, aren't we? There's always going
to be wars.'

He looks across at me, his eyebrows raised. 'Not something
I care to think about much.' He lifts up his pint. 'Ah, well. Here's
to the Forgotten Army,' a mixture of cynicism and pride in his
tone. We clink glasses.

'The name still rankles,' I say. The Forgotten Army. We're
supposed to wear that name like a badge of honour – we're supposed
to be proud that we felt forgotten back home by the powers that
be, but we carried on anyway, and beat the Japanese back.

Louie shrugs. 'It's just the way things were. Europe was more
important to people because we were fighting the enemy on the
doorstep. And it's not until you get back, and hear about
everyone else, you realise how tough it was for all of us. No-one
had it easy, did they? I'd rather have been in the jungle than the
bloody desert.'

As usual, he's right. I think of all the men here, all their
experiences repeated in whatever landscape they were in. I think
of John. And of Michael and Joe in the Art Hut. Anyone who'd
not been through it would never understand.

He leans back against the wall and closes his eyes.

'Do you ever think about it, though, Louie? The war? Burma?
All of it.'

I'm not sure he's heard me. There's a long silence and I think
he's dozing off.

Then he sits up and leans forward, focusing his gaze on the sparrows twitting about on the pub wall. 'Sometimes. God knows, I don't want to ever think about the bloody war. All the things we saw . . . all the things we did. Remember the Forgotten Army, forget the bloody war, that's what I say—'

I jump in. 'But it just ambushes you sometimes. That's the word I used with the Doc, "ambush" – you can be OK one minute, then wham! A memory whizzes in from nowhere and knocks you for six.'

I almost ask him then about the Japanese boy. About what he thinks of what I did. We've not spoken of it, ever, since the day it happened. But I can't do it. I hold back, just like I did in Tommy Duck's. Maybe I don't want to hear the answer.

He looks thoughtful, then nods. 'Sometimes I wake up in a cold sweat. Or Nuala wakes me because I've been shouting in my sleep.' He shrugs. 'Doesn't happen often, though.'

But it happens, I think. It happens to you too. It's the first time since I've been in Northfield that I've had anyone else to compare myself to – someone who has been through exactly the same things I've been through in the war, but who hasn't ended up in here, trapped in memories, going over and over them, comparing them to everyone else's.

And it dawns on me, it must happen to all of us who've been through it. So why have I ended up in here and Louie hasn't? Why am I so different?

As if he's tuned into my thinking, Louie says, 'It takes some of us different to others. Some of us just don't seem to be able to bury the past. But you've got to, haven't you? It was war. It wasn't normal life. You've got to walk away from the memories. And how can you walk away if you keep one foot in the past?'

He drains his pint, then carries on. 'Whenever the memories ambush me, I say to myself, that was then, now is now – and let's face it, what's happening now is hard enough to be getting on with. If you're not careful, the memory will stop you doing

209

what you want to do. It might not go away completely, but you have to let it lie.'

His face flushes; he's not one for talking about his own feelings.

It's what Carter has been saying all along, but it rings more true from Louie. You'll always have the memories, it's no use trying to block them out. It's how you handle them that's important. That's the difference between someone like Louie and someone like me. He handles the memories better. Doesn't let them beat him. I keep saying the memories won't let me go. But it's me – it's me that can't let them go.

He looks at me again. 'That's what I think, anyway, but we're all different.' He trails off.

I wonder if he sees how feeble I am and knows he's stronger, and feels bad about that. The sparrows get adventurous and come right up to our feet to peck away the last pie crumbs, then fly off for good.

'I'll go and get us another pint.' He won't take the money I offer him. 'Garage money,' he says, jingling a handful of coins as he heads through the pub door.

He comes back and sits down, takes a gulp of the beer, then turns to me, a serious expression on his face.

'I'm going away.' He looks at me, head on one side, a lopsided smile on his face, the caution I saw earlier back in his eyes. 'We're going away, I mean.'

'You're on the move again? Where? I thought you were happy in London?'

'I am. We are. It's been good for me, being away from Manchester, nobody knowing my business. I felt free and there's plenty of work for trades like mine. It's on its knees, poor old London, but there's so much building going on, you wouldn't believe it. Different kind of building too, interesting stuff.'

'Then why leave?'

He sits forwards on the bench again, so that he's not looking at me directly. 'I've not been able to settle since I came home. I thought I had, but I haven't. Part of the problem was Annie not being here when I got back.'

He pauses for a moment, then says, 'But it's more than that, if I'm honest. Everyday life here – Christ, it's dull, after the last five years. Everywhere is so bloody grey – the buildings, the people. And nothing's really changed, has it? The rich are still rich, the poor are still poor – we're all just supposed to slot right back in to where we were before, aren't we? I thought Ardwick in Manchester was awful but you should see some of the hovels in parts of London.'

'But you'd do well, wherever you end up – you'd make your way.' I know praising him won't make any difference, but there's a bit of me beginning to panic now.

'It's not about being able to make my way. You're going to think I'm crazy. The war – it made so many things possible for me. Going overseas, seeing those strange places – Durban, Chittagong, even Kohima Ridge – if you could look past the fighting and the war, Burma was beautiful. And coming back through the Suez Canal – do you remember? Marvellous engineering, that. I never dreamt I'd get to see any of those things except in a book, or a Hollywood picture. But I did. I never thought I'd say this, but I miss the excitement of being somewhere foreign. I even miss the tropical climate – well, some of it – not the monsoons, granted. And I survived everything Burma threw at me. Including the bloody Japs. So, I think I could go anywhere in the tropics and do the same thing, only this time it's just for me, for me and Nuala, not for King and Country. I've done my bit for King and Country.'

All this comes out in a rush. Then he turns and looks at me, the blue eyes intense and direct, as if he's trying to judge my reaction.

'So where are you going?'

'Durban. The company's expanding and there's an opening for an overseas site manager there. I've been told it's mine if I want it.' He beams as he says 'manager'.

'I remember you when we got off the ship at Durban on the way out; you were like a wide-eyed kid. Most of the lads went off on a binge and a hunt for the local girls; you spent the whole week walking about looking at the place with your mouth open.'

'I'd never seen such strangeness, such colours,' he says, a slight awe in his voice. 'Anyway, they'll pay our passages, and Nuala will easily get a job out in one of the hospitals.'

'Sounds a big move.' My voice is a bit thin, but he doesn't notice, he's so animated.

'Nothing to lose, everything to gain. I don't have much in the way of a family, and Nuala says she wants to get away from hers, so we'll create our own family.'

It's a shock, the reality of him going, knowing that I'll probably never see him again.

But I hear myself say, 'I wish you the very best. If anyone can make a go of it overseas, you can.' And it sounds genuine because I believe it.

'It'll be another three months at least, all sorts of travel documents, arrangements.'

He tries to sound world-weary, but he's excited as hell, like a little boy waiting for Christmas.

'What about you? When will they let . . . when do you get out?' He reddens a little as he stumbles over the words.

'Another couple of weeks, with a bit of luck.' It's the first time anyone has asked me when I'm getting out.

'Then what will you do?'

I look cheerful and tell him what I know he needs to hear. 'Not sure, but I'll be alright.'

We spend the next half-hour or so talking about this and that, a bit more 'do you remember when' stuff about Burma, but our hearts aren't really in it. He tells me about the Burma reunion he'd gone to in London, way back in June. I was surprised, I didn't know he'd gone. But it was the week before I came to Northfield, so I'd not been in a fit state to know what was going on outside.

'General Slim was good,' he says. 'He went through the whole campaign, telling us what we'd done, what we should be proud of. It felt strange, though, listening to it laid out like that. It seemed like it happened a long time ago to someone else, to someone else's army. It was already history. It sounded to me like listening to history you could read in a book.'

He put his empty glass down on the ground. 'All that looking back. It was bloody depressing. I won't be going to another. One reunion's enough to last me a lifetime.'

He checks his watch. 'I need to be off. It'll take a good four hours to get back, and I've a stop off on the way. A man I know has got some second-hand bricks from a demolition. I need to sort out some sort of deal; they'll do fine for a garage or two.'

We walk back to the bike. I pat the handlebars.

'It'll be a pity to leave this old girl behind.'

He looks shocked. 'I'm not! I told them, they pay passages for me, Nuala and the bike, or the deal's off.' We both burst out laughing.

He takes the goggles off the handlebars and places them round his neck while he puts his jacket back on, then the helmet. 'Hop on,' he thumbs over his shoulder to the pillion and pulls up the goggles, 'I'll give you a lift back.' This time, he doesn't leave me at the gates. He has a word with the man on gate duty and they chat about bikes. The corporal had been a dispatch rider in Normandy. Before I know it, we're trundling up the driveway to the hospital, strictly against the rules. He stops at the shark's teeth border but doesn't switch off the engine. I climb off, he puts his goggles up on his helmet. We both look at each other.

'Well, then,' he says.

'Well, then.' I offer him my hand. He clasps it tight. The callouses are still there, but not as rough. I wrap my other hand round his, then pull away.

'Keep in touch,' I say.

He nods. Goggles on, he circles the bike round, then looks back at me and grins. 'Don't let the bastards grind you down.'

I watch the bike and sidecar taxi down the driveway like a plane with one wing negotiating take off, growing smaller until it reaches the gate, then slowing down. The man on duty waves him through. He rounds the bend slowly, then he's gone.

8

Daniel could feel the sweat trickling down his back as he sat through the first ten minutes of Sargant droning on. It was, as he'd expected, little more than the key points of his book.

At last, he came to prefrontal leucotomy, suggesting it was a particularly interesting development, and that its applications had expanded over the past four years or so.

About time, thought Daniel, surely now he'll hand over to McKissock.

A note of excitement crept into Sargant's voice at this point. 'Which brings me to my paper offered to you today. It is the first case study to be published on a *leucotomy* performed on a member of the armed services suffering from chronic battle neurosis.' He looked out at the audience as he stressed the word leucotomy. 'In fact, the improvement of this patient has been among the most gratifying in the several thousand cases of war neurosis treated by physical methods at Sutton in the past seven years.'

Daniel sat up straight in his chair. He'd been expecting McKissock, not Sargant, to give some sort of additional lecture on leucotomies, most probably an updated set of *Housewife, fifty, Melancholia*, civilian cases. But leucotomy operations for battle neurosis? That was something new. And under Sargant's supervision? A buzz of interest rose in the room as people realised the significance of what Sargant was saying.

McKissock stopped doodling and turned in his chair to face the audience, his back to Sargant, his expression impassive.

Sargant paused, savouring the effect of his words. He waved his notes about in the air. 'The details of the case, the treatment and the post-operative results are all in the *BMJ* article and I propose to do no more here than give a short summary.'

He began with an overview of the patient. Thirty-six years old. Tank crew veteran of D-Day landings and the subsequent fierce fighting across Europe.

As Daniel listened, he was reminded of the high pile of files on his desk categorised as D-Day/Normandy landings. What he was hearing now could be the story of countless tank crew who'd been through Northfield. This veteran had also seen friends burned to death, and had also fought on with increasing dread that he'd be next. He'd escaped his third direct hit, crawled to safety, and ended up back in England being treated for minor physical injuries.

And that's when the battle neurosis had taken hold.

Sargant continued the case background at a brisk pace, summarising as he went along. They hadn't been able to get him fit for return to action, and he'd been discharged in 1945 with a small pension. He'd deteriorated further over the year and was admitted to Sutton Hospital in 1946.

'He was depressed and disgruntled about his pension,' said Sargant, 'and also anxious about his war experiences and convinced he would never get better. His responses varied, from superficial appreciation to sullen criticism of all efforts to help him. He would sit in the ward, watching the activities of others, doing nothing himself.'

If there was ever a textbook list of typical symptoms of chronic battle neurosis, thought Daniel, then Sargant had just covered it. This was the day-in, day-out reality for all patients. So what was so different about this man that he warranted surgery?

Sargant poured a glass of water for himself. He took a sip, then slowly scanned the audience again.

He's really enjoying being the ringmaster at this particular circus, Daniel thought.

There was a sense of deep concentration in the room – Sargant had painted a vivid picture of a suffering patient. The young students in the front row were scribbling furiously, trying to take down his every word.

After another sip of water, he moved on to physical treatments tried over the past nine months, starting with intravenous barbiturates and ether.

As he heard this, Daniel had a sudden memory of the Acute Ward in Northfield, back in 1943. It had been his first week there, and he was still finding his way around the hospital. He'd heard shouting coming from a side ward and had gone to find out what was going on.

He'd walked in to find a patient strapped down on a trolley. One of the senior psychiatrists was standing behind his head, administering doses of ether on to a large mask over the man's face and nose. The psychiatrist was shouting at his patient, in a state of high excitement – 'You're trapped in your tank, corporal, you can see your friend burning, but *you* can get out, you can escape!'

The man was shouting back, in great distress and gasping for breath through the mask: 'Yes, sir, I can see him burning. But I can't get out, sir, I can't, there's a snake, there's a snake!' He tried to heave himself up against the restraints, but an orderly forced him down and the psychiatrist applied more ether. The man howled and was given yet another dose.

Daniel left and waited outside until the treatment was over, thinking he should apologise for blundering in. He felt uneasy about what he'd just witnessed, although he'd seen it several times during his training. It was a standard physical treatment to induce what was known as abreaction, where patients are encouraged to release emotions associated with a traumatic experience by recalling or reliving it. Chemically induced abreaction, using drugs or ether, had been trialled increasingly on men suffering from battle neurosis, since the withdrawal from Dunkirk in 1940. Sargant was a key proponent of the technique. But the physicality of it always unsettled Daniel; the holding down, the raised voice of the psychiatrist, the patient struggling to breathe while being forced to speak at the same time.

The psychiatrist, a mild-mannered man when he wasn't wrestling with patients, had spoken to him afterwards. He'd been pleased by what had been accomplished. The man had been part of a tank crew in the Western Desert, at the Battle of El Alamein four months previously, and had not responded well to other treatments since being shipped home.

The physical restraint had worked well, he'd said – it replicated to some degree the patient's feeling of being trapped and therefore added to the intensity of his heightened emotional state. The results from this treatment, he suggested, showed that just one session of powerful physical and chemical stimuli could produce an excellent outcome. Daniel had thanked him for his time and said he'd found it most enlightening, then gone out for a walk in the grounds – he could detect the faint whiff of ether fumes clinging to his clothing.

He brought himself back to the Old Board Room to find Sargant moving rapidly down the list of physical treatments. Insulin sopor. Electric-convulsion treatment. Insulin coma, inducing deeper unconsciousness. All of them progressively more powerful physical treatments. And all of which, according to Sargant, only either temporarily relieved the patient's symptoms or worsened his condition.

Daniel noticed Hunter was nodding vigorously. They were all treatments he specialised in at Northfield.

'He also had many hours of psychotherapy,' said Sargant, 'but always seemed unable to gain insight into his symptoms.' There was no attempt to disguise the disparaging tone. 'At this point,' said Sargant, 'I'd like to bring in Dr Minski.' He sat down.

Minski remained seated, referring from time to time to his notes and a copy of Sargant's paper. He'd been asked to submit an independent psychiatric opinion on the patient and he skimmed through it quickly, as if he wanted to get it over with.

He began with the psychiatric assessment – the patient was a 'hysteric', was 'histrionic', but displayed 'no antisocial traits in his pre-neurotic personality'. Then he moved on to more of a behavioural assessment. Terms like 'self-centred and shallow' peppered his description, together with the observation that the patient became 'irritable and fidgety' when discussing his pension.

Anger rose from somewhere deep in Daniel – since when did showing signs of irritability and being self-centred and shallow count as appropriate criteria for a leucotomy?

If that were the case, half the staff at Northfield would be in the queue, including a number of the psychiatrists.

Minski looked up from his notes at this point, and spoke directly to the audience.

'Quite frankly, I agreed that psychological and ordinary physical methods of treatment were not likely to help him – but I didn't know what effect leucotomy would have on him.'

He glanced across at Sargant, gesturing for him to retake the floor.

Daniel noticed McKissock looking grave. That last remark of Minski's, about not knowing what the effect of the leucotomy might be, was not exactly a ringing endorsement of the procedure the surgeon was so associated with.

Sargant stood up again, thanked Minski for his contribution, and addressed the audience. 'Given these factors, this particular case of chronic battle neurosis was considered appropriate for treatment by leucotomy, with a reasonable probability of success.'

He looked across at McKissock, who still had his back turned to him. 'Mr McKissock performed the operation in June, this year. I don't know if you would like to say more about this, Wylie?'

It's 'Wylie', is it? Daniel smiled to himself. Sargant is really riding high. And it was McKissock who did this particular operation. So that's why he's here.

McKissock turned and nodded to Sargant, then faced the audience. He didn't stand up either. 'There's not much more to say. It was a straightforward operation, no complications.' He paused for a moment, then said in an authoritative and determined manner: 'One thing I must stress, however – and it's good to be invited here today in order for me to say it – I would suggest that this operation, valuable as it may be in individual cases, should be regarded still as a highly experimental procedure. It is justifiable only when all other available methods have failed and when experienced psychiatric opinion is convinced that no hope of spontaneous cure remains.'

He nodded at the other three and they all nodded back. McKissock then turned to face the audience again.

That's much the same thing he'd said at Barnwood, thought Daniel. He's still protecting his interests because he must realise he'll be mentioned in the *BMJ* paper as the surgeon who did the operation. He wants to make the delineation clear between those who decide the operation is necessary and surgeons like him who carry it out on their advice. Maybe old Wylie isn't quite as willing to be as chummy as Sargant would like to think.

If Sargant was put out by McKissock's perfunctory contribution, he didn't show it. He smiled at Slater and then at the back of McKissock's head. All three of the Sutton Hospital men began to gather their papers together, and Slater looked as though he was about to stand up to make his closing remarks. McKissock spent some time adjusting his tie.

'I have a few questions, if I may?' Daniel tried to keep a neutral tone. He had to raise his voice slightly above the general hubbub; the audience had taken their cue from the speakers and were shuffling in their seats and murmuring. 'Just a few questions after such a stimulating paper.' His voice began to sound a little steadier.

He noticed Hunter's head swivel round like a ventriloquist's dummy – he'd obviously recognised Daniel's voice and was staring at him, eyebrows raised in startled disbelief. Slater,

Sargant and Minski looked at the audience, trying to spot where the voice was coming from.

'We can certainly make time for one or two questions.' Slater had located Daniel by this time. 'The officer at the back? Would you be kind enough to identify yourself, sir?'

'Major Carter, Northfield Military Hospital.' Daniel felt the audience turn round to him as one body, a many-headed, multi-eyed gorgon, waving its neck slightly this way and that, trying to catch sight of him.

It was almost unheard of to ask questions at this type of lecture, unless specifically invited to do so, and Daniel wondered if the audience were intrigued or just irritated.

The room was devilishly hot by now and people must have been gasping for a drink. They're probably irritated, he thought. I'd better keep it short.

'Well, then, Major Carter?' Slater was his usual courteous self.

All eyes were still on Daniel, including McKissock's, who leaned back in his chair, his arms folded. As Daniel stared back, he thought he could see a face he recognised, right in the middle of the audience. Housewife, fifty, Melancholia. Wide-eyed and looking straight at him. And the others in the audience became the men he'd treated at Northfield, some of whom, if Sargant had his way, would now be suitable cases for leucotomies.

Come on, he said silently to himself. Time for some forward action.

He sat square on his chair, back upright, his knees at right angles to the floor, his hands clasped as loosely as he could in his lap. He took a deep breath.

'You seem to be suggesting that the surgical procedure of leucotomy is based upon the theory that the brain has both "a thinking part" and "a feeling part", if I may put it so simply, and that separating one from the other will "remove the sting from the mental disorder", as Freeman and Watts describe it – is that a fair summary?'

He noticed McKissock tense slightly at the mention of the two Americans. He obviously hadn't changed his opinion of them over the last six years, then.

'That's somewhat simplistically put, as you say, but yes, that's more or less the idea.' Sargant's tone was condescending, as if he were talking to one of the young men at the front.

'But isn't that exactly the point?' Daniel said. 'This theory of the brain's architecture is just that – no more than an idea, as yet unproven. And you are, in effect, deliberately destroying healthy brain tissue, all on the basis of that theory. And not only that, once such destruction of the brain is done, it cannot be undone, as you yourself have written.'

He looked straight at Sargant. 'Aren't we doing our patients the greatest harm? We, who have the strongest ethical obligation to first do no harm?' He paused for the fraction of a second then continued: '*Primum non nocere*,' emphasising these last three words as he spoke, his voice quiet but firm.

There was utter silence. *Listen to the silences, work out what they say*, and Daniel almost chuckled aloud as he heard Foulkes's voice. This silence was deafening. Shocked and hostile in some quarters, embarrassed in others. Physicians rarely challenged other physicians, at least in public, or if they did, they didn't take on four of the most eminent, all at once.

Sargant's normally sallow face was puce. Minski's bonhomie seemed to have deserted him. Slater was doubling his efforts at shuffling papers. Only McKissock looked unruffled. But at that precise moment, Daniel couldn't have cared less about McKissock. He was filled with a rush of elation. He'd done it. He'd spoken for all the patients who couldn't speak for themselves. And it felt bloody marvellous.

Just for good measure, he decided to finish with a flourish. 'As I'm sure you'll all know, Dr Winnicott has already said something similar elsewhere.' He paused to let the name sink in. 'He said that even if he could be convinced that leucotomy could be good, in terms of favourable results in some cases, he'd still believe it was a bad operation because it involves the deliberate damage of the brain which then can't be reversed.'

He knew the mention of Winnicott would be like a red rag to a bull. Donald Winnicott, one of the most noted psychotherapists of the day, was a dogged opponent of physical treatments, especially ECT and leucotomies, and his criticisms had appeared regularly in medical journals from the early 1940s.

Sargant's head went up at this. 'Ah, that explains all! We have a disciple of the inestimable Dr Winnicott in our midst!'

There was some nervous laughter at this. Sargant opened his mouth to add something else, but Slater put a hand on his shoulder and stood up. He said, as smoothly as he could, 'Thank you, Major Carter. No more time for questions, but I'm glad to say, plenty of time for sherry, which should be arriving any moment.' He brought the proceedings to a close, eliciting a special round of applause for Will Sargant who, he reiterated, would be sorely missed.

The secretary arrived on cue, bearing a large tray with bottles of sherry and glasses, which she set on a small table in front of the fireplace at the other end of the room.

Daniel sat still while the crowd scraped their chairs and rumbled past him. He was ignored by most of them, but he caught a few giving him sidelong glances. Sargant, Slater and Minski walked past, making sure they were talking as a threesome and didn't have to acknowledge him. Hunter hovered behind them, nose up, not looking Daniel's way. McKissock followed them, in his own space. As he went past Daniel, he looked directly at him. Daniel could have sworn there was a hint of a nod.

He soon found himself sitting alone on the edge of the thicket of chairs. He was slightly disorientated. He thought he'd feel angry, seeing McKissock again. But as he'd observed him during the meeting, he began to think of him as not some arrogant monster, but as a brilliant surgeon who saw the leucotomy procedure as just one aspect of his neurosurgical work, and one he was trying to guard with care. It was Sargant who was the loose cannon. He was the one to watch, a man on a self-aggrandising mission, if ever there was one. A dangerous man, powerful, and with powerful allies.

The rest of the audience had now congregated at the sherry end of the room and he was conscious of sitting with his back to them. Foulkes would have had another field day with that little insight into group dynamics. He was unsure what to do next. He hadn't thought past saying what he'd planned to say; he certainly hadn't planned an exit. The adrenalin rush he'd experienced had drained away and his body suddenly felt leaden, weighing him down in his seat, as if his pockets were loaded with stones.

He'd just have to get up and go.

He pulled himself up and turned round. Small groups stood about, holding glasses.

As he headed towards the door, determined to take it at a measured pace, he was aware that a substantial number of individuals in the groups kept their backs turned away from him. John Bain's voice came into his head. *Deserted in the arse of the enemy.* He allowed himself an inward smile. Another helpful comment from Bain to see him through – he really would be irritated if he knew.

Hunter trotted over and cornered him just as he was about to escape into the corridor. 'That was quite a performance,' he said, supercilious as ever. 'I'm going to have to spend a good part of the evening distancing myself from your point of view.'

'Something you've had plenty of practice at, I'm sure.'

'Thought you'd like to know,' Hunter said, 'I've left Northfield. I'll be leaving the army in a month's time, as a matter of fact.'

'A great loss to us all.' He knew the heavy sarcasm of repeating Slater's earlier comment about Sargant's departure would float over Hunter's head.

'I'll be starting at Sutton next week,' Hunter said loudly. 'I've arranged to do the rest of my army service on transfer there, as assistant to Professor Sargant. He's been most helpful. The Maudsley will soon get going again under the new National Health Service. I aim to be in the right place at the right time to move across there. It'll be one of the best hospitals in London.'

Daniel had a brief image of Hunter swinging from Sargant's coat-tails. 'The best of luck,' he said. I'm sure you and Dr Sargant are well matched in your vision of the future.'

Hunter paused, then said, 'There's one of ours at Sutton. In the queue for a leucotomy.'

'One of ours?'

'Similar history to Sargant's patient. A year of treatments off and on, ended up with us at Northfield this last June. Got his ticket out. Came home to London. Didn't last long. Admitted to Sutton this week. A prime candidate. The leucotomy has already been approved. Scheduled for next week. I'll be super-vising his pre- and post-operative treatment.'

'Who is it?' He started to run through a list of the latest discharges in his head.

'Simm. Corporal Freddie Simm. Tank Commander, D-Day. You assigned him to me in June. Best thing you could have done for him, as it turned out.'

There was a smirk on his face.

Daniel didn't remember Simm's details. But the thought of having a patient pass through his hands and end up on the waiting list for a leucotomy made his stomach churn. He needed to get away, before he said or did something he'd regret.

'I have to go, Hunter.' He turned on his heel. As he did so, he caught sight of McKissock. He was standing by the window on his own, staring out over Queen Square, his back to the crowd.

9

I don't want to stay in the dormitory after I watch Louie leave. It's full of men either nervous as hell getting ready for their visitors, or moping on their beds because the visit is over. I need space to get used to the idea of not seeing Louie again. I gather up my book on Paul Nash and my sketch pad, and head off to the bench under the copper beech next to the Art Hut, where John and I had listened to Mozart.

I sit and look across the field with the three oaks, thinking about Louie and me in Burma. He's right, it does feel like history, like something that happened to someone else.

I open the Nash book at a black and white plate of *The Menin Road*, and my head begins to buzz. The Menin Road. Passchendaele. My father's face. The perfect roundel of a shrapnel scar, pink and mottled, the size of a half-crown, on his left cheek. I would stroke it as a small boy. He never talked about the war but would sometimes talk about artists who painted it. 'Nash gets to the truth of it,' he would say. '*The Void of War*, he called it. He knew, he was there.'

Stripped of its colour, Nash's landscape is even more apocalyptic. Two soldiers scurry across the battlefield, their small figures stranded in the middle, encircled by emptiness. But look closer and you can see there's nothing empty about this tipped-up-tilted-down obstacle course. It's scarred with shell holes, shattered tree trunks, disjointed concrete slabs. All is distortion.

It's difficult for your eye to find its way to these men, but when you do manage to get alongside them, you look round and see what they see: there's no way back, no way through, no way out. You feel it then, the terror of being lost in such a landscape. Past the line of stripped woodland in the distance, your eye picks up two other soldiers. Little more than shadows, they are heading for the safety of a copse. The blurred outline of its trees on the horizon is surprisingly whole and unblemished. But then you realise that this foliage is a mockery, that these hazy canopies, promising shelter, aren't trees at all, they are the smoke clouds of explosions shooting skywards.

There is no place of safety for these men on the Menin Road. They are surrounded by a landscape intent on their oblivion.

Roads and valleys, ridges and rivers, deserts and mountains and jungle – scraps of landscape to fight in, over, cut through, creep through, break through, blast through, lose, win, lose again, win again, abandon, besiege, relieve, hand over, grab back. Sometimes within the same day, the same hour. Advance. Retreat. Stay put. Men fighting others they know only as the enemy. Fighting the landscape. Fighting themselves.

We know. We were there too.

I think of Louie and me in the clearing off the Imphal Road. Our road. Our landscape. I hear his voice. *Where the hell did they get red ink?*

I begin to sketch the *sotoba*. It doesn't take long. It soothes me to see it in my mind's eye then watch it appear on the paper. Their marker for the dead.

He was looking forward to meeting up with Laurence Bradbury after Sargant's lecture. He'd thought of going to see Foulkes, but he knew it would have been a more formal professional conversation. He could just imagine him listening then saying, *So what have you learned from it all?* Laurence had never claimed to be a therapist, and he and Daniel had enjoyed each other's company at Northfield, spending the time talking about anything but the patients. Laurence had left the army and was now back in London.

They met in front of the National Gallery and went to a little café nearby that Laurence knew. It served a version of sausage and mash – doubtful sausages, mostly claggy bread with a little indefinable meat – but real potato. The place was clean and full. Laurence, being a regular, got an extra spoonful of potato for both of them from the woman who ran the place.

He looked different. More at ease in his tweed jacket and well-worn corduroy trousers. If ever a man should never have been in army uniform, it was Laurence, although he'd seemed oblivious to the shambles he'd looked at Northfield. He was working now at the Tate and the National Gallery, giving lectures on art history from time to time.

Over the meal, he made Daniel laugh, telling him about the recent debacle over the conservation of pictures at the National Gallery – they were about to exhibit ten important paintings that had undergone conservation when they'd been stored for the duration at the Welsh slate quarry at Mahod. But the conservation methods used in the process were considered harsh and inappropriate by some experts and the results had caused a furore in certain Establishment circles involved in art.

'They've done everything in the name of cleaning them, bar putting them in a copper boiler and giving them a good wash with bloomin' Rinso,' Laurence said, shaking his head and chuckling. 'Some of them have ended up looking as technicolour as *Gone With the Wind*.' He threw his head back and laughed, deep and long, and Daniel laughed with him, the tension draining out of him.

But for all his grumbles about the Gallery, he sounded like a man who was doing what he wanted to be doing. He deserved to be back in his element, thought Daniel; he'd done a magnificent job at Northfield in his own quiet way. It was already being put forward as the beginnings of a new approach to therapy. Not that Laurence would have any truck with that. Foulkes had once complimented him on the results he got from his art therapy work in the Art Hut. 'There's no such thing as art therapy, Foulkes, old chap,' Laurence had replied, in his usual genial tone of voice. 'All art is therapy.'

Whatever you decided to label it, Daniel thought, he'd managed a bit of magic in the Art Hut. British and American military psychiatrists had come to visit Northfield in its heyday during the war, and Laurence and his work had always got a good write-up in official reports.

When they finished eating, they decamped to the little pub just along the street, another of Laurence's pre-war haunts. It had survived the bombings, despite being slightly battered. They sat in companionable silence over their pints. Then Laurence said, 'Hope you don't mind my saying, Daniel, but you look bloody awful.'

That was all Daniel needed. He gabbled on about what he'd said to them at the lecture, about the leucotomy at Barnwood back in 1941. And about Freddie Simm, destined for the same experience. He trailed off, wondering if Laurence would think he was cracking up.

'It sounds horrendous.' Laurence sat back in his chair and puffed on his pipe. 'I'd no idea leucotomies were still going on.

I thought that by now, they'd be seen as some sort of ghastly aberration – that the medical men would see sense and stop the practice.'

'Quite the opposite. They've grown increasingly popular over the past six years. But to my knowledge, only with civilians. Not that it makes any difference – civilian, ex-servicemen – it's still barbaric, whoever ends up having it.' Daniel took a sip from his glass of Bass. 'I tell you, Laurence, sitting there listening to Sargant sounding so pleased with himself, so smug, it made me sick to my stomach.'

'I can imagine.' Laurence finished his beer, then said, 'We need a drop of something a little stronger, I think,' and he headed off to the bar.

He came back and set down two small brandies. They both took tiny sips, trying to make them last.

Laurence looked thoughtful. 'So they still think a particular bit of the brain is separate from the rest of it, and it's that bit that controls the emotions?' he said.

'Roughly. But it's still only research, not proven facts.'

'But the brain might not be set up like that.' Laurence shook his head. 'Or, they could be right, but they've identified the wrong bit. And that's the bit they cut out.'

'Exactly. That's what I told them. Once it's done, it's done. But they can't be right. I refuse to believe it. And even if they were, just say, even if there is a specific locus of the emotions in the brain, it would still be wrong to cut it out. I quoted Winnicott at them. Whatever the benefits, you've deliberately damaged the brain and it can't be reversed. Winnicott got to the heart of things, like he usually does.'

'Men like him, they have a lot of clout, surely? He's got such a reputation as a psychotherapist of integrity. People like him could stop it going on.'

'It's not that simple. It's seen as two professional sides who see things differently, and the physical methods group are a powerful lobby, with friends in high places. Just look at Sargant.

Psychotherapy has always been outside the mainstream. It's never caught on over here like it has in America.'

Laurence puffed on his pipe again. 'It was distressing watching the effect of ECT on the poor blighters at Northfield. Far too much messing about with their minds for my liking. They'd come back to the Art Hut and you'd think at first, yes, they're much calmer, but then you'd realise they weren't calm, they were deadened down.'

He paused, then said, 'It was pitiful, really. They couldn't remember things – what they'd done in the Hut a few weeks previously, or what they'd done in the war a few years previously, come to that. Their memories were all so random.'

They sat in silence, lost in remembrances of Northfield men they'd known.

'I'm surprised the hospitals allow leucotomies,' Laurence said, 'if it's all still so experimental.'

'Not all of them do. There was a rumour going round that Sargant couldn't get the London County Council to agree to it going on in some of their hospitals. So, he discharged the patients from the hospitals that wouldn't give consent for whatever reason, and then re-registered them in the ones that would.'

Laurence sighed. 'The world's gone mad. It must be something to do with the Atomic Age. There don't seem to be any checks and balances any more. It was bad enough when all we had was ordinary bombs.' He sighed again. 'It's only since I've come back to live in London permanently that I've realised the true damage the bombing did. It's not just the fabric of the buildings that's been destroyed. It's the fabric of society. We put a brave face on it, harking back to the Blitz mentality, but everything's torn apart.'

He dropped his voice a little. 'And now we've got a bomb that can dole out death on a scale we'd never imagined. But we shouldn't be working out how to end wars with bloody great bombs, should we? We should be working out how not to start them in the first place.' He swirled the last of the brandy and drank it down, his face grim.

Daniel saw that underneath the geniality, Laurence was as exhausted and anxious as everyone else. Peace was turning out to be as uncertain as the war.

He nodded back at Laurence. 'It's as if we come up with a possible solution to a problem, and it doesn't matter if it's inhumane, we'll justify it any way we can, and use it just the same. Atom bombs. Leucotomies. It might not be the right solution – it might not even be the right problem you've identified, come to that. But you label it "experimental" and you get away with it.'

He suddenly felt very weary. It must be the events of the day catching up with him.

He took another sip of his brandy. 'It was bad enough signing our men at Northfield off as "fit for action", knowing we were sending them back to the situation that had led to their breakdowns in the first place. Now, it's worse. Once they're in civvy street, even though they're suffering from the same thing they had the day before they were discharged from the army, they're civilians. If they relapse, they may end up as a "suitable candidate" for a leucotomy. It doesn't bear thinking about.'

He thought of Freddie Simm. 'I just don't see how you mend an unquiet mind by taking a slice of it away.'

Laurence looked at him, the same compassionate look on his face as there'd been at Northfield when he was relaying some of the goings-on with the men in the Art Hut.

'No, Daniel,' he said. 'Neither do I.'

When he got back to the flat in Marchmont Street, he sat in the dark and finished off the last of Ian's whisky, hoping he wouldn't pay too much for mixing his drinks. He was exhausted, his mind dull, his body a dead weight. It had helped to talk to Laurence, but it had been a roller coaster ride of a day, and he needed to be alone, needed to regain his equilibrium.

He thought back to his encounter at Queen Square, going

over what he'd said and how he'd said it. He doubted if they'd even heard the real message he'd intended. They'd probably put his intervention down to overwork. He could just imagine Hunter, faking sympathy for his overstressed colleague, while simultaneously putting the boot in. But deep within him, it felt right to have done it. If the men from Northfield came back to visit him again in his dreams tonight, accompanied by Housewife, fifty, Melancholia, he could look them all in the eye.

But then there was Freddie Simm. He remembered the triumphant look on Hunter's face as he'd told him about Freddie. It was the randomness of what had happened that was disturbing. And the part Daniel himself had played, however inadvertently. He had to admit to himself that he'd been influenced by Hunter's unwillingness to take extra patients. He'd allocated Simm to Hunter to prove a point – '*You can take him, chock-a-bloody-block or not.*' Another thing to feel guilty about. If he hadn't put Simm on the Normandy pile and forced him on Hunter, he might not have ended up on the list for the leucotomy.

Once he'd got him, Hunter had probably marked Simm out as a suitable case for treatment from the beginning. It would have been easy to suggest to the relatives that if he was discharged and there was a relapse, admission to a specialised London hospital could be arranged. He'd put it across as a privilege.

There was also something else Daniel had to face up to, this weekend. Thinking so much about the men at Northfield, thinking about them as ordinary human beings, not just as patients, he realised he had more in common with them than he cared to acknowledge. He was traumatised himself. He wouldn't admit this to anyone else in his profession – except possibly Foulkes – it would be seen as professional weakness. Also, saying this to himself, acknowledging that he was traumatised too, felt like it was disrespecting or devaluing the experience of his patients. After all, he hadn't suffered what they had gone through first hand. But some of what he'd listened to on a daily basis must have seeped down into his own emotional foundations. That was the catch with this kind of work – you have to be distanced enough to do the job, but sensitive enough to connect with the suffering revealed to you. He had become saturated with other men's suffering.

He was almost as lost as the men he'd been treating. Whatever these men had seen or done in the name of war, they were now being asked to go quietly and fade back into the fabric of ordinary life again. They were struggling to put the past behind them, move on to an uncertain future in an outside world they were finding hard to relate to any more. He was in the same position. The role he'd been forced to play, fixing them up to send them back to war, had gone. What he did next, the choices he'd make, would affect the rest of his life, just like his patients.

That's why he'd come to London. He saw that now. He'd told himself it was to see how far he'd come after his Barnwood experience, or how he'd react to seeing McKissock again. But it was more than that. It might have been a subconscious act, but he'd set the situation up, and in so doing, had created the crisis which would bring on all this soul-searching.

Men like Sargant, who represented the very opposite of what he felt psychiatry should be, and McKissock, who was prepared to take the psychiatrists on trust, then use the situation for surgical experimental research, were in positions of real power within psychiatry and medical circles. He hated to admit it, but Hunter was right about that when he said they controlled the future.

Listening to them and observing them had made Daniel face his own anxieties. This is your profession, he told himself. You can delude yourself all you like, say you're at the Winnicott and Foulkes end, with Sargant and McKissock at the other. But we're all part of the same spectrum, whether you like it or not. When Northfield closes as a military hospital, you're going to have to go back into the mainstream, take up your position in it. For five years, you've been able to avoid making that kind of decision, hiding away in the Northfield bubble. Now you're going to have to patch yourself up and get back in action.

He sipped the last of the whisky and sat back on the sofa. His brain had jumped back into gear again and he was almost enjoying the indulgence of trying to rationalise his thoughts rather than be at the whim of them.

How did you get here, Dr Carter? He smiled at the irony of using a stock question to patients on himself.

He'd gone into psychiatry thinking he could ease the mental suffering for others, but he'd found out as much about himself as he had about the patients – his own vulnerabilities, his own limitations. No bad thing for a psychiatrist – most of us do that, he thought, we just don't admit it to anyone. But he hadn't looked after himself in the war years – he'd had to focus on men with far greater needs than his. It had left him exhausted, drained, confused. It was time to change. That might mean getting out of psychiatry altogether. He pushed this thought away at first. He had no idea what he would do if he didn't work as a psychiatrist.

But the thought kept creeping back. And the more he gave it space in his head, the less frightening it became. Do I want to be part of the Winnicott–Sargant spectrum? Do I still want to practise psychiatry at all? He realised he didn't know the answers, but at least now he knew the questions. A complete break might help with those answers.

Once he made that decision, he felt lighter, physically lighter, as though someone had reached down and lifted the dead weight from him. As the pressure lifted, he was overtaken by a sudden longing for sleep.

The trail of Sunday visitors weaves its way up the lane from the bus stop like a multi-coloured ribbon caught in the light breeze. All women, this week, by the look of it. I wait just outside the gate, like I did yesterday for Louie. My feet feel rooted to the spot. I don't see her in the first group, but the line is strung out, winding back round the curve in the road.

Some of the women at the front walk in pairs and have linked arms, not so much in the loose friendly way that women do, but more tightly, as if they need someone to help them steady their nerves, share the butterflies in their stomachs. If only they knew it was the same for us in here. On Friday nights before the weekend visiting days, the short fuses get even shorter, the flare-ups even more petty – *you took my teaspoon without asking – stop your fucking shoving in, there's a queue here.* Maybe that's the difference between men and women when they're nervous: women cling to each other, men bait each other.

There's a buzz of conversation as the women get nearer, an occasional laugh, short and sharp edged, but they all grow quiet when they reach the gate. They stand in a ragged queue at first, the usual bunch of mothers, wives and sweethearts. Then a woman at the back in a bright yellow frock and too much make-up says, 'I'm buggered if I'm queuing for me husband as well as everything else!' and there's some laughter and the tension goes out of them a little. They break up into groups, or pairs or the odd single, and mill around, glancing up the driveway as another ribbon, blue and khaki this time, snakes its way down to the gate.

A group of stragglers comes round the bend. Still no Beth.

My body sways forwards, searching the line. Then I see her at the back walking on her own.

She's wearing a simple white dress I haven't seen before, large buttons down the front, deep pockets with slanted edges on either hip, and as she walks, the light cotton catches against her, outlining the shape of her thighs. A white silk scarf holds her hair back. My heart starts to thump. My feet are still rooted. The perspiration pops out on my upper lip.

I am miserably conscious of my Blues – the delphinium more garish than ever, the too short trouser legs, this hideous red tie like a puppy dog's tongue lolling down my chest. I felt self-conscious before, with Louie, but it's the first time I've felt ashamed. I shouldn't have let her come. I shouldn't have let her come. The words bump round in my head as she spots me, gives me a slight wave and quickens her step. As she gets closer, she doesn't take her eyes off me and I study her face, watching for any little flicker of disgust.

She reaches me and we stand close, looking at each other, not touching. Slowly, she rests her face against my chest, both hands flat against me, as if she's listening intently to my heartbeat. I somehow move my arms, put them around her, drop my cheek against the top of her head.

I've no idea how long we both stand like that, swaying a little. Then she takes a step back and looks up at me.

'I've missed you,' she says, and I see the strain around her eyes.

'Beth,' I say, her name a gentle breath on my lips.

I kiss her, tasting her lipstick, my lips pressing too hard against hers, so that our teeth tap and I'm back to being a clumsy adolescent again. Her body gives slightly against me, then she steps back again and it's her turn to study my face.

She must see the anxiety, because she puts her fingers on my lips.

'There's plenty of time, we've got plenty of time.' She smiles and links her arm through mine.

I think: it's going to be alright. We're going to be alright. I allow myself to relax a little.

'There's a pub,' I say, hoping she'll say no; I don't fancy taking her there with all the other Blues. It feels important to keep them apart, as if they're two separate worlds.

She twitches her nose at the idea of the pub.

'There's a tea shop.' I sound relieved. 'It's where the men take their mothers.'

'God, no!' She laughs. 'Do I look like your mother?' Then she nods towards the driveway. 'Why don't we walk for a while? The parkland is beautiful.'

So that's what we do. I find myself crossing the boundary with her, bringing her into my world. It feels risky, but there's nothing for it, she's here. 'If we walk up to the top and round the back, there's a terrace garden,' I say, as if I'm extolling the delights of some country hotel.

She smiles. 'Sounds lovely.'

Then I go and spoil it. 'They used to call the terraces the airing courts, when it was an asylum. They'd allow the patients out there for an airing.' She nods, the smile fading a little on the word asylum. We walk up to the oak, and I hear myself saying, 'I stopped here on the first day. Almost turned round and came straight home.'

'Are you glad you didn't?' It's such a simple question.

'I feel safe here.'

'Safe from what?'

'From myself. At home, I never knew what I was going to do next. I was out of control.'

'And now?'

'I'm surrounded by men who felt the same before they came in here. It helps, knowing you're not the only one. And so many of them are getting well.'

For some reason, I think of Freddie, lying in my arms on the corridor outside the day room. Freddie, who I can't imagine ever getting well. 'And I'm not the worst either.' I start to feel a little anxious, then – telling her there are others worse than me is hardly reassuring.

She squeezes my arm and we carry on walking up to the hospital buildings in silence. The vicar from the local church has got the ladies of the parish to organise a tea and buns table on Sundays for patients and their visitors. Tea on the terrace. All very sedate.

We find a small table, joining a few other couples scattered around at the other tables.

I fetch two cups of tea and a plate with two unfathomable biscuits that look like hard tack.

As I make my way through the tables to Beth, the stocky man from the Art Hut storms past me, into the building, almost pushing me over. I haven't seen him much since the day I did my first charcoal sketch. He hasn't come back after his outburst about the VD.

'That man,' Beth whispers, nodding in his direction, as she takes her tea and the plate of biscuits from me, 'I thought he was going to hit his wife.'

The woman in the yellow dress who cracked the joke about having to queue for the men at the gate is sitting at a far table dabbing her eyes with a handkerchief. 'They had some sort of argument,' Beth carries on. 'I couldn't catch it all, something about her saying she didn't know how she got it, and him saying he didn't believe her, then he grabbed her by the arm and drew his hand back and I really thought he was going to slap her across the face, but he just got up and walked away, thank goodness.'

The woman is still sniffing into the hanky.

'There are a few like him in here,' I say. 'It gets to them, whatever it is they've gone through; it all gets stoppered up inside. It's got to come out sometime.'

It surprises me that I'm defending him, I don't even like him. Then I see Vinny's face, the bones mashed from the kicking I gave him, and me standing over him, relishing what I'd done.

The person who did that is someone else, some mad stranger. But it wasn't. It was me. I'm no better than the stocky man. I look away from Beth so she can't see my face.

The woman gets up and stuffs her hanky in her bag. Head down, she makes her way round the corner of the building towards the driveway leading to the gates.

I suddenly want to be away from this goldfish bowl where we all seem to be struggling to behave like normal people. Tea on the bloody terrace. Another test I've failed.

'Let's go somewhere more private,' I say, thinking about the Art Hut. 'I know a place, there's never anyone there on Sundays. We'd be on our own. We could talk.'

As soon as we walk through the archway leading to the walled-off area of lawn on the way to the Art Hut, I begin to relax a little. The hospital seems miles away. The small rose garden laid out along the path is past its best, but Beth spots a late blooming climber on the wall and drags me over to have a closer look. 'A Madame Carrière,' she says, burying her nose into the white-pink flower, looking like a Bisto kid as she sniffs up its scent.

We sit down on a little bench in front of the rose, my arm around her shoulder, our heads together. I'd forgotten how good it feels to be so close to a woman. I stroke the bare skin of her lower arm, feel the silkiness, breathe in the soft jasmine of her hair.

I look across at the Art Hut. 'I spend a lot of my time in there.'

'In that ugly old Nissen? Whatever do you do in there?'

'That ugly old Nissen is a regular artists' studio,' I say. 'All manner of things artistic go on there, courtesy of good old Sergeant Bradbury.'

I find myself telling her about Sergeant Bradbury and *The Island*, and the thousand-yard memory, all the memories, and about the arguments, though I deliberately tone down the language, don't mention the VD or the more graphic sex, or the cruder comments about some of the women. Steve's *Jane* makes her smile, and Joe's comment about her scanties, and then her lack of scanties, makes her laugh out loud.

I'm surprised I choke up when I mention Bradbury's name. He left some weeks ago – left the army altogether and is back working at one of the London galleries. He said his goodbyes to us, wished us luck. The Art Hut's not the same; it's lost its soul somehow.

'Do you actually get around to doing any painting, or is it just a free-for-all?'

'We can please ourselves. It's surprising what gets done. Would you like to see?'

As soon as I say it, I feel panicky again. Maybe it's not such a good idea. It's my inner sanctum, the Art Hut, and I'm allowing her in. It's not just mine, either; it's all of our memories, for our eyes only. Outsiders might not understand. But it's too late now.

She turns to look at me. 'You mean there's somewhere we can be on our own? Without the rest of the world watching us?' I nod and she stands and tugs at my hand to pull me up.

The Hut is empty as usual, so we go in and I lock the door behind us.

A velvet curtain, old gold and faded in patches, is spread over the trestle table. It's draped with a deceptive casualness, the folds creating interesting shadows as they fall over the edge of the table to the ground. The chipped vase holds some drooping Madame Carrière roses in it, rather than its usual hogshairs, and there is a pewter plate, an old green wine bottle and a long-stemmed glass arranged on the velvet.

'It's the still life lot, they're in on Friday nights,' I say. 'Sergeant Bradbury got hold of some bits of canvas and some oil paints the last time he was up in London. He said it was a leaving present for us. He's responsible for all this.' I sweep my hand round the walls, with the stacked scrolls and the easels, some still with half-finished work on them.

'Can I see?' Beth taps one of the scrolls.

I roll out a short stretch of the nearest scroll on the floor.

'We all take a turn on *The Island*, then we can talk about it if we want.' I'm surprised at the note of pride in my voice. It's not so long ago I was dismissing it all as futile. I hadn't realised until now just how much work we'd all done.

She looks at the various scenes and is quiet for what seems like a long time.

'The bloody war,' she says, 'the bloody, bloody war.' She takes my hand and holds it to her cheek. There are tears in her eyes.

I stare at the work on the stretch of paper, see it as Beth must see it, and it strikes me for the first time the loss and the fear and the shame and the guilt and the chaos and the bewilderment of it all.

And anger. There's so much anger in our memories, I realise. Beth's tears are tears of anger, too, not sadness.

She says she'd like to see some more and I say we could roll it out on the trestle. I take off my jacket and tie, and there's a sudden surge of release, as if I've shed an unwelcome part of myself. I clear away the still life objects onto the low table with the hogshairs and other art paraphernalia.

She leans forward to reach the vase of roses, her dress pulling tight over her breasts as she stretches. I feel a pulse of desire, a need to know the softness of her again, breathe her in. I take hold of her arm to pull her close. She is still holding the vase and there is a moment of clumsiness between us as she turns and bends to put the vase on the low table, and a petal from a wide open bloom floats down into the wide gape of her dress pocket. I think of the silky petal nestling deep inside it, resting on a thin layer of soft cotton stretched over the skin of her thigh.

I turn her towards me and slide my hand into the pocket, my fingertips searching out the petal. It's already warm to the touch from the heat of her. The Hut is suddenly so still, so quiet, I can hear the faint whisper of my hand over the smoothness of her dress as I begin to stroke her thigh. My fingers follow the slight dip leading to the soft swell of pubic hair. Her breath comes in small sips, warm on my ear, and she pushes up against me. Then she pulls away slightly, guides my hand from the pocket, kisses my fingers and lays them on her breast, as she always did.

I reach behind her to pull the velvet curtain off the table. We fold our bodies down so we are on our knees. I begin to work my way down, button by button, peeling back the dress, and she unfastens my shirt and edges it off my shoulders, both of us swaying slightly, the motion and the touching almost hypnotic. We stretch out on to the curtain. She lies back, her slender body in a slip of ivory silk, the white dress spread like soft wings round her. I rest on my elbow, taking in the curves and hollows of her, the paleness of her skin, the faint flush across the rise of her breasts. I've missed this, I've missed all of this.

There is another moment of clumsiness as I kick off those stupid plimsolls and fumble with the buttons of my trousers and work my way out of them and then the rest of my clothes. I lie there for a moment, savouring the cool air on my body. My naked body. Stripped of the Blues. With a woman lying by my side. The thought of that. The freedom of it. For the first time since I've been in Northfield, I feel like a human being. I feel free.

I turn back to her and inch up her slip. Her skin is hot as I stroke it through silk and lace and she wriggles a little, lifting her hips off the ground to make it easier for me to slide the flimsy material down. I'd forgotten the sheer bloody physicality of sex – the hardness, the softness, the slipperiness of our sweat, as we close into each other and around each other.

I begin to lose all sense of myself as the rhythm becomes more intense.

She closes her eyes, I keep mine open, I want to see her face. Then, for one moment, I look up over her head. And I freeze. Just behind her, I can see the low table, and on it, a thin wooden box full of charcoal sticks. I try and look away, look down at Beth's face again, but I can't. My gaze is locked on to the sticks.

I sense what's coming and try and fight it back but it's useless. A thumb-smudge of grey-black rises up from the box, and a mocking cloud drones towards me at a leisurely pace. It can only be there for a second, this filthy image, but it seems to flit by in slow motion, filling my head with blackness and buzzing and putrifying flesh.

It's a physical pain, this death of sexual desire, a skitter of sharp pulses, a sense of the strength of me ebbing away. Then a dull ache. I groan a little. Beth mistakes the sound I make for pleasure and grips me tighter, and I panic. I'm desperate to withdraw before she feels the truth. I push her away and I roll over, my back turned to her. I whisper, 'I'm sorry, I'm so sorry.' I am the loneliest man on earth.

Both of us lie completely still for what seems like an eternity. I hear rustles, feel her move as she dresses. I keep my back turned. I expect her to walk out of the Hut. But she sits back down on the floor next to me. I stand up and gather up my clothes, afraid to look at her.

I get dressed slowly. The flannelette shirt, delphinium trousers, the schoolboy plimsolls. As each ridiculous item of clothing goes on, I feel myself diminished again. I don't know if she's watching this pathetic metamorphosis back to the specimen I really am. I sit back down on the curtain.

I'll have to turn round and face her. When I do, if she looks at me, and if the look she gives me is one of pity, then it'll be all over between us. I can stand anything but pity. I can deal with the shame and the guilt and humiliation – they're all mine to deal with. But someone else's pity, especially Beth's, I couldn't bear that. I don't deserve pity and even if I did, I don't want it.

I turn towards her. She's fully dressed, the silk scarf wound into a band around her head slightly crooked. She has her knees drawn up, hugging them, her head resting on her arms, looking directly ahead at the scrolls stacked against the far wall. She sighs, a long, soft exhalation through her nose as if she's trying to expel something painful from deep inside her. It's me. She's trying to get rid of me, the smell of me, the feel of me. Then she moves closer to me, close but not touching.

'Beth,' I say, 'I'm so sorry. I'm not sure what happened.' That's not strictly true, of course. I know it's something to do with the memories, but I can never share those memories. She would be revolted by them – who wouldn't be? – but worse than that, she'd be revolted by me, knowing they were part of me, in my head. I want to touch her, but I know I couldn't bear it if she should stiffen, move away again, freeze, like I did. So I sit there, listening to the silence closing in and around me.

And then, she slides her arm gently under mine and leans her head on my shoulder. 'This bloody war,' she says, more sadness in her tone than anger.

The chorus of the art group flits into my head, then out again and echoes round the room – *it's the bloody war, making us into something else, something less.*

She turns to look at me, touches my cheek, turns my face towards her.

I don't see pity. Her gaze is intense, almost as if she's challenging me to keep looking at her. There is sadness in her face, in her eyes, around the downturned mouth. But there is something else too. There is determination.

'Whatever you've been through,' she says, her eyes still on mine, 'we can't let it beat us. If we do, what has it all been for?' She gestures round the Hut again, with its scrolls and easels full of memories and misery. 'All this, it's just memories. It happened, but it's not happening now. You can walk away from it, leave it all here. Lock it away in this room.' She kisses me then, soft and gentle, so gentle, our lips hardly touch. 'You can come home,' she says.

She gathers up the curtain on her side and wraps it round her shoulders and I do the same on my side. We are cocooned in faded gold velvet and I can smell old dust, mixed with the faint scent of jasmine.

'We'll be alright.' I don't look at her as I say this.

'You can come home. Come back to me. We're the lucky ones, remember?'

'We'll be alright,' I say again.

12

He got back to Northfield late Sunday afternoon. On a whim, he asked the taxi driver to drop him off at the gates. He felt like a walk after the stuffiness of the train from London. The gates stayed open until five, for Sunday visiting, although there was no-one around. The weather had been changeable all day, more noticeably so as he'd travelled up from London. It had rained here recently, dampening down the dusty ground and freshening up the trees. He breathed in the cool air, his head clearer than it had been for weeks.

He couldn't remember the last time he'd walked up this driveway. The staff who lived in tended to drive or cycle from the hospital. He and Foulkes used to go out together for a drink in a pub at a nearby village, the opposite way from the Crown, to avoid the patients. They'd get a lift there and walk back, a good five miles, a satisfying way of finishing off their pub conversations. They'd always fall into a silence when they'd turned in the gates, as if they'd passed through some sort of airlock separating them from one way of breathing to another.

He didn't stop at the oak. He was more puffed than he liked to admit, but his small suitcase wasn't heavy and he was determined to do the drive in one stretch. He came to the shark's teeth border and stopped. He looked at the hospital and noticed how dilapidated it was, with its rotten window frames and battered front doors.

He had the peculiar experience of imagining himself at the tea room window, observing himself as he stood there. He'd been right in his theory about the gravel path – it did feel like a no-man's-land. His gaze followed the run of the long, low buildings and was stopped by the water tower, backlit by the sinking sun. It singled him out, casting an admonishing finger of shadow over him. The whole building seemed to be watching him, sizing him up, throwing down some sort of challenge, determined to intimidate him into submission.

It was such an obvious thing to do, put himself in the position of the countless men he'd observed standing here, and yet he'd never done it. He wished he had. It was definitely his weekend for learning things about himself. He squared his shoulders and walked round the back to Reception.

13

I spend the next few days rerunning images of what happened with Beth. I find myself cringing both inside and out, physically hunching over, diminished by the memory of the humiliation. What if it happens every time? What if the memories keep coming back? It's the last thing I think about at night, the first thing I think about when I wake up, if I even manage to fall asleep.

There was no pity. At least I have that.

On Friday, the letter comes. I think of the men in Burma, opening their *Dear Johns* and slinking away like wounded animals. I think of Louie, reading his on the day we left Bombay, and never speaking of it. The envelope is flimsy, light blue. *Treatment means the Blues.*

I take myself off to the Art Hut beech tree. An ache, a real ache, solidifies and lodges just under my heart. I open the envelope. There's only one thin folded sheet of paper with something thicker enclosed in it.

A watercolour, postcard size. A miniature version of Beth's three demoiselle cranes. Ethereal, impressionistic, like they might take flight and fade into the distance. There's a lightness of touch about them, as if she was holding her breath when she painted them.

One line on the notepaper, in her loopy handwriting.

Come back to me. Come home. We'll be alright.

My memory goes back to her studio, to the vibrant demoiselles on the wall, to the brass bed bathed in a wash of blue-green light, and our first-time, stumbling, fumbling sex. How it got better. How we got better at being together. How she was always there.

The tension within me begins to ebb away, leaving me light-headed and dizzy. I look across to the oaks in the field, and this time I focus on the first, the greatest of the three, its leaves still deep green against the late August morning light.

My eye takes in its spreading outline, not quite symmetrical, down to where it curves back in, its lowest branches seeming to cradle the whole of the canopy, taking the weight of it, able to cope with whatever happens above. There's a sense of endurance about it, a stoicism I find calming. I must draw this tree before I leave Northfield.

I fold Beth's message around the watercolour and put them both in my breast pocket. Those words I've just said to myself. *I must draw this tree before I leave Northfield*. It's the first time I've acknowledged the inevitability of my leaving. I take a long look at the tree again. A sketch in charcoal, perhaps. A charcoal sketch of an oak in full leaf, whole, unblemished.

14

He spent Monday catching up, and was grateful that it had been a quiet weekend while he'd been away. No-one had gone AWOL, no suicides or attempted suicides, thank the Lord.

Tuesday, he did his ward rounds and had individual sessions with his more severely depressed patients. He was down to one full session a month with each patient now, the staffing ratio was so bad. The situation was as chaotic and hopeless as ever, but it didn't seem to affect him in the same way it usually did.

It wasn't that he didn't care, he'd always care. But there had been a subtle shift within himself. He couldn't quite pinpoint what the change was – maybe something to do with not taking on so much personal responsibility for trying to make a doomed institution like Northfield work. And not feeling guilty about it. Whatever it was, he felt less anxious, more open physically, more able to take a breath in and use it to centre himself, feel calmer.

It was a small step, but he sensed it was permanent, it would stay with him.

On Friday, two pieces of news put this new-found sense of equilibrium to the test. The CO called an emergency meeting in the afternoon at 1600 hours. He'd had confirmation that the hospital would be ceasing to operate as a military hospital in March 1948. It would be absorbed into the new National Health Service as a civilian facility. He read the details out as though it was a battle plan. The hospital would be vacated by the military in December. The schedule for evacuating the premises would be posted in due course.

There would be no more admissions and those awaiting

assessment would be transferred to other hospitals. Current patients would be signed off immediately, at the latest by the end of September, or moved elsewhere for further treatment. Medical staff could apply to stay on when the hospital became part of the National Health Service, or apply for transfer within the military.

There was nothing new in all this; it confirmed the rumours. But giving it a date meant it had at last been rubber-stamped, it was really happening. To some, it was unsettling, but to Daniel, it seemed like a validation of his decision to move away from what he'd been doing for so long. And it felt good *not* to know what his next step was going to be. It felt like freedom.

The second piece of news shook him up more, even though he was expecting it. After the meeting, there was a memorandum waiting for him in his pigeonhole, typed on official Sutton Hospital Neuropsychiatric Unit headed paper.

Re: _Corporal Frederick Simm_

    Leucotomy operation undertaken on 26 August.

    I would be obliged if, in your capacity as initial Admissions and Assessment Officer, you would ensure the transfer of Simm's records at the earliest convenience.

    (signature) Major Hunter, Assistant to Professor W. Sargant

He had never known Corporal Simm. He was only a name on an admission file to him. But he would take up his place deep within Daniel next to Housewife, fifty, Melancholia. Voiceless. Powerless. But unforgotten.

15

Dr Carter spends the first few minutes talking about the hospital closing.

'I already know,' I say. 'Jungle drums.' The hospital is buzzing with the news. Joe and Derek and Michael from the Art Hut have already had their last sessions, and leave tomorrow. Joe and Derek are going home. Michael will be taking his unresurrected dead to a London hospital.

'This will be our last session,' Dr Carter says. 'I'm sorry our work together is going to be cut short. I can arrange for you to be referred back to the psychiatrist in Manchester, if necessary. You'll be in good hands.'

Mention of Manchester gives me a little jolt; it's another confirmation that I will be leaving Northfield. I finger my breast pocket with Beth's watercolour in it.

'Although, you've done some of the groundwork on your own.' He taps my work on his desk. 'A lot has gone into this. A lot of thinking and reflection.' He takes off his glasses and rubs behind his ears. For a moment I see John mimicking his gestures, wickedly accurate.

He lodges his elbows on the desk and rests his chin on his clasped hands. 'I wondered what it felt like to sketch your memories, to write them down.'

I have to think back to doing the drawing and the writing. It seems a long time ago and my mind now is full of Beth. I wonder if I should ignore his question and bring up the problem I had in the Art Hut, but I know what happened to me isn't normal. He might not understand, and anyway, it would be too embarrassing; I'd not be able to find the words to describe it.

I look at the pile of sketches and notes and remember when I started to draw, after my session with Carter. The sense of myself diminishing. Of abandonment. Of isolation. Of becoming *The Empty House*.

'When I looked at the sketches, the words – it seemed to be about someone else. That boy at the MG before the war, then the man who came back – they're both me, but they're total strangers.'

Mentioning the MG reminds me of the times with Mrs Tipton in that airless room, drinking tea, our heads together, poring over the staff lists. 'I can't believe I was that naïve, that I was such a dreamer. You'd think I'd have more sense after four years of war, believing I could ever go back, fit in there again. Fit in anywhere. I'd changed. They'd changed.'

He nods, as if he understands. We settle into silence. I don't feel the urge any more to jump in and fill it up.

He speaks first, tapping my papers again. 'There's so much we could talk about here. But I'm aware this is our last session and we only have a limited amount of time. I wondered, out of all the experiences you've set down, which one feels like the most painful one for you to remember?'

I think of the hurt look on George's face when I was sarcastic about the roundel on the front of the *Odyssey*. The Penguin paperbacks, their covers curling up in the flames of the fire. The anxiety around my mother's eyes when she looked at me. Beth sitting on the edge of my bed and me turning my face away from her. The images fade in and fade out.

But one keeps coming back and stays.

'Beating Vinny up.' As I say this out loud, I see myself in the alleyway, Vinny prone on the ground, my foot crunching into his face. *Kill me, would you?* I think I can even smell the stink of piss around us.

'He was only a boy, eighteen at most,' I say. 'He thought he was a tough guy, but he was all mouth. He may have been in fights, but I don't think he'd ever set out to kill anyone.'

'You describe Vinny's face turning into the Japanese soldier's – that you thought it was really the Japanese soldier you were beating up?'

'I kept seeing the Japanese soldier's face in the faces I passed in the street – that was so frightening. Then when I got Vinny in the alley, one minute I was looking at his face, and he looked so young, the next it was the Japanese soldier. He was no more than a boy too.'

'So beating Vinny always leads to the memory of what happened to the Japanese boy?'

My chest is beginning to tighten with anxiety. 'That boy was the only Japanese I killed, close up. We weren't infantry or artillery, we were communications. We'd fixed our bayonets – you never knew what you'd come across when you went in after the action had finished. But it was a shock to be so close to him and realise he was deliberately trying to kill me. He must have known it would be the last thing he'd ever do on earth – kill me. Captain Evans was right, he would have shot himself after that. That was what I was left with. I've never felt such rage.'

Carter puts his head on one side. 'That's what they were there for, to kill British soldiers. That's what you were there for. To kill Japanese.'

'I know, I know. That's war. I know.' I pause to catch hold of my words, then they come tumbling out. 'It wasn't war, though, was it, that night with Vinny? Just some pathetic insults in the pub.'

'Who was the rage really aimed at?'

I have to think about this. 'There was real anger at Vinny. But when I was thinking about it, writing it down, the Japanese boy came back and all these other thoughts took over.'

'What kind of other thoughts?' He's gentle, but insistent.

I look past him, down the driveway to the gravel wasteland. See the boy soldier lying there and the three of us, standing over him. I blink the memory away. But it comes back. His eyes locked on to mine. Then the hole in his head.

'The boy was dying anyway. Louie said I put him out of his misery, gave him a quicker death. But there was nothing humane in what I did. It was all about revenge. He tried to kill me and I wanted revenge. Captain Evans understood that. He could have finished him off himself, but he gave me the pistol. He gave me the choice. I took it. I killed a dying sixteen-year-old boy. It was as primitive as that.'

I have to pause and sort my breathing out. Carter leans forward, waiting.

'But as I thought about it to write it down, I realised it was more than that. We'd had four years of being forced to live like animals, fight like animals, in some godforsaken jungle. That Japanese boy, lying there, he somehow became the war itself, if that makes sense. He became everything it represented. Things that had been done to me and men like me. Things that it made me do, things that had been taken away from me. That was what my real rage was about. What the war had made us.'

I look out of the window again. See myself taking the pistol and shooting the boy.

There's a long silence. The boy with the hole in his head turns into Vinny with his caved-in face.

'It frightens me,' I say, 'what I did to Vinny.'

'What is it about it that frightens you?'

'Like you said before. The violence . . . what I'm capable of.'

'What we're all capable of. In certain circumstances.'

'But we're not in those circumstances now, are we? I can rationalise what I did to the Japanese boy. Like you said, he was there to kill me, I was there to kill him; that was war. I know that. What happened with Vinny wasn't war. It was a grubby brawl in a filthy alley next to a seedy backstreet pub. What if I'd kicked him to death?'

'But you didn't.'

'As far as I know. I scoured the papers for weeks after, expecting to see him as a murder. You do it in war, you can tell yourself it's allowed. But it's still killing, isn't it?'

'From what you've just said, what you did to Vinny is tangled up in specific memories of war.'

'Doesn't mean to say it's right, or that I'm not capable of doing it again.'

'No, it doesn't. But you recognise that. And you're also able to see the memory of the Japanese soldier for what it was. What it means to you. And what happens when you remember it. And why you might have done what you did to Vinny.'

He places his hands down flat on my sketches and notes. 'There's so much remorse and shame and guilt here. It might not feel like it, but that's progress. I'd be more worried if there was no remorse or shame or guilt.'

'I hope to Christ you're right.'

'That's not a bad thing for all of us to hang on to, in the end,' he says. 'Hope.'

I feel drained, wrung out. There's nothing else I want to say.

He seems to sense this. He looks down at *On Not Recalling War*. 'I see what you mean about the title – the irony of it.' He hands back my papers and shakes my hand. Wishes me good luck. I think of Sargeant Bradbury doing the same thing when he left. And Louie. So many goodbyes, so much moving on.

I head for the door and realise that in the general awkwardness of taking back the notes and saying goodbye, I've forgotten to thank him. I turn to say something, but he has swivelled his chair round and is sitting back in it, staring out of his window, massaging behind his ear lobes.

16

Monday, he spent time on his paperwork. Signed several discharges, including the one for David Reece. Located Freddie Simm's clinical notes and arranged for them to be sent on to Sutton. Returned the patient assessment files to Admin. He felt a twinge of guilt as he deposited them on the clerk's desk. The patients were someone else's responsibility now, but it didn't come easily to him to think like this.

The rest of the morning was taken up with Medical Boards. John Bain got his ticket out, to the relief of all concerned. Daniel signed him off shortly after the Boards had ended and told him he could leave immediately. There was no thanks from Bain, not that Daniel expected any. Hardly half an hour had passed before Daniel, staring out of the tea room window, saw Bain walking purposefully down the driveway towards the gates. He was in civvies – he must have brought them with him when he arrived, probably planning to leave for good, either legally or illegally, if necessary. Standing there, watching him, it occurred to Daniel that it had been a week of endings. For Northfield, for all the men, for everyone.

He watched the figure go through the gates, then he turned back to the last of his case notes on the desk. He hoped Bain would find peace of mind in his quest to become more human again. He was a survivor, his war record and his skill as a deserter had shown that. But he was deeply wounded within himself, Daniel was sure of it. So many of them were. John Bain. David Reece. Spence. All carrying the burden of terrible secrets hidden in their hearts. The walking wounded.

Just like our own fathers when they came back. And he

wondered how many of his own generation would hand on the legacy of these secrets to the next. And how the next generation would fare, carrying the weight of all these legacies, until it was their turn to create their own.

17

He left yesterday, when I was out sketching the oak. The word was he'd planned to go anyway, whether they gave him his ticket out or not. There were no awkward goodbyes or handshakes, no good luck wishes for the future. It hurt, not seeing him. But he left me the box file on top of my locker. Inside was the copy of *Tribune* with his own poem in it. And Graves's *Collected Poems* with *Recalling War*. No note.

When I opened Graves's poems, there was an oval inked stamp on the inside cover. *Leeds University Library*. It made me smile.

Carts have been brought down and parked near the orderly's desk at the end of the dormitory, in preparation for the extra discharges. I fetch one and begin to pack my things. Clothing, flannel, shaving brush. The Moore and the Nash. John's poetry. My own sketches.

I'm not sure I've captured the oak as I'd have wanted, but it's good to work with charcoal again. *On Not Recalling War* goes on top with Graves's collection.

They expect us to make our own way, unescorted, back down those endless corridors to Reception, via the kit store. I walk towards the junction of Pall Mall and Petticoat Lane, and stop when I get there and look back. The vanishing point is behind me.

I pick up my suitcase at the kit store and get changed out of the Blues. For a moment, I'm reminded of stripping off in the Art Hut with Beth. But there's no feeling of humiliation, just the same sense of freedom I'd had then, before things went wrong. I take off that stupid demeaning uniform for the last time and it's like shedding an outgrown skin.

I've put on a little weight – my old shirt collar feels tight, the trouser waist a little snug. My mother will be pleased. My Oxfords feel heavy after the canvas plimsolls. I transfer the cranes and the oak to my suit breast pocket.

The storeman collects the Blues and the enamelware, nods at me, ticks me off his list.

I arrive at reception. They tick me off another list. I sign a form and notice Dr Carter's signature in the space above mine.

Then I'm out into a cool, blustery afternoon. A maple tree near the guard room is already on the turn, the leaves still green but edged with gold, giving in at last to the stress of the hot, dry summer. I suddenly realise it's the first day of September. This time last year, I was beginning the journey home from Chittagong.

The gravel path is mussed up and dusty. Many pairs of feet have trodden on it, moving quickly, and no-one thinks it's worth-while smoothing it over. A few of the shark's teeth have come loose and fallen over and someone has kicked them away, leaving gaps, so there is no need to step over them now.

I begin the long walk down the drive and when I get to the oak I don't stop. It's Saturday, and I'm catching the visitors' bus back to the station. No-one to help me on my way. That's how I've planned it. There's already a little group of Blues and khakis waiting for their visitors at the entrance, but there's no-one I recognise.

I pass through the gates and keep walking until I've gone round the curve in the road, then stop to change my suitcase over. I breathe in the cool air, the freedom. I place my hand over the breast pocket of my jacket. Beth's fragile demoiselles rest there, still in their flimsy blue envelope.

Acknowledgements

My thanks to the staff at the Imperial War Museum, the Wellcome Library, the Guardian Archive at the John Rylands University Library of Manchester, the Medical School archive at Queen's University, Belfast, and the Royal College of Surgeons, Dublin. Special thanks are due to Hilary Mantel and Sebastian Barry for their guidance on the research aspects of the novel and to Henry Marsh for his insights into leucotomies. Thanks also to Vernon Scannell's two literary executors, Jeremy Robson and Martin Reed. I owe a great debt to Ian Sansom, Sinead Morrissey, Andrew Pepper, Damian Smyth, Cathy Galvin, and the late Professor Keith Jeffery, and also to David Park, whose comments on what I thought was the final draft were invaluable. Thanks to friends and colleagues at the Seamus Heaney Centre for Poetry, and to others dotted about in Northern Ireland, Ireland, and elsewhere, who read drafts or extracts of the novel, or provided support and encouragement – in particular, Malachi O'Doherty, Maureen Boyle, Tim Loane, Glenn Patterson, Darran McCann and Garrett Carr.

Drummond Moir, my editor at Sceptre, together with Jenny Campbell, have both shown enormous flair and patience in working with me on the novel. Bill Hamilton made the whole thing happen. My husband Ken, together with my in-laws, Liz and Dougie, helped me through the times I thought it would never happen. Special thanks to Edward Nash, who was in Burma, and to all those who found themselves in other theatres of war during the Second World War, whose experiences I have been humbled to learn about during the research for this novel.

Copyright permissions